C.

Charlie McCoy has three rules. The first rule is don't associate with idiots. But here he is, sitting with Moe Baker in a corner booth in a pancake house, talking about committing breaking and entering. Moe has a wispy goatee and wears sunglasses with small rectangular lenses. The goatee and the glasses make him look like an idiot. Today Moe's added a black porkpie hat to his ensemble, which makes him look more like an idiot than usual.

"Linda's got this job, working for this rich guy," Moe says, looking around. "He keeps a bunch of cash in a safe in his house."

Charlie stirs his coffee, watching the sugar slowly dissolve.

"How would she know that?" he asks.

"She was walking by his study. Saw the dude stuffing big bundles of cash in the safe."

Charlie picks up his coffee cup and raises it to his lips. He uses his left hand because his right hand is in a cast. His hand shakes, spilling some coffee on the green linoleum table top.

"Cash is good," Charlie says, putting the cup down and wiping the spill away with a napkin. "But right now, the job is a non-starter. I'd need information on this safe before we can even think about it."

"It's not a combination lock. It's a key lock. The guy doesn't trust his memory."

Charlie leans over the table, lowers his voice, and looks Moe in the eye.

"What's your point? Key lock, combination lock, doesn't make any difference. If you want me to crack the box, I need to know the manufacturer and model number of the lock and the safe, just for starters. And keep your voice down."

"Linda can get me the key."

Charlie's thinking--Linda. Moe's old lady. Full-time stripper. Part-time hooker.

"She screwing him?" Charlie says. "This old man, I mean."

Moe doesn't say anything. That tells Charlie all he needs to know.

"I don't understand something," Charlie says. "You know where the safe is. You've got a key. What do you need me for?"

"The security system. You can take it out. It's Mickey Mouse. And there are some small-time locks that need to be picked. Doors and stuff."

"I don't know anything about this job. Are there motion detectors? TV cameras? Heat sensors? Door alarms? Are we going to have to go through any walls?"

"None of that stuff. Nothing. Linda's cased the place."

"How much are we talking? You know, if we do this job."

"I'm guessing five hundred large. Or more."

Charlie studies Moe, trying to see if he's lying.

"Who keeps that kind of cash lying around?" he asks.

"Phil Adonis."

Charlie lets this sink in for a moment. Typical Moe. He leaves the most important information to the end.

"Little Phil or Big Phil?" Charlie asks. As if it makes a difference.

"Big Phil."

That explains the key. The guy is three-quarters senile, from what Charlie's heard. Big Phil couldn't remember a combination if his life depended on it. Big Phil Adonis also has the Justice Department up his ass big time. Money laundering and tax evasion are the rumor. It makes sense to stash your money where the feds won't find it, although sticking it in a safe in your own house isn't the world's brightest move.

"So I understand you correctly, your proposal is we rob the Godfather of the Adonis crime family?"

Charlie looks around for a waitress so he can pay the bill and get the hell out.

"You need the money, Charlie." Moe points at the cast. "What happens when Goran breaks your other hand? Tough to do the kind of work you do with two broken hands."

"I'll get Goran his money before he breaks anything else of mine."

"That must've hurt, what he did. But you had it coming. You're a degenerative gambler, man. You should've known better than let Goran get into you, especially a guy your age. Those Russians are the worst. Even worse than the Italians."

Charlie shrugs. "Actually, I think Goran's a Bulgarian."

"You accepted his money. You'll never be out from under him. You shouldn't have done it."

"It seemed like a sure thing at the time."

"How you gonna get twenty grand in three days?"

Charlie looks away, out the window, at the cars on the Interstate.

Moe says, "Your problem is, you don't study all the angles, man. You need to study the angles if you want to get anywhere in life."

Charlie says he'll think about Moe's proposal and get back to him. Moe tells him not to wait too long. Jobs like this don't come along every day.

***

Charlie's in the parking lot, sitting in his pickup truck, staring, wondering how things got so screwed up. He hates being called a degenerate gambler by an idiot like Moe Baker, especially since Moe doesn't know why he borrowed the money.

Charlie met Moe in county lock-up while Charlie was waiting to make bail on a B&E. Moe was high on something. His eyes were glittery, the pupils enlarged, and he talked non-stop, mostly about punking, a word he'd learned from a stupid TV show. Moe explained that punking was like spraying starch on a hundred dollar bill.

"Why would you do that?" Charlie asked, just killing time, not because he cared in the least. "Because you like them extra crispy?"

Moe leaned against the metal bars.

"No, man. It's like this. You know those pens they use in stores to see if a hundred dollar bill is real? Those pens detect starch. You see, phony money is paper, but real money is fabric. Paper's a starch. Fabric isn't. So if the mark turns black, it means it's paper and it's a phony bill. You can make a real bill look like a phony by spraying it with starch."

Charlie sat up on his cot. Making a real hundred-dollar bill look like a counterfeit. That's something you didn't hear every day.

"What's the point?" he asked.

"As soon as the mark turns black, store security is called and the guy's taken into custody, and then the cops are called. He could end up spending a weekend in stir before people figure out the bill isn't phony. Maybe they search his house, looking for counterfeit bills and find drugs or something and he gets busted for that."

"Still . . . not seeing the point."

"I only do it when somebody gets on the wrong side of me. Like they've been bugging me about some money they say I owe them. I slip them a couple of Moe specials--that's what I call them--to teach them a lesson. You don't want to get on my bad side, believe it."

Charlie said he'd keep that in mind.

That was three years ago. Charlie got his charges dismissed. Moe spent six months in stir for possession with intent to distribute. Since then Moe has called him with ideas on how they could get rich quick. Charlie turned him down because Moe's ideas were always stupid. Charlie's a little surprised that Moe's been able to stay out of the joint this long given how stupid his ideas are. But this time he agreed to a meeting.

Reaching across with his left hand, Charlie shifts his truck into drive. He doesn't like the job. A lot of unknowns and, including Linda, there are two other people involved. His second rule is never pull a job if more than one other person is involved. More than that, things get too complicated too quickly.

He could ignore his rules, just this once.

Or maybe find another way out of this box. One that didn't involve breaking into the home of a powerful mob boss.

Chapter Two

Goran Ivanov is small and deeply wrinkled with walnut-colored skin and a shaved head.

"You got my money?" he says.

"No, I don't," Charlie says.

"So what you want from me, Charlie?"

"A little more time."

"Time to do what? To fuck around some more? You already wasting my time, man."

"It's not like that. I need more time so I can get your money."

Goran leans back in his chair. They're sitting in his office, which is in the back of the Happy Dayz Club, Goran's night club and meth distribution center. The office is small, with just enough room for a small metal desk, a couple of metal chairs, and a metal filing cabinet. A half-eaten sandwich lies on a paper plate on the desk. Goran's pit bull sits on the floor next to Goran's chair. It eyes Charlie with unrelenting malevolence.

There's a knock on the door and a man sticks his head in. It's the guy who held Charlie down while another guy broke his hand with a hammer. He's a huge man, his head almost touching the low ceiling. Just looking at him causes Charlie's hand to ache.

"Sorry, to bother you, boss," the man says, speaking with a heavy East European accent. "They need you up front to sign for some booze."

Goran says, "They'll have to wait a minute. I'm speaking with my good friend Charlie McCoy. Milos, your remember Charlie. He's begging for more time to pay his bills."

Milos laughs and shakes his head, as if in amazement.

"I'll tell them you'll be a while," Milos says. "Let me know if you need me."

He glances at Charlie, then steps out closing the door quietly behind him.

"Now where were we?" Goran says. "Yes, we were talking about Goran's money."

"I'm looking for work right now, but I need a little more time." Charlie holds up his right hand. "How do you expect me to earn with my hand like this?"

Goran's face settles into a look of disdain.

"And whose fault is that, I ask you? Yours. You don't do what you're supposed to. Pay me back. You said you'd pay me back, but you didn't. You know problem with you, Charlie?"

"No, I don't know," Charlie says warily. "What's the problem with me?"

"You haven't suffered enough. You're soft, like all Americans. You have everything given to you. I not have anything given to me. I work for what I have. Made me tough."

He strikes his chest with his fist.

"I grow up under communists," he continues. "Fucking communists. I stand in line in freezing cold for hours just to get loaf of bread. I am little kid. When I get in store, all bread is gone. You ever stand in freezing cold for loaf of bread, Charlie?"

"No, Goran, I never--"

"Of course not. You have bread given to you. So what my guys did to you, it'll toughen you up. Make you a man."

He strikes his chest again.

"You don't have to thank me," he says.

"I'm already a man," Charlie says.

"You think so? Really? Look at this."

He takes a shred of ham from the sandwich and holds it a couple of feet above the dog's head. The dog stirs itself.

"Look at this," Goran says again to Charlie. "Look at me."

The dog jumps, trying to get the meat, but it's just out of reach. Goran holds it higher and the dog jumps higher.

"You're like dog, Charlie. I tell you I forgive your debt, if you jump in air, you do that. Wouldn't you? And I tell you to jump higher, you do that, too."

"No, I wouldn't."

"Sure you would. Cause you're not a man, Charlie. You're a dog." He looks at Charlie. "You're my dog. Woof, woof."

He drops the piece of meat on the dirty concrete floor and the dog gobbles it up.

Goran laughs, a high-pitched tinny sound. "Now be good dog and pay me my money. You got three days, to July Fourth. Think of it as Independence Day."

* * *

Charlie drives south, out of the city, to a small strip center. It's a gray, heavy, mid-summer day and he's sitting in a pool of sweat on account of the broken air conditioner in his truck.

The strip center is in a depressed suburb, mostly rundown apartment buildings, foreclosed homes, and payday lenders. A pawn shop--EZCash--is squeezed between a Walgreen's and a Chinese restaurant. Outside the pawn shop is a row of bicycles--men's, women's, children's--all chained together and padlocked. Charlie eyes the bikes. Who were the people who rode these bikes? Why did they pawn them? Because they needed the dough. Thinking about the bikes makes Charlie feel dispirited.

Inside, it's dark and cool and crowded with merchandise. Power tools, musical instruments, and firearms mostly. Billie Joe Fish, a tall, skinny guy with shoulder-length hair and a gray beard is behind the counter. He's eighty pounds lighter than when Charlie first met him twelve years ago. An extended bout with lung cancer will do that to a guy. Fish wears a large-caliber revolver in a holster on his right hip, just in case anybody's got the foolish notion to try and rob his pawn shop.

"Charlie, my man," he says. "What can I do you for this good day?"

Fish has a loud hoarse voice that can probably be heard outside in the parking lot. He takes a long pull on a cigarette, a look of bliss briefly flitting across his face.

"Thought you gave those up," Charlie says.

"I've got it taken care of," Fish says with a laugh. "Since I have only one lung left, I've cut my smoking in half."

"How's that working for you?"

"So far, so good. How's the family?"

"They're well."

"And your daughter, uh . . ."

"Amy? She's fine."

Charlie glances at the front door.

"Can we go in the back?" he asks, speaking softly. "I need to speak with you."

Fish's face creases into a frown.

"Is it about work? Cause I don't have anything right now. Sorry, man."

"You have anything coming up?"

"Not at the moment. Check back. Maybe a couple of months. If I hear anything I'll keep you in mind. You know how this business works."

"I need some work right now. Not in a couple of months. You know of anybody else who has work? I'll take anything. Even a penny-ante job. Even a smash-and-grab."

An expression--is it pity?--flashes across Fish's face.

"I haven't heard of anything lately," he says. "You know how it is. Good jobs are to find nowadays. With all the security systems and cameras and all."

Charlie nods, turns to leave.

"You doing okay, Charlie? You don't look so good."

"Yeah I'm doing great. Never been better."

Fish points. "You do something to your hand?"

"I was careless. It was an accident."

Fish casts him a doubtful look.

"Should be healed soon," Charlie continues. "It's not a problem, though. I can still work."

"I understand. Like I said. I just don't have anything for you."

Charlie takes a small nickel-plated pistol from his pants pocket. A look of apprehension from Fish and his hand creeps toward his revolver.

"What will you give me for this?" Charlie says.

Fish eyes the gun.

"Beretta Minx," he says. "Don't see many of those anymore. I'd give you seventy, eighty maybe. If it's in good condition."

"That's all?"

"Not much call for guns like that. You can get a nine millimeter that's just as small and has more stopping power." He holds out his hand. "Here, let me look at it. Maybe I could go ninety."

Charlie puts it back in his pocket.

"Never mind," he says. "It's not a big deal."

Fish takes a large roll of bank notes from his pocket.

"Listen, Charlie. You've always been straight with me. I haven't forgotten that you did me a solid on that warehouse job."

"Yes, I did."

"That could've been bad for me. Real bad. Don't think I'm not appreciative. You need a few hundred to see you through, I can manage that."

He peels off some hundreds.

"Don't worry," Charlie says, waving him off. "I'll be all right."

Charlie steps through the door and into the gray sunlight. Standing next to the chained-up bicycles, he thinks, you need a few hundred to see you through?

Thanks for nothing.

Chapter Three

They drive slowly past Big Phil Adonis's house. The Ford E-150 van that Moe stole needs a ring job. Charlie can feel the shaking through the latex FoodHandler glove he's wearing on his left hand.

Moe looks alert, sharp. Charlie's disappointed. He was hoping that Moe would show up stoned and out if it, and that would give Charlie an excuse to quit this job. But no such luck.

"You already got your cast changed," Moe says, pointing at Charlie's right hand.

"Yeah, just a splint with an ace bandage over it."

"That's fast for a broken bone."

"Always been a quick healer."

Chez Big Phil is a Tudor-style in the middle of the stockbroker belt. There's a ten-foot-high brick wall with a wrought iron gate in the front. A little plastic sign attached to the gate reads AAA SECURITY. Charlie loves it when they do that. The sign is supposed to be a deterrent, but it tells him the exact system they're using and how to wire around it.

"Where is everybody?" Charlie says. "It's only three-thirty."

"Tuesday. It's Senior Citizen's Night at Luby's."

An alley goes up the back of the house. Charlie likes alleys for the same reason homeowners like alleys. Lots of privacy. And with their white tradesmen's van and gray overalls, they're easily mistaken for a couple of repairmen.

He drives slowly, examining the power poles and overhead lines.

"We've got a problem," he says.

"What's that?"

"I don't see a telephone line."

"I know it's not a wireless system."

"It wouldn't be. Not Triple A. They're strictly old school. I did some work for them. They must've put it underground. I hope I can find it or we're out of luck."

Charlie pulls over and stops the van. He gets out and stretches his long legs. Moe's already around the back when Charlie gets there. They slide a ten-foot aluminum extension ladder out the back and prop it up against the wall.

They slip on masks. Charlie's mask is George W. Bush. Moe's mask is Dick Cheney. The masks are Moe's bright idea.

Charlie surveys the top of the wall. This is the point of no return. He hasn't broken any laws yet. He can still change his mind and turn back.

He can still walk away.

Instead, he cinches up his tool belt with his left hand and then scrambles up the ladder as fast as he can. It's a hot July afternoon and he's sweating like a big dog inside his gray overalls. Moe follows. He also wears gray overalls, and he's carrying a big navy-blue duffel bag. How much money is Moe really expecting to find? The bag could hold a half-million and change, just like Moe said. Charlie's thinking his share of five hundred large would be okay.

"We're splitting this fifty-fifty," Charlie says. "Like we said."

"That's right, buddy. Fifty-fifty, just like we said."

From the top of the wall, Charlie studies the back of the house. There's a pool with a flagstone surround, a hot tub, and a gazebo. French doors lead into the house.

No sign that anybody's home. And no dogs.

Sitting on top of the wall, they drag the ladder over to the other side and climb down.

The alarm will be connected to the phone system. Standing by the pool, Charlie looks around, trying to figure out where the telephone line comes in to the house. He mentally draws a line from the telephone pole to the side of the garage, the closest structure, and there it is. A four-inch length of black telephone cable snaking out of the ground and into the side of the garage. Charlie severs it using a pair of wire cutters.

He looks at Moe.

"We're good."

Charlie follows Moe around the pool to the French doors. Charlie glances at the lock, and then takes a torsion bar and a lock pick from his tool belt. Using his left hand he holds the torsion bar with his pinky, while he operates the pick with his thumb and index finger. With two good hands he would have the door unlocked in under twenty seconds. Today it takes a full minute.

Moe says, "It enriches my soul to watch a master at work."

Charlie turns the knob, pushes open the door.

No alarm sounds. No dog barks.

"This is almost too easy," Charlie says, his face feeling hot under his George W. Bush mask.

"Big Phil probably never imagined anybody would rob him."

Charlie nods. "There's a good reason for that," he mumbles.

They trot through the den, Moe leading, Charlie following. The blood is suddenly warmer in his veins, his senses more acute. It's the familiar adrenaline rush, fight-or-flight, and the exhilaration that accompanies every break in. But there's something else. A vague feeling of dread that he's felt only once before, when a job went horribly wrong.

But what can he can do now? He's inside.

They turn left into a paneled hallway, and then turn right into a large study. The room is lined with leather bound volumes, which Charlie figures nobody has ever opened. The furniture is dark and heavy looking. The wooden blinds are drawn and only a sliver of light peaks through.

Moe pulls back the corner of an oriental rug, revealing a large floor safe.

"What do we have here, Charlie?" he says.

He takes the key from his pocket, inserts it, and twists. The sound of sequential clicks of tumblers opening echoes. He turns the recessed lever clockwise and heaves the door open. Inside there are a number of computer discs.

"Where's the cash?" Charlie says.

Moe removes the computer discs and hands them to Charlie. A CD is labeled ADONIS FLYING PIZZA. Another CD has a label that reads ADONIS VENDING COMPANY. Another reads ADONIS DRY CLEANERS. Moe hands him more CDs: one for a restaurant, another for a night club, some more that Charlie doesn't even look at. Big Phil's companies. His legitimate ones. The businesses he uses to launder his dirty cash.

Another CD has nothing written on it, making Charlie wonder what's on it.

Moe holds up a large bank bag. It's a beige canvas sack with the words HOBOKEN BANK AND TRUST in red letters on the side. He dumps out the contents on the floor. Three large bundles of bank notes. Eyeballing the money, Charlie figures thirty grand at most. His share won't even pay off Goran.

"Where's the rest?" he says.

Moe looks in the bag. "That's all there is, Charlie. Big Phil must've taken the rest."

Charlie doesn't like the way Moe is throwing his name around, even if nobody else is present. A cardinal rule on any job is No Names.

Charlie looks around for something worth stealing and sees nothing.

"Let's get the hell out of here," he says. "Now. Before it gets any worse."

Moe stuffs the money in the duffel bag. Pointing at the CDs, he says, "We need to take those computer discs with us."

"What for?"

"We can use them. The government's looking for this stuff. The discs probably got all kinds of financial information on them. That's why he hid them here. It gives us leverage."

"Leverage for what?"

"Stop talking. We're getting the hell out of here and we're taking this stuff with us."

Ten minutes later, they've changed out of their overalls, and they're in the van, headed west. The bright afternoon sun is in Charlie's eyes, almost blinding him.

An abandoned Taco Grande is up ahead and Charlie turns into the right-hand lane. The plan is to ditch the van and the overalls behind the Taco Grande and complete their getaway in a stolen Toyota Corolla. There are still a million things that could go wrong.

A lot of risk for not much money.

"You tell Linda I was involved in this?" Charlie says, pulling into the restaurant's drive and past a faded sign advertising half-off coupons.

A hesitation. That means a lie is coming.

"No," Moe says. "Why should I? She didn't need to know."

"I've been thinking. Linda's the weak link in this operation. You need to talk with her. Big Phil's going to sweat her big-time. She needs to be prepared."

"She won't be a problem, believe me. She knows to keep her mouth shut."

Charlie drives around to the rear of the Taco Grande and pulls up next to the Toyota.

He shakes his head, thinking, I've made a big mistake.

"You're kidding yourself," Charlie says. "This has inside job written all over it. Somebody had to know where the money was. They're going to suspect her."

"I'm telling you. It's not a problem."

"And I'm telling you --"

Moe gives him a shit-eating grin.

"You got other things to worry about, man. You don't mind me saying."

Charlie hears a clicking noise. Moe has a snub nose .38 in his right hand. It's cocked and pointed at Charlie's belly.

"What the hell are you doing?" Charlie says.

"It's a set-up, Charlie and you're the patsy. Big Phil had to get rid of them computer discs. He couldn't just destroy 'em. He'd get charged with obstruction of justice, for sure. Now the feds think some burglars took them, so he's off the hook."

"Why the hell would the feds think that?"

"That house is bugged. They heard us talking. The FBI has us on tape. With you dead, that'll seal the deal. They'll figure we fought over the cash. And you having a record for burglary is icing on the cake." He giggles. "You always thought I was stupid. But you were really the stupid one."

"I never thought you were stupid, Moe," Charlie says with all the sincerity he can muster. "Now, put the gun away and we'll talk about this. You can keep all the money and the other stuff."

"Think about it, Charlie. You been punked. By dumb old Moe Baker of all people."

He points the gun at Charlie's head. Charlie raises his right arm as if to shield himself from the bullet. He squeezes the trigger of the Berretta hidden in the ace bandage. The recoil causes the pain from his broken hand to ratchet up his arm. A bright red, dime-sized hole, brown around the edges, blooms in the middle of Moe's forehead, and he slumps backward against the passenger door.

Charlie snatches the duffel bag and shoves the driver's door open. The third rule is the most important. Always have a backup plan.

Chapter Four

Assistant United States Attorney Russell "Rusty" Prescott pushes open the glass door and ambles into the conference room. He's wearing tan khakis with dirt smudges on the knees and a lime-colored Izod shirt that barely covers his paunch.

"What's this all about?" Prescott asks, slumping into a chair.

FBI Special Agent Mike De La Torre sits at the head of the table, surrounded by stacks of manila-colored files. He's wearing a custom-tailored charcoal gray suit, a dark blue Charvet tie, and a white twill shirt, heavy on the starch. The brilliant white shirt perfectly sets off his mocha-colored skin.

"You didn't take the time to get cleaned up, I see," De La Torre says.

"I was working in the yard. On my vacation. In the middle of the summer. After five. This better be damned important. And let me say up front, however. Nothing can be sufficiently important."

"It's about Phil Adonis."

Prescott's big slab of a face goes blank. Then a little muscle under his left eye twitches almost imperceptibly. This delicate tic first developed soon after Prescott was passed over for the office of US Attorney, which happened shortly after a four week trial in which Big Phil Adonis was acquitted of murder and racketeering charges. The trial featured an important witness turning up hacked to pieces and stuffed into a fifty-five gallon oil drum and two other witnesses recanting their testimony. According to the medical examiner the guy was still alive when he was cut up. De La Torre always figured the outcome of the guy in the drum influenced the thinking of the other two. Ever since that trial, anything related to Phil Adonis brought the twitch on.

"What about Adonis?" Prescott asks. "Is there a development at long last? Did we finally catch a break?"

De La Torre thinks for a moment.

"Development? Definitely yes. Break? Not exactly."

"You mind getting to the point?"

"Some thieves apparently broke into Adonis's house this afternoon."

"Somebody broke into Phil Adonis's house?" Prescott laughs. "That's funny. Not for them, I mean. But still funny. I guess they never heard of the Wonderland Murders. As a rule of thumb, it's never a good idea to break into a mob boss's house. But why should we care? It's a local police matter."

"They made off with some computer discs. Apparently, it's Adonis's financial information. He was keeping it in a safe in his house."

"Is that the stuff we been looking for?"

"The info that accountant Lisk downloaded. Sounds like it. Apparently it ended up in Big Phil's safe."

"Who was in the van?"

"Wally and Frank."

"What were Wally and Frank doing as this burglary went down?"

"What could they do? They listened and recorded. You want them to call the police and let everybody know we have the Adonis mansion bugged?"

Prescott stares at the floor.

"I suppose not."

De La Torre nods. Prescott's father is the managing partner at one of the largest law firms on Wall Street. Now, his son makes eighty grand a year as an assistant US attorney, a job his father obtained for him. That is called regression toward the mean.

"The timing is interesting," Prescott says. "Tomorrow morning we were getting a search warrant signed by Judge Ellis for Adonis's house. We would've been tossing the place by noon. And whatever was there would've been in our possession. And now it's been stolen."

He makes finger quotes just in case De La Torre missed his point.

De La Torre says, "Makes you think doesn't it?"

"So we have this fortuitously timed break-in," Prescott says. "And now all of Adonis's financial information has gone missing."

"I smell a rat. Somebody sold us out. It's the only explanation."

"Jesus, this isn't the first time--somebody had to tell Phil Adonis that Lisk was an informant. But who is the leak? Could be somebody on the judge's staff. Somebody in the clerk's office. Or even somebody in the Bureau." Prescott pauses. "Or it could just be a coincidence."

"I don't believe in coincidences. And, by the way, you left out the Justice Department. It could be somebody in your shop. It took forever to get that damned affidavit from your guy on the inside to support the search warrant. I don't think it was even necessary. We could've moved on this a week ago."

Prescott grimaces. He doesn't like having the integrity of his department called into question.

"That's above your pay grade," Prescott says. "Leave that kind of thinking to the law school graduates."

That one stings. Prescott must've heard the story about how De La Torre was set to start Columbia Law School when his mother died, leaving him as his family's sole provider and forcing him to forgo law school.

"If we move quickly maybe we can recover this stuff," Prescott says. "What do we know about these thieves?"

"Nothing, except one is named Charlie."

"That's it? Has Adonis reported it?"

"Not yet."

"What if Adonis doesn't call it in?" Prescott asks.

"He will. That was the whole point of staging this break in, right?"

"So we have two losers running around with some CDs with a bunch of accounting information that could be very valuable to us. And to Phil Adonis."

"That's about the size of it."

"These discs are probably back in Adonis's hands by now," Prescott says, a tinge of bitterness in his voice. "They're hidden away somewhere. Or, worse yet, destroyed. We'll never find them. And he'll be able to credibly deny there was anything incriminating on them."

"I don't know about that. One of the burglars talked about using them for leverage. Maybe they're thinking of going off the reservation."

"Leverage? Do these guys have any idea what Phil Adonis will do to get these discs back? They'll leverage themselves into early graves if they try to screw with Phil Adonis. Jesus, they may just throw the stuff away. Then we'd have a real problem. There goes the whole case against Adonis. Eight years down the drain. And we were so close this time."

"You do realize this is going to be a big problem for us, right?"

"Of course. It means we've wasted eight years."

De La Torre shakes his head.

"I don't mean that," he says. "This is going to make a big stink. There will be investigations right and left. The Inspector General's Office will be up our ass so bad it'll feel like a proctologic exam."

The twitch under Prescott's eye has turned into a quiver.

"You're right," he says. "I hadn't thought about that. They're still bugging me about what happened to Lisk and that was three weeks ago. They keep reminding me. It's not every day you're able to turn a mob accountant and we lost him. Now this. It'll definitely be a problem."

"They're going to have to find somebody at fault, otherwise they won't have done their job right. There will be a scapegoat for all this. Rest assured."

"What do you think we should do?"

"What about your guy inside the Adonis family? Get in touch with him. Maybe he knows something that'll help."

"It's not as easy as that. I can't just call him up. Our asset is very skittish. For good reason--when you think about what happened to Lisk. Our meetings have to be set up well in advance."

"Maybe now's a good time to bend the rules a little."

"I can't. There must be something else we can do."

"I'll contact local law enforcement," De La Torre says. "See if they can give us any leads on this guy named Charlie. If we can get ahold of that information quickly, it'll be no harm, no foul. We'll be in the clear. Hell, we'll look like heroes."

"Might just be a wild goose chase," Prescott says gloomily. "Probably any number of thieves named Charlie out there."

"It's a place to start."

Chapter Five

Jerry O'Brien waddles across the street toward Luigi's, glancing at the sign above the window with disgust. God, he hates Italian food. His father was Irish, but his mother was Italian—Sicilian, even. And Italian food was all he ate growing up. Linguini. Ravioli. Spaghetti, of course. Gallons of spaghetti. Pasta. And more pasta. And even more pasta. He trembles at the memory of it.

He eases his bulk inside the narrow doorway and without hesitation Luigi, himself, comes over to greet him. He grins and bows and shakes O'Brien's hand until O'Brien thinks it'll fall off. He's not surprised. This is the sort of respect the lawyer for the Adonis crime family expects from the older generation of dagoes. That generation still respects the Cosa Nostra, what remains of it. And they know how to keep their mouths shut. O'Brien is standing on the very spot where Sammy "Big Chicken" Graziano was gunned down by Big Phil Adonis in 1963--except back then the place was called Sal's. Two shots in the back of the head as Sammy walked toward the door after a meal of eggplant parm. The picture of Graziano lying face down in a pool of blood was in every major paper around the world. Pravda had it on the front page, calling it evidence of America's criminal-capitalist culture.

The shooting occurred in front of a half-dozen witnesses, but Big Phil was never prosecuted. Nobody saw nothing--not even an eighteen-year-old Luigi who was standing in the doorway--so what were the cops to do? Big Phil had made his bones with the Graziano hit.

The good old days. 1963. Sam Giancana. Salvatore Trafficante. Carlos Marcello. Back then, not even the president could afford to get on the wrong side of the Cosa Nostra.

It's hard to believe how far the mob has fallen.

O'Brien blames modern society. Porn used to be a big business. Now you can get it online for free. There was a time when the mob made a fortune off the numbers racket but now the government does it, except they call it the lottery. Casino gambling is everywhere, much of it run by the red Indians, of all people. In the old days there were clear lines between what was legal and what was illegal, between what was moral and immoral. Now there are no boundaries, so it's harder to make a crooked buck.

O'Brien and Luigi wind their way through the restaurant to the back room. O'Brien takes his customary seat in a booth in the rear, where he can see both the back door and, through the tinted windows, the front door. The back room is dark and the dining room is well lit, so he can see out but people in the dining room can't see in. He surveys the crowd, looking for anybody who doesn't belong. But it's just a bunch of young yuppies. The kind of people who don't mind paying thirty bucks for a veal scaloppini and some pasta.

"I'm expecting one guest," he says to Luigi. "He'll probably come through the back, as he usually does. Is it unlocked for him?"

"Of course."

"And I don't want to be disturbed."

Luigi backs away nodding and bowing. O'Brien half expects him to tug at his forelock.

O'Brien flips through the menu. What he really wants is a two-inch thick porterhouse, creamed spinach, and a baked potato with all the trimmings on the side. A tasty Pinot Noir to wash it all down. Maybe some bread pudding with whiskey sauce for desert. O'Brien's great-great-grandfather had come to America to escape the Potato Famine. He supposes that somewhere in his genetic makeup there is an insatiable desire to stay well-fed, just in case another famine comes along.

A noise and the back door swings open. Mike De La Torre slips into the room, quietly closing the door behind him. He sits opposite O'Brien.

"Busy day," De La Torre says aggressively. "Real busy. Kind of surprising. The middle of the summer and all. I thought everybody would be taking it easy. Instead I hear about a mysterious break-in at Big Phil's house."

"You know what they say. No rest for the wicked."

"I would've appreciated a head's up."

"This was Little Phil's plan. He didn't see any reason to include you in the loop."

De La Torre pauses. He's never liked being put in his place.

"So, is everything taken care of?" De La Torre asks.

"No, not exactly."

"What does that mean?"

"Two guys were involved. One was a sap, a guy with a history of breaking and entering. The plan was the sap would get terminated. Make it look more like a real robbery, only a robbery that went bad when it came time to split the loot."

"Makes sense."

O'Brien puts the menu down.

"An hour ago the local PD found the getaway vehicle with a dead guy in it," he says.

"So, everything went according to plan."

"Not really. The dead guy wasn't the sap."

"He was dead, wasn't he?"

"Okay, he was a sap. But he wasn't the sap."

"You mean the guy who was supposed to be the sap killed the guy who wasn't supposed to be a sap."

"That's about the shape of it. Things didn't go entirely as planned."

"So who is this guy? The one that's still alive."

O'Brien sighs. "It's a guy who Moe Baker found to take the fall. I'm not telling you anything more than that because you don't need to know. You just concentrate on the Moe Baker end and leave this guy to us."

"Who is Moe Baker?"

"The guy who ended up dead."

"The guy who ended up being the sap."

"Pretty much."

"And now this other guy has got all this information. Payroll accounts, receivables, payables, everything. All that stuff that doesn't jibe with what you've been telling the IRS all these years."

"It's worse than that, in fact. Much worse."

"How do you know that?"

O'Brien looks up at the ceiling.

"From what I understand, we obtained the information about what's on one of the discs somewhere around hour two of Lisk's session with Little Phil. Toward the end, somewhere after the electric drill and before the blow torch. Lisk apparently thought that telling Little Phil about the discs and where they were hidden would end the pain."

"Did it?"

O'Brien shakes his head slowly. "Just pissed Little Phil off even more. That's what I understand. This is all rank hearsay, I don't know it of personal knowledge."

"So what's on this disc that is so important?"

O'Brien checks his watch. "I could tell you. But then I'd have to kill you."

"Ha-ha."

O'Brien lets his face go blank.

"Let's put it this way," he says leaning forward. "It wouldn't be good for you if the authorities get their hands on that one particular disc."

De La Torre stares, obviously processing this information.

"Do you have anything to go on?" he says. "You want me to put out feelers for this guy?"

"No. We'll take care of that. What we want you to do is to slow play any investigation into this break-in and the death of Moe Baker. Give us time to find this guy before the authorities figure out who he is."

"A burglary investigation. That's not going to be our jurisdiction. That'll be the locals."

"You can talk to them. Tell them the FBI is interested. You know, Phil Adonis, the organized crime angle. Tell them you want to be involved. Throw a few roadblocks if it looks like they're getting anywhere. We're only talking a day or two."

"Don't you have a guy in local PD who can take care of that?"

"Don't ask stupid questions."

De La Torre nods.

"Anything you find out, and I mean anything, you let me know. Immediately. After all, that's what we pay you for."

There is an awkward silence.

"While we're at it," O'Brien asks, "any information on who our rat might be?"

"No, I'm not in that loop, either. But I tried to push Prescott into contacting him, whoever this rat may be. Told Prescott we needed all the information we could get related to this break-in. So you may want to keep an eye on your boys. See if any of them start sneaking out to take mysterious phone calls."

"That's a lot easier said than done. The Adonis family is still a large organization."

"Let me tell you, all this talk about a rat has me concerned."

"You don't have to be worried. There are only three people who know that you work for us. Big Phil. Little Phil. And me. I know that none of us are working for the Justice Department. And if you're so concerned about this rat, maybe you should be doing more to find out who he is."

"You know this phony break-in may create a lot of trouble for me," De La Torre says.

O'Brien says nothing.

"We're looking at a major internal investigation," De La Torre continues. "First Lisk and now this. I don't know how we dodged the bullet on Lisk."

"And this is my problem--how exactly? I mean, you're not going to be telling anybody about our relationship, right?"

De La Torre's jaw clenches, then releases.

"So, I guess I'm out of here then," De La Torre says. "On the way over, I phoned in an order for three extra-large pizzas and a dozen cannoli. The order should be ready."

"Enjoy."

De La Torre opens the door to the main room of the restaurant, sticks his head out. Looks around. Steps though the doorway, closing the door behind him. He moves with grace and fluidity. O'Brien wonders what it must be like to be that slender and athletic. He was always the slow fat kid. Always the last chosen at stickball or basketball, if chosen at all. The butt of many unkind jokes.

O'Brien waits, giving De La Torre time to pay for his order. De La Torre is laughing with Luigi, as if he doesn't have a problem in the world. De La Torre is typical of the younger generation. No shame. Betraying his country in exchange for a lousy eight grand a month paid into a Bahamas bank account, and it doesn't bother him in the least. No sleepless nights. No second thoughts. O'Brien can tell. He's bought plenty of cops. He knows when a cop is comfortable in his corruption. De La Torre has rationalized his immorality. He's told himself it's the best thing for his family. That everybody does it. If he doesn't do it, somebody else would. Crap like that.

O'Brien's father was a corrupt cop, crooked to the bone. But he spent every day hating himself for his sinfulness, sure that his moral trespasses had consigned his immortal soul to everlasting hell. Things were different when O'Brien was a kid. There was no win-win. Everything came at a cost. People did wrong and suffered for it. The best you could hope was to come out even in the end. Things were better then.

But De La Torre is useful. He told them about the bug in Big Phil's house, and about Lisk, and about many other things over the years. What would've happened if Lisk got his information to the feds? It would've been the end of everything. The end of Jerry O'Brien, for sure.

The situation is still precarious with this guy running around with the information. There are a lot of moving parts to this puzzle and they all have jagged edges. Just thinking about it depresses O'Brien. But he knows what to do when he's depressed. He leaves the restaurant and gets in his Cadillac SUV and points it toward his favorite steak house.

Chapter Six

Phil Adonis, Jr., a small, impeccably dressed man, with jet black hair, graying at the temples, stands just inside the front door of the Pink Pussycat Lounge, letting his eyes get accustomed to the dark. A gorgeous brunette is on the main stage, wearily gyrating to Led Zeppelin. She's wearing only a black G-string. Strobe lights alternated red, white, and blue. A bunch of guys, probably a bachelor's party, surround the stage. They're hooting, hollering, waving dollar bills in the air, and pushing each other in an attempt to close to the dancer.

A scene straight out of hell.

A bouncer hurries over.

"Mister Adonis, something I can do for you today?"

"Where's Marco?"

"In the VIP room."

Phil nods, almost imperceptibly. "I'll go get him."

"He's not alone."

"I understand."

Phil points at the dancer. "And Marco and I will want to speak with Linda as soon as she gets off the stage."

"She's got some customers lined up. Upstairs, you know. Some real big spenders."

"So?"

"They're some of our best customers. Guys who drop a couple of grand a week in here."

Phil doesn't say anything. He just contemplates the bouncer. The bouncer looks puzzled and checks his fly. Phil cocks his head to the side, like a lizard aroused by a curious sound, and the bouncer nods his head vigorously.

"Y-Yes, sir, Mr. Adonis. I do understand. Where do you want to see her?"

"The dressing room will be fine."

The VIP room is up a staircase that is next to the men's room. Upstairs, he pushes open the door, expecting to see Marco, but the room is empty. Then a desperate gasping noise comes from behind another door. He pushes open the door, which leads to a little room, the size of an office cubicle. Marco, a steroidal-enhanced hulk of a man in a tight black T-shirt and black jeans, is seated on a high-backed chair that is shaped like a throne. A little blonde, dressed only in a pink G-string, is on her knees in front of him, her head bobbing up and down. Phil watches. Both participants are so engrossed, they don't even know he's there. It's not the woman he's interested in but Marco, his head thrown back, his massive hands clutching the sides of the woman's head. Phil's breathing quickens. His knees weaken.

"Come on, Marco," Phil says, his voice hoarse. "Playtime is over. We've got work to do."

"Almost finished . . . here," Marco says.

Phil steps forward, gives the blonde a sharp shove with the heel of his boot and with a shriek she stops what she's doing.

"Now."

Phil strides out of the room, closing the door behind him.

Fornication. It's a sin of the flesh that clouds the mind and causes poor decision making. Later, he'll have a discussion with Marco, although he doesn't think it'll do any good. This is a man who has the names of his children tattooed on his right bicep. Four children. By four different women who were located in four different states. None of whom Marco bothered to marry.

Marco asked for the manager's job at the Pink Pussycat, even though there were higher earning jobs available to him. Jobs that demanded respect. But he wanted the bar for the sex. Phil shakes his head just thinking about it.

Linda has been replaced by a light-skinned Hispanic on the center stage. Phil makes his way to the dressing room through an entrance behind the stage. The dressing room is the size of a racquet ball court with lockers in the middle. The walls are covered with mirrors.

Linda stands next to a locker, still dressed only in a black G-string. A faint sheen of perspiration glistens on her breasts. She looks up, sees where he's looking, and smiles.

"Freddy said you wanted to talk with me," she says. "He seemed upset."

Phil spies another dancer in the back of the dressing room, gazing at herself in the mirror.

"You," he says, jabbing a finger at the dancer and then at the door. "Get the hell out."

The girl squints. She must need corrective lenses and is too vain to wear them, even in the dressing room. Then she realizes who is yelling at her, and she rushes out the door, clutching her clothes to her chest, her butt cheeks wobbling.

"I've got some bad news for you," Phil says. "It's about Moe."

"Jesus, what happened? Did he get busted again? The next rap could be a long stretch, with his record."

"No, he hasn't been arrested. He's dead."

Her hands fly up to her mouth.

"Oh, my God. What happened?"

He thought about how he should handle this. There's no telling how much she knows. Best to be cautious, keep it simple, keep it direct. Don't give anything away.

"He was doing a job. He had somebody with him. We think the other guy killed him."

A look creeps into her eyes. Phil's seen it before. It means she's working the angles. It means she's thinking. Always a tricky proposition for a stripper.

"We're looking for the other guy," he says. "I thought you might know who he is."

"Why are you looking for him? Can't the cops handle it?"

Phil gives her the granite stare. He's practiced it many times in his bathroom mirror.

"Don't you know who the guy is?" she says, a little uncertain.

"No, I don't know. How the hell would I know? I turned this over to Moe to handle."

"I thought it was your plan. To get that stuff out of Phil's safe and get rid of it. That's what Moe said."

A moment of silence as Phil tries to contain his rage. Moe always had a big mouth and he talked to this stripper, who also has a big mouth. This can't be anything but bad.

"The plan was Moe's," he says slowly, as if he were talking to a retard. "And he shouldn't have told you about it."

She shrugs, turns away from him, and takes a pack of cigarettes from her locker. The rage surges through him again like a liquid inferno. She knows she can get away with this shit because she is Big Phil Adonis's current comare. One in a long string dating back fifty years. He remembers being introduced to "Aunt Jane" when he was six. She was blonde-haired and blue-eyed and didn't resemble any of his other aunts, but it wasn't until a couple of years later that he realized who she was.

You'd think his father would know better by now. Nothing more sickening than an old man chasing after a much younger woman. Phil blames Viagra. At his father's age, you don't have enough blood flow for sex. You send too much one place, you don't have enough for other places where it's needed, like your brain.

He's trying to get his temper under control when she lights a cigarette and blows a perfect smoke ring, and then bends over as she shimmies out of her G-string.

He slams his fist hard into a mirror. The mirror shatters and several large shards fall to the floor. Blood seeps from a half-dozen small wounds on his knuckles.

"Look at me when I'm talking to you!" he screams. "This is important. I'm not doing this for my health!"

She steps backward, her hands covering her face.

"Now that I have your undivided attention," he says, panting. "Maybe you would kindly answer some questions for me."

The door opens and Marco wanders in, a satisfied look on his face. His massive bulk fills the entire doorway.

"What's going on?" he says, looking at the broken glass on the floor, and then at Linda.

"Linda and I are having a little conversation here," Phil says. "I think we're beginning to come to an understanding."

Linda starts to slip on a red G-string.

"No!" Phil screams. "I want you naked when I speak to you."

Her face reddens, a tear rolls down her cheek.

"W-What do you want to know?" she asks.

"Who was the other guy?" Phil asks. "The guy with Moe."

"A guy named Charlie McCoy," she says.

"Good. Now we're getting somewhere. Do you know how one might locate this Charlie McCoy?"

"I don't have a clue. Really."

Phil bends over, picks up a large shard of glass, and walks toward her. He holds the piece of glass next to her left eye.

"I don't know where he is," she says breathlessly. "Why would I lie?"

"Beats me. I don't know why you would lie to me. Doesn't seem like a good idea at all. Maybe you got something going on with this Charlie McCoy. That would explain a lot of things."

"I don't. I wouldn't."

"I don't like you, Linda. I don't need much of a reason to cut you. Then what would you do? Not much demand for a whore with a cut up face. Maybe you could give blow jobs over on the docks for ten bucks a throw. In the dark, so the customers wouldn't have to see your face because it would make them sick."

She waves her hands, as if signaling him to be quiet. She's afraid, of course. Phil knows this but doesn't quite understand it because he has never been afraid. Never. When he was a child, he wasn't even afraid of his father, who beat him frequently and severely.

"Or maybe I'll just cut your pretty eyes out," Phil continues. "We'll call you blind Linda. How does that sound?"

"I-I know how you can find Charlie McCoy," she says. "He owes Goran Ivanov a lot of money. Goran broke Charlie's hand because he didn't pay him back. Goran would know where he is. Right?"

Phil scratches his head, looks at Marco. It's not exactly the information that Phil's looking for but it's close.

"Goran Ivanov," Phil says. "He's the guy that owns that club."

"Happy Dayz," Marco says.

Linda nods, tears in her eyes.

"Okay," Phil says, his voice calm. "It's a start. Linda, you gonna take care of the arrangements?"

"Arrangements?"

"For Moe's funeral."

She pauses. Her eyes glaze over, as if she's trying to remember who Moe was.

"I guess so. If I have to, I mean. He's got a brother in New York. Maybe he can handle it."

Phil drops the piece of glass and pulls out of his pocket a wad of bank notes the size of a softball.

"Here's about six grand," he says, shoving the bills into her hand. "Call Testa's funeral home. Make the arrangements. Get it taken care of. Tell them to make it real nice. When they need more money, have them to call me." He pauses. "You know what to say if the cops ask you about Moe."

"I don't know nothing."

He pats her on the cheek. "Good girl."

Chapter Seven

Charlie drives around the block twice and doesn't spot any strange cars or guys standing around on the sidewalk or anything else out of the usual. He parks his truck down the street and, carrying Moe's duffel in his good hand, comes in the back way by hopping a short wall, crossing through a backyard, and going up the fire escape.

He dumped the stolen Toyota a couple of blocks from where he he'd left his truck. As he walked away, he heard somebody shouting at him, a woman. But he didn't stop. He wanted to put as much distance between himself and that Toyota as possible.

Something's bothering him. He's forgotten something, but he doesn't know what. He has so much on his mind he can't even think straight and that's dangerous. That's how you make mistakes.

He unlocks the deadbolt on the back door that leads into his kitchen. Before opening the door, he examines the lock, looking for tell-tale scratches that would tell him it was tampered with. It looks okay. He pushes the door open. Here's where he finds out whether Big Phil Adonis has identified him as a person of interest. He stands in the doorway, listening. There's nothing. Treading gently though the small kitchen, the Beretta still in his right hand, hidden under the ace bandage, he thinks about what he'll do if he finds a couple of Big Phil's knuckle crushers in the living room. He softly curses himself for not taking Moe's little revolver. Two little guns would be better than one.

But the living room is empty, not a knuckle crusher in sight. He checks the locks on the front door--they're solid. The Adonis family must not know he was involved. Not yet, anyway. But if--when--they find out, they'll be after him. There's something important on those discs, he's sure of it. Why else go to all this effort to set up a phony burglary? These discs are important. They're all he has.

And they'll know who he is as soon as they speak with Linda.

He needs to get away. Far away.

He shoves some underwear, socks, and blue jeans into an overnight bag and places it on the floor next to Moe's duffel bag. Where to go? A place where he can't be found. Thirty grand will be enough to get him there, but what happens when the money runs out?

He'll worry about that when the time comes.

He looks around. He's sure he's forgetting something. What else do I need?

Then, a sound. Footsteps are coming up the stairs. Sounds like more than one person. Crap. He needs to go. Now.

He's half-way to the kitchen when a loud knocking comes at the front door. Dammit! How did they find him so quickly? He grabs the bag and walks backward toward the kitchen, holding the gun out and pointed toward the front door.

"I know you're in there, Charlie. Now open up."

A woman's voice. It's his ex-wife, Carol. What's she doing here?

Then he remembers.

"You can't fool me by parking down the street," she says, her voice strident. "I know all your little tricks. Open up."

He opens the front door. Carol is standing there with Amy, their thirteen-year-old daughter.

"This is the week," Carol says pushing Amy toward him. "Remember? I told you."

Charlie backs away.

"Honestly, I forgot all about it," he says. "I'm sorry."

"One week every summer. Don't say it's not, just because you've never used it before."

"This is kind of a short notice. I have a lot going on right now. It's not the best time."

"I would've called you on your cell phone. But you don't have one. Of course."

"I'm sorry about that, but--"

Carol gives Amy another shove in his direction.

"Amy's staying with you for the next four days. There's no alternative. I can't afford a sitter for that long and all of Amy's friends will be out of town for the Fourth, so she can't stay with them. Four lousy days. It's the least you can do for your daughter."

"I--"

"I'll pick her up Saturday afternoon, so she and I can go to church Sunday morning."

She says the last words with a smirk, as if attending church makes her something special.

"This really isn't a good time, Carol."

"You said that already. It never is a good time for your daughter, is it?"

He glances at Amy, who is hugging a teddy bear to her chest. Isn't she kind of old for a teddy bear? Her little mouth is turned down in a scowl and she's staring at the wall in front of her.

"I mean this really isn't a good time," he says. "I've got a lot of things going on. It's kind of complicated. I can't have a kid hanging around right now."

"Too bad. I've been looking forward to this week. I have plans. And by the way, you owe me three-fifty for this month's child support, as agreed."

She holds her hand out, palm up. It's a gesture he remembers from their marriage. She's hoping he'll have nothing on him and that will make him look bad in front of Amy. He'll be a deadbeat dad, just as she has undoubtedly told Amy all those times over the years.

He feels like telling her he doesn't legally owe her child support, not anymore, but he isn't going to say that in front of Amy. And given that a couple of mobsters might show up at any moment, this isn't the time to get in an extended argument right here in the hallway.

He needs to get rid of Carol.

He jams his hand in his jeans and triumphantly pulls out four one-hundred dollar bills and drops them into her hand. For a moment she looks surprised. She starts to say something but decides not to. She hurriedly tucks the bills down the front of her blouse.

"Keep the change," he says.

"Have her ready by two on Saturday."

She leans over, kisses Amy on the cheek.

"You be good, sweetie. Are you going to miss mommy?'

Amy nods.

"Mommy's sure going to miss you sweetie. Take care of yourself."

Carol turns and strides off in the direction of the stairs.

Charlie glances down at Amy, who looks small and alone. He must make one last appeal to Carol before he's saddled with Amy. But what does he say? You can't leave Amy with me because the mob's looking for me?

Carol would really enjoy hearing that.

He'll just take Amy back to her mother's house later this evening, in a couple of hours. Maybe Carol won't be there and he can just drop Amy off and then beat feet.

Inside his apartment, Charlie finishes stuffing his toiletries in his overnight bag. Amy gazes around at the apartment. She's small for her age and willowy and has pale blond hair like her mother. She has a neon-yellow backpack in her left hand, and a tan purse over her shoulder, and in her right hand is a small red-and-green plaid suitcase. The teddy bear is under her arm. The bear is wearing a coat and boots and a hat.

She puts everything on the kitchen table.

"I need to go to the restroom," she announces.

Charlie realizes she's never been here before. He points to the bedroom.

"It's through there."

He examines the teddy bear. On the coat is a pre-printed tag with lettering that reads PLEASE LOOK AFTER THIS BEAR THANK YOU.

Cute. He turns over the tag. Amy's name and address are written on the back in a childish scrawl. He tosses the teddy bear on the sofa.

He checks his watch. He can't just take off. What if she's here and the mobsters show up? But he can't wait much longer, either.

He takes another look out the window and sees nothing out of the ordinary.

The toilet flushes and a few seconds later she appears.

"Dad, are you going somewhere?" she asks.

He thinks for a moment.

"Yeah, I am. But not just me. Both of us. We're going to the Shore. How about that? The beach. The ocean. It'll be an adventure."

"I didn't bring a bathing suit."

"We'll get you one. Maybe two."

He pulls the blinds up, glances out the window, and sees nobody. He turns. Amy's staring at him. She's smart enough to know that something is wrong. He can see it in her eyes.

He slings his overnight bag over his shoulder and picks up the duffel bag in his good hand.

"Are you taking all that stuff?" she says.

"Yeah. I've got a lot of work to do."

"At the beach?'

"Among other places."

Chapter Eight

De La Torre jabs a finger into the elevator call button so hard that he feels the pain radiate into his wrist. A meeting with O'Brien will do that. O'Brien always acts like he owns him, talking down to like he does.

Worst thing is, he does own him. Lock, stock, and barrel. The thought makes De La Torre even angrier.

He's going to see the one person he can talk to at a time like this--his brother, Malcolm. He takes the elevator to the third floor and turns right. He gives Lenore and Wendy at the nurses' station a wave as he walks by. They give him big smiles. He tipped them each a grand at Christmas.

His brother's where he's been for the last fifteen years--room 312b, the last room on the right. Malcolm's bed is in the middle of the small room. The room is darkened. The cardiac monitor--registering the last vestiges of life that remain in Malcolm's body--and the IV pump, which supplies his nutrition--provide the only light. De La Torre drags a chair over next to the bed and sits.

Malcolm's eyes are open, he's awake. He has sleeping and waking cycles just like anybody else. But if De La Torre were to speak to him, he wouldn't hear a word.

Malcolm was a senior at Fordham studying biomechanical engineering and living in a public housing hellhole in the South Bronx because it was all he could afford--even with the money he received occasionally from his brother. He came home late one night to find two guys camped out in the north stairwell. They were waiting for a small-time dealer named Tavaris Washington, who owed them some dough. They mistook Malcolm for this dude Tavaris, put a bullet in Malcolm's head, and took off.

It took De La Torre two weeks to find them and get even.

But that did nothing for Malcolm. The surgeons saved his life. But the intracranial swelling had destroyed a large part of his brain that controlled higher functions, leaving only the lower brain stem intact and functioning. He's been in a permanent vegetative state ever since.

The eerie thing is that he looks almost normal. He blinks his eyes and he breathes normally and without the aid of a machine. Sometimes his arms or legs move, although De La Torre understands this is involuntary--at least that's what he's been told by the doctors. He even saw Malcolm smile once. De La Torre half expects Malcolm to just sit up one day and ask, in one of those funny voices he always did, where he is and what he's doing here.

But that's not going to happen.

He wonders what it's like in there for Malcolm. Is it a permanent darkness? Is it like a never ending dream? Is he aware of time passing? Does he re-live that last moment before he was shot over and over again, in a never ending loop? De La Torre sometimes thinks that Malcolm might be better off dead, but he knows that kind of thinking is wrong. There's nothing more important than life.

De La Torre often talks to Malcolm about when they were kids. Christmas. Trips to the park or the movies. Sometimes he talks about their mother. Or about how Malcolm used to copy him. He copied Mike's clothes, copied his walk, and copied his jump shot. All Malcolm ever wanted to do was be like Mike.

Talking with Malcolm helps him work out his problems. And the nurses said the talking might be good for Malcolm. External stimuli, they call it. Patients had been known to recover from vegetative states. And having people talk to them might help with the recovery. Nobody knows.

And he prefers talking to Malcolm than to anybody else, including his wife. Malcolm never interrupts or argues with him or belittles him.

It was a win-win, in a sad way.

De La Torre tells Malcolm about his meeting with O'Brien. O'Brien seemed different than usual, less sure of himself. Something has Big Jerry rattled. And that concerns De La Torre.

"There's something going on here," De La Torre says. "That's for sure. And I need to figure out what it is."

He sits silently, thinking. Even after the charity price break he receives from the Holy Sisters of the Incarnate Word, the hospital care costs him three grand a month. He doesn't mind paying it because Malcolm's family, and as his mother always said, "You don't have family, you don't have nothing."

And Malcolm's all the family he has, other than his wife and daughter that is.

But it makes him think, what if he were not around to pay that monthly bill?

It would be the end of Malcolm, that's for sure.

***

It's a half-hour later when De La Torre pushes open the front door to his house, a fully renovated Colonial on an acre. A Mercedes sedan and a BMW SUV are parked by the curb. The sleepover must already be in full swing.

De La Torre's father was a Puerto Rican who, after getting his mother pregnant for the second time, disappeared. He went out for a pack of smokes one night and never came home. De La Torre was five at the time.

When De La Torre was ten he found out that his name meant "from the tower" and was a name associated with the aristocracy in Spain. He liked that. It made him feel special. He imagined himself as a medieval knight in armor who slew dragons and had a castle with a moat.

Now this is his castle.

He steps into the kitchen carrying the three boxes of extra-large pizzas and the two smaller boxes of cannoli. His wife, Cynthia, is in the kitchen with two other women, one blonde and one brunette. He can't remember their names. They're both married to guys who work in finance, and their daughters go to the same private school as De La Torre's.

He gives Cynthia a hug, smells alcohol on her breath. A half-full bottle of white wine is on the counter. An empty bottle is next to it.

"So Liz Cheng is on my blacklist from now on," Cynthia says, a little too loudly.

"I'm sure she'll come to regret that," the brunette says.

"That's for sure. Always talking about how her husband's this big-shot heart surgeon. I tell her that's nothing compared to a husband who is head of the Organized Crime unit of the FBI."

She gives De La Torre a squeeze on the arm.

"Only in this state," he says.

"But that'll change." She nods to the two women. "We'll be in DC soon enough."

De La Torre smiles. Washington is her dream. It's where her father is a federal judge and where she went to school and grew up and went to college. Before she got swept up and taken away to New Jersey by a tall, slender, good looking man in an expensive suit, that is. She'll never be satisfied until he's working at FBI headquarters. Hell, she won't be satisfied until he's sitting in the director's chair.

But his dream is to work his way up to an assistant director's position, and then leave for a cushy six-figure job in the private sector. He can see himself in a large corner office with his name on the door, taking consulting gigs for Fortune 500 companies at $600 an hour. The problem is that he needs three more promotions before he'll be an assistant director and time is running out.

"Where have you been?" Cynthia asks. "You're home late. I expected you two hours ago."

De La Torre doesn't mention Malcolm. Once, when Cynthia had been drinking, she said some things about Malcolm and the cost of his medical care. Ever since, De La Torre has stayed away from that subject.

He gives Cynthia a peck on the cheek.

"You know what they say," he says. "No rest for the wicked."

"Were you busy catching bad guys?" the brunette asks, a twinkle in her eye.

"Ma'am, I'm always busy catching bad guys."

She leans over the island, exposing some cleavage.

"Sounds fascinating. What can you tell us?"

She says this with a grin. She flirted with him hot and heavy at the school gala a couple of months ago, even going so far as to caress his arm while waiting in line at the bar. Then he remembers. Her name is Sandy.

"I can't tell you much, Sandy." He winks. "It's top secret."

"Is there much organized crime left now?" the blonde says. "I mean other than on TV. I thought the Mafia was put out of business long ago. All those informers."

De La Torre says, "La Cosa Nostra, as we call them, are still there, especially in this part of the country. And there are other crime cartels as well. The Russian Mafia. The Latin American drug cartels. The Asian Triads. It's truly global now. A lot of cybercrime. Identity theft. Credit card fraud. That sort of thing."

Cynthia says, "Don't let him fool you. There's a lot of old fashioned organized crime. Mike's been chasing after the Adonis family for years."

"There's an Adonis girl in the kindergarten class," the blonde says. "I thought they were in the garbage business."

De La Torre chuckles.

"That's one of the fronts they use to launder cash from their illegal enterprises."

He flashes a broad smile.

Sandy, the brunette, says, "Do you even have to carry a gun anymore?"

"I surely do."

De La Torre pulls back his jacket, exposing the Glock 23 on his right hip.

Sandy says, "Cynthia, aren't you scared for your family? I mean, the Mafia might seek retribution for something Mike does to them."

De La Torre gives Cynthia a hug.

"That's nothing to worry about. No way do they go after the family of a law enforcement officer. They know better than to do that." He steps toward the family room and flashes a big smile. "Now, if you'll excuse me, ladies, I'm going upstairs to get changed."

He trots up the well-lighted staircase with the photographs of his wife's family lining the walls. He passes his ten-year-old daughter's room and hears giggles. His perfect little girl's first sleepover. It makes him feel good to think about it.

You don't have family, you don't have nothing.

He knocks on the door.

"There's pizza downstairs," he says. "And cannoli."

Squeals of delight come from inside behind the door. Pizza! Cannoli!

They'd want to use the pool later. Maybe he should check the water for bacteria again. He shakes his head. That's just silly. He checked before he went to work, just twelve hours ago.

He likes the idea of his daughter's friends coming to visit. It seems so . . . so normal and healthy. So different than his own childhood. He grew up in a rat infested tenement with a single mother, who worked two, sometimes three jobs to keep food on the table. He parlayed his all-state quarterback skills into a scholarship to Rutgers, where he majored in criminal justice. To the surprise of everybody, including himself, he became a straight-A student and the dean let him know there was a scholarship waiting for him at Columbia Law School.

It was a couple of days after that conversation that his mother suffered a stroke while cleaning a white family's bathroom. They found her face down in the toilet bowl, scrub brush still in hand. Suddenly he had a little brother to support and law school was out of the question. Six months later he was a Newark PD rookie driving a patrol car.

Something is still nagging at him. Something he needs to be worried about. He can't figure out what it is, but he's always trusted his feelings. His instincts never let him down.

Then he realizes what it is. Jerry O'Brien said he could tell him what was on the disc, but then he'd have to kill him. A tired old line and not typical of O'Brien. O'Brien warned him off, told him to stay away but he feels in his gut that he has to do something. Then it hits him. O'Brien doesn't know who the guy is they're looking for. He's out there in the wind with a bunch of incriminating shit. If I remain passive, things might get out of control. His control, anyway.

And he learned early on to always stay in control.

Chapter Nine

Happy Dayz is a dingy hole-in-the-wall crammed full of bikers and tweekers and hookers and a few frat boys who are definitely out of their element. Phil motions to Marco and they head toward a hallway behind the bar.

Phil could've shown up with a couple of dozen soldiers and intimidated Ivanov into giving him the information he needs. But if he did, that would send a message that there's a big problem, big enough to call out half the Adonis family, and Phil doesn't want anybody else in the organization knowing there's a big problem. This can still be taken care of quietly. The trick is getting the information from Ivanov without making the problem worse.

"What do you figure Goran clears in a month?" Phil asks, heading toward the bar.

"A hundred large," Marco says. "After expenses. Maybe a little more."

Phil shakes his head. "And he operates out of a dump like this."

A guy steps from behind the bar. He's big, but he's still a head smaller and fifty pounds lighter than Marco.

"You can't go back there," he says, his voice unexpectedly high pitched. "It's private."

"I'm here to see Goran Ivanov," Phil says.

"He's not seeing anybody right now. He's busy."

"Tell him it's Phil Adonis."

"Phil Adonis? I thought you were a lot older."

"That's his father," Marco says, his voice a deep growl. "Now get Ivanov."

The guy's eyes stray toward the bar. Phil figures there's a sawed off under the counter. Marco apparently thinks the same thing, as his hand slips under his jacket.

The guy does the math and his expression changes.

"Let me see if Mister Ivanov is available," he says, stepping away from the bar, his hands in the air.

He goes down the hall and disappears behind a door. A few minutes go by.

"Goran's calling for reinforcements," Phil says.

Marco nods. "You think we should call a couple of crews over? You know, a show of force."

"Don't worry. I can handle the Russian by myself."

The door opens and the guy waves them in.

Ivanov, a greasy little prick is sitting behind a metal desk, a beer bottle in hand.

"Hello guys, so good to see you. Not often I get visit from the Adonis family. To what do I owe the honor?"

"I'm looking for Charlie McCoy," Phil says.

Adonis's face slips into a quizzical expression.

"Who is this Charlie McCoy?" he asks.

"Missus McCoy's little boy, I'm guessing."

"Still not ringing the bell."

Phil looks up at the ceiling.

"That's funny," he says.

"What's funny?"

"I hear bells ringing. Now, just do me this favor. Don't bullshit me. You know how I can find him."

Ivanov leans back in his chair. "Why you want Charlie McCoy? He owe you money, too?"

"He's got something that belongs to me."

"Not surprised. Guy is thief, man. What is it he has, anyway?"

The door opens and two guys step through. These two are each as tall as Marco, although not as muscular. Ivanov is looking for a confrontation, which isn't surprising. The Adonis Family has always had a weak hold on this side of the river. Russians, Columbians, Nigerians, even some Asian syndicates, all have a piece of the action. It's a real wild-west free-for-all down here. It'll give Ivanov some major street cred if he were to run off a couple of members of the Adonis family, including the consigliere.

Ivanov says, "You were about to tell me what Charlie McCoy stole from you."

"No, I wasn't," Phil says.

"Then you get out of my place."

"I want to know where McCoy is. Then I'll leave."

"If wishes were ponies, beggars wouldn't have to walk. I think that's how that goes. You're outnumbered, man. I've got more guys out in the bar."

Phil glances at the two apes.

"Hold on just one second," he says. "Maybe we just got off on the wrong foot. I apologize. What was I thinking?

What we need to do is look at this situation as rational businessmen."

"Certainly. I am rational businessman." Ivanov thumps his chest with his fist. "What do you propose?"

"It doesn't cost you anything to tell us where McCoy is. On the other hand, not telling us could prove very expensive."

Phil says this in a voice that's calm yet menacing. He's practiced it many times using a tape recorder.

Ivanov laughs. "You trying to frighten me with that mean voice of yours. You can't hurt me. The Adonis family don't mean shit down here. Now, get the fuck out. Before I hurt you. Bad."

Goran's dug in his heels and he can't afford to lose face in front of his men. He needs a way out. Phil puts his hands up, palms out, in a gesture of surrender.

"All right, I'm going. But you're going to need to find a new methylamine supplier. That chemist in Philly is about to stop doing business with you."

Ivanov's expression changes.

"Chemist in Philly? I don't know who you mean. You're rambling, man. I don't know any chemist in Philly."

"Yeah, you do. No methylamine and you'll be back to using junkies to scrounge Sudafed. That's no way to do business."

Ivanov shifts in his seat.

"Why would chemist in Philly suddenly stop doing business with Goran?"

"Just guessing, he probably wants his little girls, ages nine and eleven, to keep on breathing, that's why. And when he stops selling to you, there goes your little meth enterprise. And there goes Goran."

Phil makes a fluttering motion with his right hand, like a bird in flight.

Chapter Ten

"Your apartment is kind of creepy," Amy says. "You know that, don't you? I'm sorry to say it."

Charlie ignores her and concentrates on the highway ahead. She messed with the air conditioner for fifteen minutes before finally accepting that it was broken. She told him she couldn't believe he drove a truck with no air conditioning. She asked what was wrong with it. She inquired as to why he didn't get it fixed. He ignored her. She complained about the smell in the truck. Charlie took a sniff. He didn't notice a smell.

"I said your apartment is creepy."

"I heard you the first time. We're not staying there, so it's not going to be a problem."

"Why do you live there?"

"I was sort of between places when I moved in. I needed a place in a hurry and I got it on a month-to-month lease and I just kind of stayed on."

"When was that?"

"About five years ago."

"That's a long time. And it smells funny, too. Like sweaty underwear. Is that you or the apartment?"

"The apartment's okay. It's all I need."

"You don't need very much. Can't you afford anything nicer?"

"Not on the money I make."

"There's not much money in being a lock pick?" she asks.

He glances at her. She's just looking straight ahead, no change of expression. Carol's always said that she wouldn't tell Amy about him doing a six-year stretch in the state penitentiary for felony burglary. He figures she was telling the truth because there's no way she's ever going to admit to her daughter she married a thief. She'd do it for herself if not for him.

"I'm a locksmith," he says. "Lock pick is something different."

She nods her head and he gets the feeling she just misspoke. Her tone of voice didn't sound as though she was accusing him of being a crook.

"What's the difference?" she asks.

"A lock pick is thief. He picks locks so he can break into places and steal stuff. A locksmith installs locks, makes keys, stuff like that."

"Do you like being a locksmith?"

"It's okay. Locks keep people secure. Or at least they feel secure."

"You don't sound very excited when you explain it like that."

"It's not what you would call exciting work."

"Mom's always complaining that she can never reach you. She said you don't have a cell phone. Is that true?"

He glances at Amy. God, she looks like her mother. Large gray eyes, high cheekbones, thin bloodless lips, and skin so pale that it would show a smudge mark if he were to touch it.

He can't see anything of himself in her.

"That's right, I don't have a cell phone. I haven't had one in years. I don't see the point. Nobody had them when I was a kid and we managed to survive."

"You're not into change are you?"

"Still don't use ATM machines."

"Seriously?"

"They charge you fees to get your own money. And don't get me started on crunchy peanut butter. Who came up with that idea?"

"You're making fun of me. But what if somebody needs to talk to you and it's an emergency?"

He slows down for traffic ahead that's exiting.

"If somebody wants to speak with me, they can call me on my house phone. Look, having a cell phone puts you at the mercy of somebody else's agenda. Wherever you are, they can get to you. You see what I'm saying?"

She gives him a quizzical look.

"That's an unusual way of looking at it," she says. "Isn't that kind of antisocial?"

"With a cell phone, you're never alone. There's always somebody there, somebody wanting to talk to you."

"You like being alone, don't you?"

"And you ever notice that with all these gizmos we have today, that people still can't communicate? In fact,

I think communications skill are worse than they've ever been."

"Don't take this the wrong way, but I'm not sure you're the best person to speak about communication skills. Sorry. At least from what Mom tells me. What was it you needed to do?"

"What do you mean?"

She gives him a steady, opaque look.

She says, "You said now was not the best time for you to look after me."

"Don't worry about it. It's not a problem anymore. I got it taken care of. Say, are you hungry?"

Without waiting for an answer, Charlie pulls off the Turnpike and into a McDonald's. He orders two Number One Meals—Big Mac with fries and a drink--from the drive-through window.

"I'd like three packets of mayo with that," he says. "And a coffee with one of those, not soda."

"I would prefer a chicken sandwich, not a hamburger," Amy says. "Grilled chicken, please. I never eat red meat. And bottled water, not soda."

He changes the order. A minute later their food comes. Charlie pulls over to the side and parks near the exit to the highway on-ramp.

She examines her sandwich.

"I don't often eat at fast food restaurants," she says. "And I never eat in the car."

"I do. All the time."

She looks in the rear of the king cab at the empty Wendy's, McDonald's, and Burger King bags, wrappers, Styrofoam coffee cups, and French fry containers.

"I can see that," she says. "Your back seat is full of garbage."

"I'm in my truck a lot. And that stuff could be valuable one day. Do know people sell old McDonald's stuff on eBay?"

"I get it. You're holding onto that stuff as an investment. For your retirement, no doubt." She peels the top off her sandwich. "This doesn't look very appetizing."

"It's what you asked for. You shouldn't ask for something if you're not going to eat it."

"I didn't know it would look like this."

He takes a bite of his burger. His mouth full, he asks, "You don't have any kinds of allergies I should know about, right? Like peanut allergies or something else that would cause your throat to close up?"

"Nope, no allergies."

He removes the lid from his coffee and dumps in sugar and creamer.

"You drink coffee with a hamburger?" she asks.

"Sure. I drink coffee with everything. It's cheap and it tastes good."

"How many cups of coffee do you drink?"

"Per day? Seven or eight."

"That can't be good for you."

He takes a big gulp of his coffee.

"No," he says, "that's not true. Drinking a lot of coffee helps prevent liver cancer. I read that somewhere. Or maybe it was pancreatic cancer."

He takes a mayonnaise package and squeezes it on his French fries.

"What are you doing?" she asks.

"I like mayonnaise on my French fries. Are you going to criticize everything I eat? If so, you can stop right now."

She wrinkled her nose. "Sorry, but that's soooo gross. I don't believe it. Are you going to put salt in your coffee, too?"

"It's how people in Europe eat their French fries. With mayonnaise. Some even put mayonnaise and onions on their French fries. Except in France they call them pommes frites."

"Still gross." A pause, and then an inquiring look. "How do you know that people in Europe put mayonnaise on their French fries? Did you read it in a book?"

"I lived in Europe for a while."

"Where in Europe?"

"Italy, mostly. And some time in Germany. And some time in other places."

"How did you get to go to Italy?"

"When I was in the Marines I was stationed at the US Embassy in Rome for a few months. That's one of the things the Marines do. They guard our embassies. I was at another embassy for a while, too."

"Rome. It's so romantic there. I'm thinking of changing my name to Aimee, with two Es because it's more European."

"What's wrong with Amy with a Y?"

"It's so common. How did you decide to name me Amy?"

"That was your mother's idea mostly. It was a character in a movie she saw."

"Yeah, that's what she said. Did you have any ideas? For my name?"

Broken condom.

"None that I can recall."

She asks him what it was like living in Europe. He says he liked Italy.

"I'm going to go to Europe after I graduate from high school," she says. "Go backpacking. That's the only way to really see Europe. What did you do in the Marines?"

"Tried to stay out of trouble"

"Did you ever kill anyone?"

He looks up at her. Searches her face for a clue of some sort and sees nothing.

"What the hell kind of question is that?" he says.

"I meant did you kill anybody while you were in the Marines."

"No, I didn't kill anybody. It was one of those times there was no real war going on."

"So you weren't a real soldier."

"Of course I was a real soldier. They even trained me to be a sniper, but I didn't like that."

She nibbles at her chicken.

"Why was that?" she asks.

"I didn't like the idea of killing a guy I didn't know from long distance because I was ordered to by some officer. A guy is just standing by the side of the street minding his own business. I shoot him from six hundred yards away and I don't even know why. With a ten-power scope, I can practically see the pimples on his forehead before . . ."

"Before what?"

"Before, you know, I pull the trigger."

He takes another bite of his hamburger.

"We had to shoot two thousand rounds a week," he continues with his mouth full. "At targets shaped like human beings, and I started to think what it would be like to shoot a real human being. Breathe in, breathe out, squeeze the trigger, and watch his chest explode in a pink mist. When I started thinking like that, it became harder to hit the target, and I failed sniper school. The Marines weren't happy about that."

"Why? You could do something else."

"From their point of view, they'd wasted a lot of time and money training me. That put a crimp in my career as a Marine. Some of my other experience as a Marine wasn't so great but I don't want to talk about that so don't ask me."

"Why did you want to become a Marine?"

Charlie pauses, looks out the window.

"I did it to prove to my father I was a man. Back then if you could survive the Marines basic training without washing out it meant you were a man."

"Did you ever want to go back?"

"Where? You mean to Europe? Yeah, I guess so. I went to the Amalfi Coast once, on leave. That's in Italy. They have small fishing villages there that overlook the Mediterranean Sea. White stucco houses that go up the hillside from the sea. Windy roads that go along the coast. Beautiful clear blue water. Very picturesque. You can sit by yourself in a café all day, sipping a cup of coffee, reading, looking at the harbor, and nobody bothers you."

"Didn't you get lonely? Being alone all the time?"

He holds up a French fry, dips it in the mayonnaise, and holds it out to her.

He says, "Here, try it."

She grimaces.

"Go on, don't be a big baby. It won't kill you. Try it."

She takes a bite. Then smiles.

"It's not too bad," she says.

"Remember that. You should always be ready to try something new."

Chapter Eleven

De La Torre pulls into the parking garage. He's breathing hard. The steering wheel is slick with his sweat.

On the drive over, he convinced himself that what he suspected was true. The information taken from Adonis's house contained records of bribes taken and paid, including the payments made to him over the last sixteen years.

That's the only thing that makes any sense.

If that information gets out, he's looking at a twenty to thirty year stretch in a federal penitentiary. Of course he'll never last more than a few months before some gang banger seeking to earn his colors sticks a shiv in his back.

But then he's overwhelmed by a sense of reassurance that sweeps over him like a wave. He can get through this. He will get through this. How many times over the years has he almost been discovered? But something always happened. Like Lisk and that information of his. If Prescott hadn't left Lisk's DOJ file laying around in the conference room where anybody could see it, he would've been toast months ago.

It's always the same pattern. He worries himself to death but things always work out in the end. Why? Because he's smart. And careful. He just needs to keep his wits about him and not collapse under the pressure.

And remind himself of what he's accomplished. A black man raised in the ghetto by a single mother, by all rights he should be in state prison serving a lengthy sentence or in a crack house, a needle in his arm. But he's making two hundred grand a year and he has a big house and a beautiful wife and daughter. He just needs to trust in himself.

And maintain control. He learned the importance of being in control--of his circumstances, of himself, of others--when he was a child and he had control of nothing.

He enters the federal building, walking quickly, swiping his card at the entrance. Inside, a federal marshal, an old guy named Mitch, waves to him and types something into his computer. There is now a duplicate record in the security database that he entered the building at 8:57 P.M.

On the fifth floor, he swipes his card again to enter the FBI offices. He logs onto his computer and pulls up a report on Serbian credit card fraud he's been working on.

So far, if anybody checks the computer security logs, it looks as though he's come in to burn a little midnight oil. So far so good.

He takes an elevator to the sixth floor. This is where it might get tricky, since the lawyers often work late, and he could be discovered--and it'll be difficult for him to explain his presence on this floor at this hour.

He swipes a key card he took from the effects of a DOJ lawyer who was fired a few months ago. He's tested it a couple of times and it's always worked. Nobody has seen fit to disable it. Yet.

And it works again this time.

He steps into the lobby and listens. No computer keys being tapped. No printers whirring. No footsteps on the terrazzo tile floor. Nothing to indicate the presence of a hard working government lawyer or two.

Prescott's office is a fourteen by twelve foot corner affair, much larger than De La Torre's office. De La Torre logs onto Prescott's computer, which isn't a problem since he has Prescott's password. Prescott used to keep it taped to the top of his desk until some security-minded soul told him that wasn't a good idea. But he evidently still hasn't changed it because when De La Torre enters the password, he gets the DOJ homepage.

He could do this search on his computer, but if he does, he'll leave a trail on his hard drive that could be found by a computer forensics expert. That could prove embarrassing. So he'll do it on Prescott's computer, instead.

He checks the NCIC reports for homicides committed in the state in the previous twelve hours. In less than half a second he gets a drug deal gone bad, a husband who shot his wife, a convenience store hold-up that turned into a shooting, a wife who set her husband on fire while he slept, a hit and run, and a shooting victim discovered in an abandoned vehicle. He's betting it's the latter and pulls it up.

The victim's name is Maurice Baker.

He hits print.

Chapter Twelve

They're back on the Turnpike, forty miles out of town, when Amy says, "I forgot Paddington. I left him in your apartment."

"Who is Paddington?" Charlie asks.

"My teddy bear. We need to go back to get him."

"Can't go back, honey. I'm sorry."

The plan is to drive to the Shore with Amy. They'll hang out there for a couple of days. Let things quiet down. Get to know his daughter a little better. Then return her to her mother.

"We simply have to go back," she whines.

"I'll get you another teddy bear. I promise."

"He's a very special bear. I got him in the hospital. He makes me feel better when I'm nervous."

What the hell does she have to be nervous about? Being with me? Really?

"When were you in the hospital?"

"When I had my appendix out. And I got a bad infection and I was in the hospital for two weeks. The

77

doctors thought I might die. That's what Mom says. Don't you remember?"

He's forgotten about that. He was in the middle of his six-year stay in the joint when she had the surgery. He didn't learn about it until after he was out of prison.

"We still can't go back," he says.

"Why not?"

"Just can't."

"Are you afraid to go back?"

"Why would I be afraid? I just don't want to waste the gas driving back and forth in the middle of the night for a teddy bear. You'll get it when we go back."

"You sound nervous. Your hand is shaking."

"Being around your mother does that to me."

This is actually true.

"Mom thinks you have problems."

"Everybody has problems. That's part of life. The trick is solving the problems. When you get knocked down, you gotta get back up again, learn from your mistakes, and move on. That sort of thing."

"Why were you looking out the window before we left?"

"To see if it was raining. Whether we'd need an umbrella."

She pouts. "If you're not running from anybody, why don't you want to go back to get Paddington?"

He slams his hands into the steering wheel.

"Jesus, just stop, will you? All right. We'll make a return trip. Waste a bunch of gas. Just to get your precious Paddington."

As he drives, he works the muscles of his jaw, which are sore. It must come from talking a lot. He's probably talked more in the last three hours than he did in the previous three weeks. As a general rule, he doesn't like talking.

He's changed his mind. After they pick up the teddy bear, he's taking Amy straight to her mother's house and leaving her there, no matter what Carol says. Amy's safer there. And she's really starting to get on his nerves.

On the way back he spots a pawn shop. He stops and tells Amy to stay in the car. Inside, he buys a pair of small binoculars. A collection of combat knives are on display. They have rubber grips and serrated blades. Thirty dollars to eighty dollars each. He has the money for one, but he can't imagine sticking somebody with a knife. Of course up until a few hours ago he couldn't imagine shooting somebody in the head, either.

Twenty minutes later, they're back in town. When he gets back to his apartment building, he drives past without slowing down.

Amy says, pointing, "Dad isn't that your apartment?"

"That's right."

"Aren't we going to stop? What about Paddington?"

"I'm going to get Paddington. Just wait a minute."

Up ahead, a late-model Mercedes SUV, black, with blacked-out windows, is pulling away from the curb. It's very large and very square and vaguely militaristic. He's never seen it before. And in this neighborhood you'd notice a new Mercedes.

He slows down, not wanting to get too close to the Mercedes. A hundred feet back, he makes a quick right turn onto a side street, maybe too quick.

Did he catch the attention of the driver of the Mercedes with that turn? He goes a couple of blocks, keeping a watchful eye on his rear view mirror, waiting for headlights, expecting to see the Mercedes round the corner in pursuit. He keeps going and then makes a right. He drives for a couple of miles, keeping a constant watch in his rear view mirrors.

"Where are we going?" Amy asks.

He doesn't say anything, just keeps driving. Taking a right, he goes a few blocks and takes another right and keeps going until he's made a big circle. He turns into a parking lot that's in the rear of a burned-out warehouse and drives behind a dumpster, turning so the front of the truck is pointed at the open gate. He waits for a couple of minutes to see if anybody followed them.

"What are we doing here?" Amy says.

"I want you to stay in the truck. I'll be right back."

She says something, but he doesn't hear her because he's closing the door. He walks toward the building and up to a pair of solid wooden double doors, an entrance big enough that you could back an eighteen wheeler trailer in and have room to spare. The doors are secured by a chain and a Master padlock. A four-year-old bankruptcy court notice is glued to one of the doors.

He opens the padlock in less than twenty seconds. He's getting better at working with one hand.

Inside, the building still smells of smoke and the floor is covered with soot. He remembers the fire. It occurred shortly after he moved into his apartment. Five alarm fire, people said. What happened here? Bad maintenance? Bad luck? Insurance fraud? His great-grandmother died in the Triangle Shirtwaist Fire. That was the family legend. A hundred and forty-six garment workers died because the owners had locked the stairwells and exits. None of the owners went to jail. That story was re-told at least a couple of times a year. There were many family legends and Charlie suspected most were baloney, but, still, he learned a valuable lesson from that story. It ain't breaking the law if you get away with it.

It's so dark--the only light is coming from the open door--he can barely see. He finds some stairs in the far corner. They're iron and don't appear to have been damaged by the fire. On the second floor the lighting is better because there are three large openings in the far wall where windows used to be. A smaller open area--probably clerical--is directly ahead and doorways are along the wall on the left. This is where the managers' offices were located.

A small hole is in the center of the floor with burn marks round the edges. He takes a slow, circuitous route around the edge of the hole, leaving a couple of feet of clear distance. As he puts his weight on his right foot, the wooden floor gives way with a crunching noise, and his leg falls straight through, up to his knee. Looking down, he realizes that the whole floor may give way at any time and it's a forty-foot drop. Gently, being careful not to put too much weight on his left foot, otherwise it'll go through as well, he slowly extricates his right leg. He drops to his knees and crawls over next to the wall. Staying as close to the wall as possible, he edges up to where a window had been and looks up and down the street. The Mercedes SUV is nowhere in sight. Maybe it was nothing, just his nerves getting to him. He directs the binoculars at his apartment.

The apartment is a mess. Drawers are pulled out, furniture overturned, the mattress pulled off the bed. For all their effort, they won't have found anything except his winter wardrobe--a couple of moth-eaten sweaters and a faded fake-leather jacket.

They found him in a hurry and the Mercedes was something after all. What will they do next? Look for known associates, what else?

"Oh, Jesus."

With a sick realization, he suddenly knows where they're going next. His winter wardrobe wasn't the only thing left behind.

Going as fast as dares, he circumvents the hole in the floor, runs down the iron steps, jumps into the truck, and floors the accelerator, causing the worn rear tires to screech in protest. Amy asks him about the teddy bear.

"Sorry, honey, no Paddington tonight."

Chapter Thirteen

Charlie drives slowly past Carol's house. They bought the house for sixty grand. The real estate agent called it a fixer upper, which Charlie soon learned was another word for dump. Charlie painted the inside. He replaced the rotten fascia on the outside. He rewired the house so they could put in more lighting, brighten it up a little. He changed out the kitchen cabinets. Installed new plumbing fixtures. Put down wood floors, wide planked hickory. He figured if the house was nice, Carol would be happy. She got it in the divorce.

He drives down the alley in the back. Amy's been nagging him the whole way about her fricking teddy bear. He's pointedly ignored her, hoping she'd shut up.

He rolls past the house. The back door is open just a sliver. A light is on. Not the kitchen, probably the dining room. He glances at Amy. She seems not to have noticed the open door.

No way in the world Carol leaves the back door open. She always nagged him if he left the front door open while he got the mail out of the mailbox, which was only twenty feet from the door.

He parks down the street, switches off the headlights, and leaves the engine running.

"I'm coming, too," Amy says, reaching for the door. "I want to talk to Mom."

"No," he says, a little too loudly. "Stay here. Keep the door locked. Don't get out. I just need to speak with your mother. Grown-up talk. I'll be right back."

He jumps out and jogs down the alley to the back door, looking in all directions as he runs, his footsteps echoing in the dark. He steps inside what was the family home and calls out his ex-wife's name.

No response. He walks through the den, his right arm extended, his finger on the trigger.

The walls are covered with black and white photographs of the Maine woods, with the trees bare of leaves, branches reaching skywards like skeletal fingers. They were taken by Carol's brother-in-law. The guy is a real outdoorsmen. Hunting, camping, fishing. And a renowned nature photographer. His photographs are hanging in art galleries around the country. Charlie always found them too damned depressing for words.

He turns into the front hall. Half a bloody heel print is on the floor. He squeezes the butt of the gun inside his splint and feels pain radiate up his arm. He rounds the corner to the dining room. His ex-wife is in a chair, her hands cuffed behind her and duct tape over her mouth. Cigarette burns run up and down her left arm. Just above her temple is a small black hole with a ring around it. An abrasion ring. The shooter pressed the cold steel of the barrel of the pistol into her flesh before pulling the trigger. On the right side, where the bullet exited, the head is gone from the eye to above the ear. As the bullet tore through her brain and skull, it slowed down, and the bullet's head deformed making it less aerodynamic. Instead of penetrating bone and tissue it pushed it out of the way, making its pathway larger and larger until it exploded on exit. On the far wall--brains, blood, bone and a small bullet hole.

All of this took a micro-second.

They wanted to know where he was. She didn't know, so she couldn't tell them. They tortured her. Unsuccessful, they killed her.

Her single eye stares out into space, wide-eyed with an expression of amazement. What was the last thing she thought?

Why is this happening to me?

He touches the skin just above the small entrance wound. It's still warm. The shooting must've happened just minutes ago.

A guy is in the kitchen, lying face down in a pool of blood. It looks as if he made a break for it but didn't get far.

He looks back at Carol. He should be feeling more. Sorrow, remorse, loss, even grief. But he doesn't. He's cold, unfeeling. Is he a monster? Prison, a life of crime, all the crap that's gone on in his life, have destroyed most of his normal emotions. He had them once—now all he has are survival instincts.

I wasn't always this way.

He startles at the sensation of movement in his peripheral vision. A man standing a few feet to his right, in the dark. He turns, raising the pistol. He's squeezing the trigger when he realizes it's his reflection in a mirror. The mirror, an antique, had been a wedding gift from Carol's aunt. For a brief moment, he sees himself, scared and desperate.

There's a noise from outside. Have they come back? Or did they never leave? Or is it Amy? Has she grown tired of waiting in the car? He can't let her see any of this.

I have to get out of here.

He goes back the way he came, tripping over a chair leg in his hurry and falling on his broken hand, and crying out in pain.

Outside, the truck is in the same place. Amy's door is open. As he jogs toward the truck she climbs out.

She didn't listen to me.

"You can get back in," he says. "We're finished here."

"That wasn't very long," she says after they're in the truck and he's pulling away. "What did you talk to Mom about?"

"Nothing important. Just confirming arrangements. Making sure we're on the same page."

"Is something wrong?"

"No. Why do you say that?"

"You look really pale. And your hands are shaking. And you're sweating."

"I told you. Your mother has that effect on me. But it's okay now."

He drives east, away from the city and toward the Shore. Soon, Amy is asleep, snoring gently.

Chapter Fourteen

"It wasn't a question of making her talk," Phil says. "It was a matter of making her shut up."

They all laugh. After leaving Happy Dayz, they picked up Taco and Dutch, so now there's four of them. Dutch got his nickname because his last name is Aalbers. Taco got his nickname because his last name is Bell. Now there's more than enough manpower to take care of this rat McCoy. As soon as they locate him, that is.

"So he's got his daughter with him," Phil says.

"That explains this."

Dutch holds a teddy bear above his head with both hands, shaking it as if it's a trophy.

"Where's he going to run to?" Phil asks. "No family. No friends. No regular job. No connections to anything."

Dutch says, "That bitch had a sister. That's what she said. I think that's what she said. Hard to tell with all the screaming."

"Doesn't sound like the sister is too crazy about him."

"His ex-wife said the guy doesn't even have a cell phone," Dutch says. "What kind of prick doesn't have a cell phone? This day and age."

"Yeah," says Taco, agreeing, "Two-thirds of the world has cell phones. Peruvians have cell phones. Fucking pygmies in the jungle have cell phones. But this guy has no cell phone. What's up with that?"

"Guy must be broke," Marco says. "Did you get a load of that dump he was living in? Disgusting. No white man should be living like that."

Phil looks at the photo of McCoy. It's a grainy copy of his DMV license photo, but Phil can still tell that it's the picture of a loser. He can see it in the eyes. This is a man accustomed to being defeated. To making bad decisions. To being betrayed. To coming out on the short end. It is the face of a man who expected to lose and so he will lose. He will find a way to make a fatal mistake.

Eventually.

But Phil doesn't have enough time to wait for this worm to eventually screw up. He needs to force McCoy into the open. But how? The secret to controlling a person is knowing what they value and threatening to take it away. Linda valued her looks. Ivanov valued his little meth business. What about this creep McCoy? He doesn't seem to value anything.

That could be a problem.

"So what are we going to do, boss?" Dutch says. "What's the next step?"

"Maybe we should see what the cops know," Taco says. "They might have a lead or two."

"We've already contacted our friends in law enforcement," Phil says quietly. "They had some helpful information. But we don't want them finding this guy before we do. He's carrying around some highly sensitive shit. So don't go talking to any cop buddies of yours without checking with me first. Understand?"

"So what are we gonna do?" Dutch asks. "Sit and wait?"

"Something will come up," Phil says. "I can feel it. We just have to be patient. Don't panic. Don't do anything stupid that will attract attention. Just wait."

Chapter Fifteen

De La Torre steps through the double doors of the police station and looks right and left. Against one wall is an ATM machine. The wall itself is cinderblock covered thinly by a pea-green latex. A heavy-set black woman in a uniform with sergeant's stripes sits in a booth, behind a thick clear-plastic barrier, similar to the kind you see in banks. The booth occupies one-half of the wide hallway and on either side is a door. Over the door on the left a sign says ENTRANCE. Over the door on the right is a sign that says EXIT. The EXIT door appears to be broken, the metal bent and the glass broken out. Somebody wanted to leave in a hurry. Above the booth, a sign reads INFORMATION.

"I need to speak to a robbery-homicide detective," he says.

He flashes his badge and ID and tells her he's from the FBI.

She makes a gesture with her hand, telling him to come closer.

"Let me see it."

He slides it to her though a slot. She spends a moment examining it, and then slides it back.

"What can we do for the federal government this fine evening?" she says with a flirtatious smile.

"I'd like to talk to one of your detectives about a homicide."

"Who was the victim?"

"A guy named Maurice Baker. He was killed this afternoon."

She glances at a clock that's over the doorway.

"I'll see if I can find you somebody," she says. "But I'm not making any promises."

He takes a seat as she speaks on the phone. He hasn't been in many police stations in the last twelve years, not since he joined the Bureau, and the feelings that well up inside him are decidedly mixed. Things were a lot simpler when he was a cop.

The policewoman hangs up the phone, gives him another smile. A few moments later, a buzzer sounds and then the sound of the door on the right unlatching.

"You can go on back, Mister G-man," the woman says. "Second door on your left. You'll want to speak to Detective Jackson. Remember there's no exit, that door's not working. You've got to come back the way you went in."

The squad room is the size of a basketball court and is divided into a dozen cubicles. An older, obese white guy sticks his head out of one of the cubicles.

"Over here," he says, waving. "I'm Jackson."

De La Torre pulls a chair over from another cubicle and takes a seat.

Jackson is eating a cheese steak sandwich, and he's dripped grease all over his desk. He takes a moment to wipe it up with a small paper napkin before holding out his hand. They shake hands. Jackson's hand is soft and greasy. De La Torre wipes off his own hand with a clean linen handkerchief.

"You are inquiring about the late unlamented Maurice Baker, commonly known as Moe," Jackson says, wiping his mouth with the same napkin he used to wipe off his desk.

"That's right. I understand he was murdered this afternoon."

"Yes indeed," Jackson says, doing a bad W.C. Fields imitation. "A single shot to the head with a small-caliber round from close range. Tell me, why does the FBI care about a low-level hood like Moe Baker? Especially at eleven-thirty at night."

"That's strictly on a need-to-know basis right now. Baker's linked to a high-level ongoing investigation." De La Torre pauses, then says, "How do you figure it happened?"

"The shooter drove his utility van into a parking lot behind a closed Taco Grande. Ah, yes, Taco Grande, I knew it well, back in the day. The van had been reported stolen this morning. Anyway, Baker drives up in a Toyota and gets into the van. We know this because Baker was found in the passenger's seat. They were sitting in the vehicle. Baker had a .38 Smith & Wesson, but he was too slow, and the shooter capped him. Whoever did it, didn't leave any prints in the van. A single shot to the head with a small-caliber weapon. Looks like a set-up."

"Any information about the shooter?"

"He was long gone by the time we got there, needless to say. Funny thing, though. Although the Taco Grande was closed the camera in the drive-through still worked. Security purposes. It caught the Toyota Corolla leaving shortly after the shooting."

"Has the Toyota been recovered?"

"Yes, indeed. It had been stolen. Subsequently re-keyed and wearing stolen plates."

"And you think that was Baker's car."

Jackson nods.

"Did the camera get a photo of the driver?" De La Torre asks.

"No, the camera for customer service was out because with the Taco Grande being closed and all, there were no customers. But here's the good part. A waitress in a coffee shop saw a man park the Toyota and walk away, very quickly. He was almost running. Tall, skinny white guy in his fifties. He was carrying a duffel bag. And his right arm was in some sort of cast."

De La Torre leans over the desk, his face less than a foot from Jackson's, so close he can clearly see the broken blood capillaries in Jackson's cheeks and nose, what his mother used to call "gin blossoms."

"Was anything recovered from the van or the Toyota?" De La Torre asks. "Anything at all?"

"Some overalls. That was it."

"I'm going to want to look at the Toyota and the van."

"When?"

"Now."

Jackson starts to say something but De La Torre cuts him off.

"After I leave, call impound and tell them I'm on my way."

"You think this guy with the cast was the shooter?"

"That's my theory."

"Interesting. He drives up in this van. Meets Baker, shoots him, and then drives away in Baker's car?"

De La Torre says, "It sounds like a hit to me. That's obvious."

"Don't you want to know who I suspect for the shooting?"

De La Torre pauses, not sure if he wants to hear the answer.

"Who do you suspect?" he says. "A known associate?"

"I don't actually have a suspect. Baker was just a low level punk. Could've been anybody."

"Did Baker have any known ties to the Adonis family?"

Jackson shoots him a sideways look as if he's surprised by the question.

"Baker was reputed to be a soldier for Phil Adonis," Jackson says. "But I doubt if it's them. Not exactly their style. "

De La Torre remains silent.

"Still want to know why the FBI is so interested in this shooting," Jackson continues. "I've got a whole file cabinet full of unsolved shootings. Maybe you'd like to help me with those while you're at it."

De La Torre slides a business card across the desk and tells Jackson to keep him informed of any developments.

"Were you the first detective on this case?" De La Torre asks.

"No. I volunteered to take it over . . . since I'll be working through this weekend."

"That was mighty kind of you. We'll touch base tomorrow morning. If anything happens call me on my cell. The number's on the back of the card."

Jackson turns the card over.

"How long you been with the FBI?" he asks.

"Twelve years."

"What section?"

"Organized crime. Like the card says, I'm Supervisory Special Agent in Charge of the Organized Crime Unit of the local field office."

A broad friendly smile stretches across Jackson's face. It makes De La Torre uneasy.

"We probably know some of the same people." he says. "I'll be doubly sure to keep you informed."

Jackson does everything but wink. De La Torre gets up to leave.

"One other thing," Jackson says.

"What's that?"

"I do have a composite drawing of the suspect. You'll want it. The witness from the coffee shop got a real good look at the guy."

***

On the way out, De La Torre stops at a pay phone. The purpose of the phone is made obvious by the large bulletin board next to it that's littered with flyers advertising bail bondsmen. Some folks who are looking to make bail for a friend or relative don't have a working cell phone.

He dials O'Brien's number and it goes straight to voice mail.

De La Torre says, "The guy you're looking for has a cast on his right arm. And he's a tall skinny white guy in his fifties. That should help."

He hangs up and heads out the door.

Chapter Sixteen

Phil eyeballs Marco, who is driving the Mercedes SUV. Marco's five o'clock shadow has darkened. He's the kind of guy who was shaving five times a week when he was in eighth grade. Phil didn't shave for the first time until he was sixteen.

Phil rubs his forehead. He's getting the crown-of-thorns feeling. That's what he calls it when he feels the pressure circling his forehead, as if it's digging into his skin. He saw a shrink about it. The doctor said it was caused by anxiety and had a fancy name for it, but Phil always liked to call it a crown of thorns. The doc gave him a prescription for Prozac, but he never got it filled, figuring it wouldn't be good if word got out that he was taking a drug for nutballs--and he never believed anything that doctor said, anyway. He knew a lot of people referred to him as Crazy Phil, which, everything considered, was better than being called Little Phil, but it still wasn't too great and he doesn't want to do anything to encourage it.

He should be happy. He handled that crumb Ivanov perfectly. He got the information he needed without having to call in reinforcements. So far, he's kept the circle small. He's kept the damage contained.

But he's not happy. He's thinking about the New York mob. The guys in New York provided protection, which allowed the Adonis family to operate without interference from the authorities and other crime organizations. In exchange the Adonis family kicked up twenty percent of their take. But the boys in New York didn't like it when things went wrong--like what happened with the Schenectady outfit. A Schenectady capo squealed to the feds, implicating some higher ups in the New York mob. This wasn't well-received in New York. On a Friday, a dozen hitters came to town. By Monday the Schenectady outfit's boss, his brother, both his sons, his son-in-law, his underboss, and a half-dozen others were all dead, and the New York mob was firmly in charge of operations.

Phil's problem is that many of the crooked politicians on those CDs were also in the pocket of the New York mob. If word got out about the bribes, it would be bad for everybody. And that would make things much worse for the Adonis family.

He suddenly realizes Marco is eying him and he stops rubbing his forehead. He can't let them think he's worried.

"You okay, boss?" Marco says.

"You got this truck checked for trackers, right?" Phil says aggressively. "Like I told you?"

Marco nods. "Yeah, boss. I already told you. I had it checked a couple of days ago."

"Good. I found one on the BMW yesterday. Looked under the wheel well and there it was, blinking red. It hadn't been there the day before. The feds, they never let up. You should have this vehicle checked every single day. Sometimes twice a day."

"I'll do that boss."

 Phil points at the curb.

"Pull over. You guys wait here."

A white Escalade is parked thirty feet down the street, under a burned out street light. Phil notices that mud has been wiped on the Escalade's license plate, making the plate unreadable.

Jerry O'Brien is in the Escalade. Big Jerry. Uncle Jerry. Phil has known him his whole life. When Phil was small, Uncle Jerry bounced him on his knee. Jerry was a penny-ante fixer back then, already as big as a house. He handled small stuff for friends of the Adonis family. Speeding tickets, health code violations, building permits. Stuff like that. Now he is his father's lawyer, although he acts more like the boss because of his connections to the New York mob.

Phil steps up next to the driver's window, so close he can smell the spearmint gum Jerry's always chewing.

"How's it hanging, Jerry," he says.

"Straight up and hard. As always. I made the burglary report."

The Escalade sits high and Phil's head barely reaches the window sill. He's uncomfortable with O'Brien looking down at him.

"Good work, Jerry," he says. "You made a report to the police. Most excellent. How much you gonna charge us for that? A couple of grand? For twenty minutes work? Must be good to be a lawyer."

"Just following the plan as you laid it out."

Silence.

"So, Jerry, you called this meeting. What's on your mind?"

"How are you doing with finding our friend?"

"We know who he is. A guy named Charlie McCoy. We know where he lives."

"Good. So take care of him. Get our stuff back. Wrap this up, for Christ's sake. Before it gets any worse."

"Not that easy. He wasn't at his place. The guy's in the wind."

The corners of O'Brien's mouth turn down.

"Should I worry about that?" he says.

"No, no need to worry. We expect to have him very soon. He can run but he can't hide. You know what I mean?"

"You have any good leads?"

"I expect to. Soon. Very soon. It's as good as done."

O'Brien scowls. "Phil, please. Don't piss in my ear and tell me it's raining."

"We've put out the word, okay? That's all I can do."

"Maybe we should get Niko involved. A little more manpower."

"We don't need Niko. I can handle this. By the way, where're you at on locating the traitor in our midst?"

O'Brien sighs. "Stay on topic. Our friends in New York are looking to you to fix this."

Phil doesn't say anything. O'Brien is so tight with the New York mob, it's tough to tell where his loyalties lie.

"How do the guys in New York know about this already?" Phil asks.

"I didn't tell them, Phil, if that's what you're thinking."

"So how do they know? It only happened six hours ago. They're way up there in New York."

"You said you put out the word. You didn't think they'd hear? They've got ears everywhere."

"I didn't provide any details about why we were looking for this guy. I'm not that dumb."

"Then it's somebody from inside your organization you have to worry about. You shouldn't be too surprised about that."

Phil points at the Mercedes. "It ain't any of my guys. They're completely loyal to the family. They'll do whatever I say. They'd give up toilet paper if I told them. Understand?"

"You gotta get this problem fixed. It was your plan that created this mess."

"It wasn't my plan to keep all that information."

"Let's recount the bidding. You were the one who hired Lisk. That--"

"He came highly recommended. I didn't know he was a rat."

O'Brien chuckles.

"He owed the feds almost a million in back taxes," he says. "You didn't think they could use that to squeeze him? You hire a guy for a sensitive position, you should check him out first. You didn't do your due diligence."

"I took care of the Lisk situation. It was Dad's idea to keep that information on the discs. He wanted it for leverage on those people. That was not my idea."

"But it was your idea to stage this phony break-in."

"It was Moe Baker's plan. They'd take the stuff. Moe would let this moron take the fall."

O'Brien's mouth hardens.

"You trusted Moe Baker's judgment, which was problematic at best. You approved the plan, as consigliore. You have to take responsibility for your actions, Phil, if you want to be a leader."

"And it was a good plan. A smart plan. It should've worked. I didn't know Moe would screw it up."

O'Brien brushes a piece of lint off his sleeve.

"This isn't getting us anywhere," he says. "It's all history now. You need to know that the guys in New York are very upset. You're going to need to make this right, Phil. And fast. Think of it as a test. A chance to prove yourself. And, by the way, you should know that your Mister McCoy has a cast on his right arm."

Chapter Seventeen

Charlie drives through the darkness, not knowing what to do about Amy. He doesn't even know how to act around her. Everything he says makes her angry. It has been this way for a long time. Two Christmases ago they went out to a late dinner at a Chinese restaurant. He ordered Mongolian beef. She had the steamed vegetables and miso soup.

"Chinese food," she said. "Really? On Christmas?"

"It's good Chinese," he said, chewing on an egg roll.

"I think it's gross."

"No other choice. Chinese restaurants are the only ones open on Christmas Day."

She pointed at his Mongolian beef.

"Do you know what makes beef tender?" she said. "It's decomposition. The best beef is the most rotten."

He shoved a piece of beef in his mouth.

"So what?" he said, his mouth full. "Everything that's dead is decomposing. Those vegetables that you're eating are decomposing. And everything that's not already dead is heading toward death. So, what's your point?"

She scowled and went back to her soup.

At the end of the dinner, he pulled a big K-Mart bag from under the table. With a flourish he tugged a backpack from the bag. Her eyes narrowed, and then she laughed.

"What's so funny?" he said. "It's your Christmas present."

She scrunched her face up. "Hello Kitty? Are you serious? I'm not, like, four or anything."

"It's a good backpack. Strong. Durable. You can still use it, right? For your school books and stuff."

"I wouldn't be seen dead at school with that. My friends would never let me forget it."

He pointed out again that it was a perfectly good backpack that cost perfectly good money, and she said she again didn't want it and shoved it back across the table, knocking a water glass onto the floor. That was more or less the end of dinner.

Merry Christmas.

Last year they didn't go anywhere at Christmas. He just pulled up outside the house, twenty minutes late. She flung open the front door to the house, raced down the steps, and peered in the passenger window.

"Don't you want to come inside?" she asked. "Just for a few minutes."

"What for?"

"Everybody wants to see you," she said, with a smile. "Come in. You'll be surrounded by family."

"Whenever I hear that phrase, surrounded by family, I think of Custer. On the North Dakota plains, surrounded by the Sioux. Except the Indians were a lot less bloodthirsty."

He reached inside his jacket and pulled out a thick envelope.

"Look, I didn't get you anything for Christmas this year. Truth is, I don't know you well enough to get you a present that I knew you'd like, you being a girl and everything. I guess you figured that out last year."

"You mean Hello Kitty."

"Right, Hello Kitty. It's my fault. I should know you well enough to know what you want, but I don't. And I didn't want to repeat what happened last year. So, instead of getting you something you wouldn't want, I figured you'd just prefer cash." He handed her the envelope. "There's a thousand dollars in there. Spend it on whatever you want. Get something nice for yourself. Put some away for a rainy day. But don't let your mother know about it."

She stepped away from the truck, looking in the envelope.

He quickly stuck the truck in gear and pulled away. As he drove down the street, he glanced in his rear view mirror. She was still standing by the curb.

That was the last time he'd seen her until a few hours ago.

So, he saw her the last two Christmases. When before that? When he took her to the circus for her third birthday and she got chocolate ice cream all over her white dress. The next day the cops broke down the front door and took him into custody.

What do I tell her about her mother? That's a problem. She'll think it's his fault her mother's dead. And in a way she'd be right. If he hadn't broken into Adonis's house, Carol would still be alive.

It's two hours later when he pulls into the parking lot of the motel with a flashing neon sign outside. The Pink Flamingo.

He figures this Shore resort will be a good place to lay low for a few days. It'll be a whirlwind of activity with hordes of people--teenagers, college students, and families with small children--coming and going. Nobody will remember a middle-aged guy and his daughter. They'll be invisible.

He didn't figure it would be quite so hard to find a room, though. It's the third motel he's stopped at. The first two were full up with July Fourth vacationers.

A pudgy middle-aged guy is behind the desk. For a moment, he looks at the splint as though he's never seen one before. Charlie asks if he has a room available.

"You're in luck," he says. "We just had a cancellation. The room has two double beds. That okay with you?"

"Perfect. How much?"

"Just yourself?"

"And my daughter. She's thirteen."

"You're in luck again. Children under fourteen stay free. It'll be a hundred and twenty-nine a night, including tax."

Charlie says he'll need three nights, counts out the bills, drops them on the counter.

"Three nights in advance. You won't have to register. You're good with me." He points. "Out the door and to your left. Second door down. Room number two."

"If I decide to stay longer," Charlie says. "I'll let you know."

Amy's fast asleep in the back seat of the car. He carries her to the room, her breath warm and humid against the back of his neck. He pulls back the top sheet, blanket and comforter with his good hand. He takes her shoes off, and tucks her into bed.

The A/C unit under the window is making a wheezing noise, but the room's cool. And the sheets are clean. They could've done worse, everything considered.

He's thankful the guy at the desk didn't ask for a credit card because he doesn't have one and he didn't want to get drawn into a long explanation about that.

He checks the bathroom. Above the commode is a small window. Standing on the toilet seat, he opens the window and looks out on the swimming pool and Jacuzzi that are in the rear. Amy's skinny enough to wriggle out the window, but there's no way that he could. Still, it's a good thing to know the window's there in case they have to leave in a hurry.

He takes his clothes out of his bag and opens a drawer to put them away. The drawer's full of porno magazines and porno CDs. Strange.

Why didn't the maid throw this stuff out when she cleaned up?

He takes the pornography and dumps it in a trash can outside. Then he drags a chair from the room and walks past two units and into a breezeway where a coke machine and an ice machine are located.

He sets the chair where he can see the well-lighted office, but, sitting in the darkness, he won't be seen.

The night is still warm. Insects buzz and sing. In the distance somebody is setting off firecrackers, jumping the gun on the Fourth by two days. From a distance the sound is indistinguishable from gunshots, and the noises make Charlie nervous.

He listens carefully, but he can't hear the roar of the surf even though it can't be more than a quarter-mile away.

He closes his eyes and thinks about everything that's happened. He can't get the image of Carol out of his head. If he can stop thinking about it, maybe the image will disappear. He's always been good at that--suppressing thoughts and feelings, especially feelings—until they no longer exist.

But he can't get the image of Carol out of his mind.

He unwraps the ace bandage and removes the gun from his broken hand. He examines the bandage. He left a space for the barrel but the bandage is slightly singed in one area.

He turns the gun over in his good hand. It's four inches long. Ten ounces in weight. It's a mouse gun, small enough to fit in the palm of his hand. The serial number is filed off. How long ago did that happen? The gun could be sixty years old. How many crimes has it been involved in? There's Moe Baker's shooting for one. Some would consider that a crime.

It's a pea shooter, really. Inaccurate beyond twenty feet. Six rounds total in a .22 short caliber. Not much stopping power.

It did stop Moe, though.

And it saved Charlie's life.

He puts the gun in his pocket and re-wraps the ace bandage around his hand. He needs a plan. If he thinks long enough and hard enough, he can always find a way out of any bad situation, that's been his experience. There must be a way out of this mess. In the meantime, he has to figure out what to do with Amy.

He thought Amy could act like a disguise. The Adonis family will be looking for a guy matching his description, but alone, not with a young girl. But not anymore. He has to figure Carol told the mobsters about Amy. Now he and Amy will stick out like a sore thumb.

Should he call the cops? Tell them what he has? Turn it over to them? He'll probably be indicted for Moe's murder. He could argue self-defense, and it might work since Moe had a gun in his hand when Charlie shot him. But he can ID where the discs came from, and with information that incriminates the Adonis family his life expectancy in jail would be less than a fruit fly's.

So what's the alternative? Call Phil Adonis and say, Big Phil, I got some stuff here that belongs to you. How 'bout we trade. I give you what you want and you let me keep my life. Do we have a deal?

Hardly. Adonis would have no way of knowing if he had made copies of anything. The only way to handle this is for Phil Adonis to get his stuff back and then torture Charlie until he's sure there's nothing else incriminating still out there. And then kill him.

Charlie wants to know what's on those discs. What makes them worth killing for?

There's a rumble of a car engine and a late-model Jaguar pulls up next to the office. A tall slender blonde in a very short skirt, high heels, and a halter top gets out of the passenger's side. She strides into the office. There is some arguing from within. She's unhappy that there are no rooms available. This goes on for several minutes. The woman comes out and gets in the car, which drives off, tires squealing.

What just happened?

Was the woman a hooker? Why was she pissed off? Because the manager told her all the rooms are rented? For a hooker, doesn't that fall into the category of occupational hazard? Maybe she had reason to believe a room would be available--the room with all the porno stashed in a drawer, for example. Had the manager rented out her room, room number two? If so, why would he risk offending a regular customer?

The lights go out in the office. The manager comes out and goes in room number one. A few minutes later the lights go out in there.

Charlie checks his watch. Two-thirty. No sound of fireworks now. No sound of anything. He walks across the parking lot to his truck and using a small screw driver he removes the back license plate. He tucks the license plate under his jacket and walks out into the street, which is empty--no moving cars, no people. Three blocks away, he finds an old Nissan Altima with a flat tire that looks as if it hasn't been driven since dinosaurs roamed the earth.

He switches the plate from his truck with the one on the Nissan.

Then he walks back to the motel room, stopping on the way to attach the plate from the Nissan to his truck.

Chapter Eighteen

Mike De La Torre sits in his kitchen, the pale early yellow morning light streaming through the French doors. He's already showered and dressed--a dove gray suit, light blue shirt and burgundy tie. The suit and shirt were tailor made and the tie was bought on a trip to Rome.

After meeting with Jackson, he drove to the police impound yard. He spent an hour going over the Toyota and the Ford van and finding nothing.

He opens the paper and scans the "Local" section. He's looking for any unusual news related to somebody named Charlie. A body discovered in a dumpster, for example. Or a body found in a burned car. An article catches his eye.

A man and a woman were found shot to death in the woman's home last night. Police responding to an anonymous 9-11 call found the bodies of Herschel Adler, age 51, an English teacher, and Carol McCoy, age 47, a secretary, in Ms. McCoy's home. Both worked at the Friend's School. Police are treating the murders as a home invasion. The woman was tortured.

De La Torre folds up the paper. Torture. Of a school secretary and an English teacher. That's somewhat out of the ordinary, even for this city. Usually you torture somebody to get information. Sometimes just for fun, but usually to get information. But it wasn't the man who was tortured--and his name wasn't Charlie, anyway--it was the woman. She must've known something. For example, where is Charlie? It certainly sounded like Little Phil's MO. Toward the end, somewhere after the electric drill and before the blow torch.

So, assuming that "Charlie" is related to the woman, De La Torre's betting that the mystery man is named Charlie McCoy.

He boots up his FBI-issued laptop, enters his password, and runs Charles McCoy on the NCIC database, figuring the guy must have a record. He's not feeling good about this, not at all. The computer search could be traced back to him. If he figures out who "Charlie" is, he should report it to his superiors. But he's not going to do that. Later, somebody could ask why he didn't and that could out him in a tricky position. But he needs the information now, and there's no way he can get on Prescott's computer during the day.

So, he has no choice.

He hits ENTER and gets five guys named Charles McCoy with criminal records and addresses in the state. One is seventy-eight. One is twenty-four. He can strike them. One is in prison. One is forty-nine. He's about the right age, but he's black. That leaves Charles Lawrence McCoy, age 53. He compares the mug shot on file with the composite drawing. The photo is old, but it's him.

He scrolls down. Charlie was busted for breaking and entering when he was thirty-seven. Pleaded down to trespass and time served. Another B & E, charges dismissed. Burglary when he was forty-two netted him nine years, served six. Another burglary. Charges dismissed. That is it.

Charlie's not exactly a heavy hitter. He looked to be smarter than the average crook, though. Beat the charges three times out of four when the average is one time out of ten. He's definitely ahead of the curve on that score. De La Torre examines the composite. "How did you get involved in this mess, my friend?" he mutters.

He takes out his phone and calls the FBI office's back line. One of the younger agents answers.

"Do we still have a tracking device on Little Phil Adonis's vehicle?" De La Torre asks.

A pause for a couple of seconds.

"That's the 7-Series BMW, right?"

"That's it. Where's it at?"

"The big Beemer is in the same place it's been since six-thirty last night. The parking lot of the Pink Pussycat."

De La Torre is surprised. This information suggests that Little Phil found the tracking device and that's why the vehicle hasn't moved in thirteen hours. He's never told O'Brien about that device--he always likes to hold back a little info, keep it in his pocket just in case he needs it at some point.

De La Torre says, "Little Phil's Beemer may be there, but I'm betting Little Phil isn't. It's not the kind of place he'd choose to bunk at, that's for sure. Who's the manager of the Pink Pussycat? The big guy."

"Marco Delassandro. You figure Little Phil got a ride from Marco?"

"Something like that. So where is Marco?"

"He's got a Mercedes G-class. Damn, these boys like their toys. According to the tracking device, it's currently going south on Highway 9. About forty miles out of town. Left real early this morning. If you asked me, I'd say he's headed to the beach for a weekend of fun and frolic. Anything else?"

"I want a print-out of everywhere that Mercedes has been in the last twenty-four hours. And keep an eye on it. I'll be over in an hour. I'll check with you then."

He's pouring himself a second cup of coffee when he hears something and turns. Cynthia's picked up the paper and is scanning the pages.

"You are up early," she says, a slight edge to her voice. "What time did you get home?"

"After two."

"Where did you go?"

"The office."

"Why so late?"

"Why the cross-examination?"

"I was just wondering. A wife has a right to know where her man is. Especially after that performance you put on with Sandy last night."

He takes a sip of coffee.

"That was nothing. She just had too much vino."

"She was practically all over you with her eyes."

"Maybe she has screwing a black guy on her bucket list, a lot of white women do."

He gives his wife a wink and she laughs. He steps over to her, wraps his arms around her waist from behind.

"You sound like you know from experience," she says, moving closer.

"You know you're the only one for me. So stop with the cross examination."

She turns, stares at him with the look that usually signals bad news.

"I had to take the Lexus back in again," she says. "The air conditioning this time. They say it'll be over two thousand dollars to fix."

"Ouch, that's a chunk of change."

"I think it might be better to just buy a new car." She points at an ad for a Land Rover in the paper. "Something like that."

"The Lexus is only five years old."

"Isn't that about the time that things begin to go wrong?"

"I'll think about it," he says, pulling away.

"Don't think too long. I don't want to get stuck out on a deserted highway in the dark somewhere with our daughter. There are a lot of bad men out there, as you well know."

He smiles. She doesn't give any thought as to how they'd pay for a $70,000 SUV on an FBI agent's salary. Just as she gives no thought to how they can afford a $450,000 house or have their daughter go to an $18,000-a-year private school.

This is not a criticism of his wife. She isn't a stupid woman. No, far from it. De La Torre understands that just like everybody, there are many things she'd rather remain ignorant about. It starts when you're a kid and you think there's a monster under your bed. Do you get out of bed and check to see if it's really there? Hell, no. There's no telling what you might find down there in the darkness. You'd rather not know. Instead, you lay in bed under the covers, terrified of the unknown. Same thing when you get older. In high school you see your girlfriend riding in some gang banger's Mustang convertible. Do you think she's cheating on you? No, you figure shc's just catching a ride. You don't think about it again until she tells you it's all over.

Later you find a whole passel of things you'd rather not know about. It might be that termite damage under the deck in the backyard, or the cracks in the walls that suggest foundation problems, or that funny growth on the top of your ear.

You spend your whole life under those covers, scared to look under the bed for what you might find. Why? Because ignorance is better. Ignorance means you don't have to do anything.

He puts his laptop in his briefcase and heads toward the door.

"Remember," she says. "We've got Dad's birthday party this afternoon. You didn't forget, did you?"

"No. I'll be back in time. I swear. But we got a big break in the Adonis case yesterday. Some good information. I need to follow up on it. Right away."

"What kind of big break?"

"I'd tell you but then I'd have to . . ."

"Kill me. Yeah, yeah, I get it."

They both laugh at the thought.

She says, "So, this big break. This information. Is it going to put a lot of bad guys away for a long time?"

"Maybe. It depends on how it's handled. It's at a delicate stage right now."

"Do you think you might get a promotion out of this? If everything goes right?"

"I hear there's going to be opening for Assistant Section Chief of the Organized Crime Section."

"That's in DC, right?"

"Of course."

"That would be a big deal. Do you think you'll get this one?"

This one.

She's referring to how he got passed over last year for the position of assistant director of the local field office.

Thirteen months and still she thinks about it.

"How long until you know if you have the job?" she asks.

She's thinking about life in DC again. She's forgotten all about her anger. The woman never loses sight of her priorities, that's for sure. He gives her a peck on the cheek.

He says, "If everything goes right, DC is definitely in our future."

In the car, he thinks about what he said. He hadn't lied. DC could be in their future. He deserves this promotion and should get it. He deserved that promotion last year, when the assistant director job opened up. Just before the announcement, he'd been responsible for busting a major Asian sex trafficking ring. The information on the ring--where, who, when--had come his way thanks to Jerry

O'Brien, but his superiors in Washington didn't know that. They should've seen it as a job well done.

So, what is it? Racism? He doesn't want to think about that. Too many African-Americans blame racism for their faults. They use it as a crutch. More likely, it's just been the luck of the draw. His time is coming. He can feel it. He just needs to be patient.

And if he gets the job in DC he'll be out from under the thumb of the Adonis family. Maybe.

From the car he calls the local police and explains he met with Detective Jackson the night before. A guy answers. He identifies himself as Detective Polaski.

"What happened to Jackson?" De La Torre asks. "He leave for summer vacation or something?"

"I guess you hadn't heard. Jackson had a massive heart attack. About three o'clock this morning. He's in ICU. I'll be handling this case going forward."

"Sorry to hear that. You have anything new?"

"You called at the perfect time," Polaski says. "We talked to that witness again. She's coming in tomorrow. She's going to look at mug shots."

"You got any other leads?"

"No, nothing right now."

Polaski sounds guarded, cautious. Has he connected McCoy to the murders?

De La Torre says, "This witness will probably be a waste of time, don't you think?"

"You never know. She got a real good look at him. And she says she's got some sort of a photographic memory. Maybe we'll get something out of this."

De La Torre swears under his breath.

"So this waitress saw the guy walking down the street, that's it?"

"Pretty much. She saw him park in a no parking zone. She was going to go out and tell him he needed to move his car, but he was walking too fast."

"So she saw him from fifty, sixty feet away?"

"About that. She says she has very good eyesight."

"Good eyesight and a photographic memory. Sounds like a witness from heaven. Don't get many like that."

"Sometimes you just get lucky."

* * *

De La Torre is still swearing when he stops the car and takes a cell phone from the glove compartment. It's a throw down, untraceable. He bought in New York, in a stop-and-rob in the South Bronx. He wore a hoodie and sunglasses, in case he was caught on camera. He paid cash and used a Jamaican accent. He's figuring nobody is ever tracking the phone back to him.

He removes a tape recorder from the glove compartment. He dials Jerry O'Brien's cell phone number, and then switches on the tape recorder. A voice, not his own, but one he recorded off the Internet says, "We need to meet."

He climbs out of his Cadillac, walks to a trash can, and tosses the cell phone into it. Then he covers the phone with trash until he can't see it anymore.

Chapter Nineteen

O'Brien looks at his cell phone. He doesn't recognize the number, but figures it's De La Torre and tucks the phone back inside his pocket.

Joseph "Joey Bats" Battaglia, the Underboss of the New York family, sits on the other side of O'Brien's desk. He showed up unannounced at eight a.m. with Max Donnelly, known as Mad Max to one and all. Donnelly eyes O'Brien. They are cold, dead eyes, like the kind you see on a sea creature that's been dragged out of the deepest depths of the ocean. So, Joey Bats brought a hitter with him. That's one way of sending a message. The hitter switches on a bug detector, a hand-held device the size of a cell phone, and starts prowling the office.

"If you need to take that call," Joey Bats says, pointing at O'Brien's jacket pocket. "Go ahead. By all means."

"It can wait," O'Brien says. "And by the way. I had the place swept for bugs yesterday. So your friend can put that thing away."

"The feds ain't the only people we're worried about when it comes to bugs," Donnelly says, casting O'Brien a suspicious glance.

"Excuse us if we don't have excessive confidence in your security," Joey Bats says, wagging a finger at him. "Where are we on this McCoy mess?"

A knot forms in O'Brien's gut. Joey Bats knows the guy's name. Joey Bats is telling him not to screw with him. He knows the score. The man has up-to-date information.

"I spoke with Little Phil an hour ago," O'Brien says. "They tracked him down. They expect to have him at any moment."

Joey Bats nods and smiles. It's a cruel, mirthless smile. He didn't get his nickname because of his last name but because of his well-known ability to wreak havoc with a baseball bat on those unfortunates who failed to make their protection payments on time.

"That's good," Joey says. "What kind of information does this man McCoy have that we're so concerned about?"

"Some discs with accounting information on it. It could prove awkward. The numbers don't exactly jibe with what was reported to the IRS."

"That's all? A little IRS trouble? Sounded more serious than that."

O'Brien has three choices. He can tell Joey Bats the truth about the missing information, and he'll be killed, no doubt. It wouldn't matter that this fiasco wasn't his idea. They'd kill him, anyway. Maybe right here in his office, behind his desk, probably very painfully.

Or he can lie and maybe get to live a little longer and get this mess sorted out without being on the receiving end of a bullet to the head.

Or he can make a move for the Colt Detective Special snub-nosed revolver in his top desk drawer. But even if he successfully gunned down both men, he'll just be signing his own death warrant. Nobody kills the underboss of a major New York family and gets away with it.

He opts for prevarication.

"This isn't just a little IRS trouble," O'Brien says, sitting back in his chair. "You're looking at twenty, maybe twenty-five million in taxes and penalties. And if they go for evasion, Big Phil's looking at some serious prison time."

"With all due respect, at Big Phil's age, that's not something to be worried about. A good lawyer should be able to stretch out that prosecution four, maybe five years. And by then?" Joey Bats shrugs. "Big Phil could be gone. I hear his health isn't the best. You sure there isn't anything else going on here I need to know about?"

"No, nothing."

"Place is clean," Donnelly says, interrupting.

He grabs a chair and slides it next to the desk. O'Brien feels surrounded with the men on two sides of him.

Joey Bats leans over the desk.

"You need to listen," he says. "This is important. We've invested a ton of dough in Costa Rica, where we plan to run an online gambling operation. We're getting a law pushed through Congress to get online gambling made legal again. This could mean billions of dollars a year in legal profit. It'll be Havana in the Fifties, all over again. You understand?"

O'Brien nods. Havana. In the Fifties. The mob's equivalent of Camelot. The New Jerusalem of La Cosa Nostra.

"This is the way things get done nowadays," Joey Bats says. "You want something, you get your people in Congress to do it for you. It's not about buying off ward bosses anymore. You go right to the top now. We're running our money through a bunch of front companies so it looks legit and we've got some very powerful people in our corner."

"Look there's nothing but a little IRS--"

"Listen to me. We've got big people in the entertainment industry helping us. Big people in the communications industry. Fortune 500 companies. But we got powerful enemies, too. The casinos in Vegas and Atlantic City among others and they're looking for an angle so they can kill this thing. Understand? We can't afford any distractions and we can't afford anybody looking at us too closely, or it'll all fall apart and we'll be out more money than you can imagine. We can't be drawing attention to ourselves. You understand?"

Joey Bats leans back, puts his feet up on O'Brien's desk.

"This is a funny business this thing of ours," he says. "So many ways for something to go south on you. There are snitches. Over-zealous prosecutors. People looking to rip you off. Crooked lawyers. Even worse, incompetent lawyers. You got to be able to have people you can trust. People who've got your back, you know?"

O'Brien nods again.

"Tell me, Jerry. Be honest. You got my back?"

"I do," O'Brien croaks, the words sticking in his throat.

"Do you?"

"Yes. I got your back."

Joey Bats stands, straightens his jacket.

"That's good, Jerry. I wouldn't want anything to come between us."

Chapter Twenty

"A re you feeling all right?" Amy says.

They're sitting in a Denny's, eating breakfast. They left the room at eight and have already stopped and purchased swimsuits and some beach towels. Charlie needs to act like he has a fun day at the beach planned because that's what Amy is expecting.

"I didn't sleep so well," he says.

"When I woke up, you weren't there."

"I went for an early morning walk."

He sits up straight. His back's killing him. Sleeping all night in a lawn chair, outdoors, will do that, especially at his age.

"Can I ask you something?"

God, I hate that question.

"Sure."

"Do you love mommy?"

Charlie scrutinizes his daughter.

Do you love mommy?

Present tense. He should tell her that her mother's dead. Get it over with. Right here. Right now.

He says, "I'm afraid not, sweetie. That's finished."

"I know it's all over, but I figured . . ."

"We'd get back together?"

"Yeah. I think about that sometimes. But I know that's stupid. People never get back together after a divorce."

"You're right, it's not going to happen."

"She says she thought you were sexy. And romantic. She liked the way your eyes sloped down in the corners."

"That's news to me."

"And you brought her flowers all the time. And she said you were a good dancer."

"I used to like to dance. You know, the samba. And the tango. I liked to tango."

"Don't you dance anymore?"

"Tell you the truth, I have nobody to dance with. Haven't for a long time. Also, my knees hurt a lot now."

"Didn't you ever love her? At all?"

There's a hopeful note in her voice. She wants to hear about romance and holding hands while walking on the beach at sunset. And maybe about getting caught in a spring shower and seeing a rainbow afterward. She wants to hear that her mother and father had something special. But there is very little in Charlie's life that has ever been special, including Carol. But he can't just tell Amy that she was the product of a careless fling that turned into a loveless marriage. None of that was her fault.

"I wanted to love her, sweetie," he says. "I really did. I promise."

She screws up her face in puzzlement.

"That's not the same thing."

"I suppose not. But for a long time I thought it was."

Or you told yourself it was.

"Did you ever think about getting married again?"

The waitress brings their meals. Three strips of bacon, two link sausages, three eggs over easy, hash browns, toast, and a refill on the coffee for him. Granola and yoghurt and orange juice for her.

"No," he said, "I learned my lesson. I did my time."

"That's really funny."

"What's funny?"

"You did your time. Like you were in prison. What about dating?"

Charlie takes a sip of coffee.

"Nope. Not interested."

"It's possible Mom might get married again."

He squeezes a red blob of ketchup on his plate. Married, he thinks. That explains the dead guy on the kitchen floor. He must've been Carole's boyfriend.

He says, "Getting married. No kidding. Good for her."

"I'm not saying she will. It's possible. That's all. I thought you should know."

"Thanks for the heads up. Consider me informed."

With only one hand, he can't cut his meal. He can only tear at it. He piles bacon, eggs, and hash browns into this mouth. Some egg yolk leaks from the side of his mouth.

"You eat like a slob," she says.

"Yeah, I know. I think it's from not being around people much. At the apartment I just eat over the sink. If I make a mess, it's easy to clean up."

"That's gross."

"It keeps things simple. Uncomplicated. I like uncomplicated."

"Still gross." A pause. "Mom says you never loved her."

He wipes his face with a napkin.

"She might be right. What I mean is, I thought I could make love happen. If I worked at it long enough and hard enough. Like if you had a broken transmission on your car, you could get it working again if you replaced enough parts."

She picks at her granola and yoghurt. "I don't think you can make love happen, not real love. It can only happen on its own."

"Let me tell you something," he says, pointing a fork at her. "You might not be able to make love happen, but it's real easy to make it go away. That's for damned sure."

* * *

They're in the truck, now. Charlie's feeling jittery. Maybe it's from the four cups of coffee. Or maybe it's from all the questions she was asking about her mother. When is he going to tell Amy about her mother? She'd want to know what happened. She'd want to know why anyone would want to murder her mother. She'd want to know why he didn't tell her last night when he found out. She'd want to go to the cops. When she finds out why her mother died, she'll blame me and hate me forever.

"Are we going to the motel room?" she asks.

"I've got to see a guy first." He pauses. "Let me explain something. Your mother and I had problems. I'm not saying she's a bad person, we just had problems. I thought I could solve them. Life's all about solving problems."

"Why couldn't you solve the problems with Mom?"

"I don't know. It was my fault. Mostly. Maybe entirely."

This is true, although he's never admitted it before, not even to himself.

"Everything went bad," he says. "But you're going to have problems in life. You solve one problem, then another comes along. And then another. And that's just the way it goes. You learn by experience."

"Am I a problem?"

More like an unexpected complication.

"Course not."

She points at his right hand, which is laying in his lap.

"How did you hurt your hand?"

"I did something stupid."

"Why did you do that?"

"Because I didn't know it was stupid at the time. Now I know it was stupid. It was an example of learning by experience. It'll be better soon, and I will have learned my lesson."

"What did you do that was stupid?"

"Sometimes you ask too many questions, you know that?"

This is true. She talks too much and the talk is getting on his nerves. He thinks of his old man. If Charlie ever asked him any questions, he was liable to get a slap upside the ear that would make his head ring for a week, so he never asked any questions. Charlie learned to figure things out for himself. But he's not his old man. He isn't sure if that is a good thing or not. His father raised three children on a steam-fitter's salary and worked sixty hours a week until he died at age fifty-four of mesothelioma caused by working around asbestos for thirty years. Charlie was overseas when his father died. He's never visited the grave. He doesn't even know where it is.

"My hand, it was an accident," he says softly. "That's how I hurt my hand. I didn't mean to."

Charlie pulls into a library parking lot. He walks in carrying the duffel bag with Amy a couple of steps behind him.

"Why are we going to the library?" she asks.

"I have some things I need to take care of. You stay here. I won't be gone too long."

"I thought we were going to the beach. That's why I put my swimsuit on at the store. Under my clothes. Remember?"

"We'll go to the beach later. Promise"

"But I don't want to go to the library."

"You like books. There's lots of books here."

"Why are you carrying that bag?"

"Mind your own business for once."

He asks a librarian where the teenager's section is. She points at some stairs.

"Go on," Charlie says. I'll see you in a little while."

Charlie watches Amy go up the stairs. Then he locates the computers and finds out that it's free to use the computers but print-outs are ten cents a page. This seems eminently reasonable to Charlie.

He runs a search for ADONIS CRIME FAMILY. The Google page comes up and offers him a choice between GOOGLE SEARCH and I FEEL LUCKY. Definitely not the latter, he thinks. He looks around, concerned that Amy may sneak up on him and see what he is doing. Seeing the coast is clear, he hits ENTER.

He gets 167,000 hits. Along the right margin of the screen are photos of Phil Adonis, Sr., boss of the Adonis crime family, Phil Adonis, Jr., consigliore, and Nicholas "Niko" Falcone, underboss. He studies the photos for a second and then clicks on PRINT. Now he'll know who to watch out for.

He opens the bag and removes a disc at random. It's marked ADONIS LAUNDROMAT. He inserts it into the E Drive and clicks on OPEN. He's confronted with row after row of numbers. After a couple of minutes he's figured that the laundromat is, as he suspected, acting as a money laundering operation. About three grand a week in cash is being added to the legitimate receipts at each of the eight different locations. Undoubtedly, it is dirty money--drugs, prostitution, gambling, and extortion--going through a wash and rinse and coming out as the revenues of a seemingly honest laundromat.

If the IRS had this information, Big Phil Adonis would be up crap creek without a means of locomotion.

He figures he'll find something similar on the discs labeled Adonis Flying Pizza, Adonis Vending, Adonis & Sons Dry Cleaning, Starz Nightclub, the Pink Pussycat Lounge, La Griglia Restaurant, Downtown Car Wash, and Garden State Waste Management. How much do they launder at these other businesses? He slips in the disc for the Pink Pussycat Lounge and examines the figures. It looks like thirty grand a week is being laundered there. So what does it add up to total, for all the businesses? Ten million a year? Fifteen million? More? Is that what this is all about? Money laundering?

He picks up the other disc, the one that isn't labeled. Curious, he slips it into the computer and gets a directory of years. It goes back twenty years. The current year is the most recent. He clicks on it, expecting to more rows and columns of numbers, and he's not disappointed. It's a spread sheet but this is different. Along the left margin is a column of names. He recognizes most of them. There are a couple of mayors of large cities in the state. There's a United States senator. And a congressman. And the state attorney general who's planning to run for governor next year. A politically ambitious state senator. Some local politicians. A famous columnist for a newspaper in Philly. There are twenty-one names in all. Under each name are two rows of numbers. At the top of the page are a series of dates, each the first of the month. Under each date and next to each name is a box with a number in it. The numbers range from 400 for some guy Charlie's never heard of up to 10,000 for the US senator.

Monthly payoffs.

And the two rows of numbers under each name? Charlie's betting they're bank account and bank routing numbers. The payoffs must be wired to the accounts.

He goes back to the directory and clicks on the oldest year. Thirty-nine names. The Adonis Family had more influence back then. He recognizes most of the names. One was a two-term governor who eventually ran for president.

Twenty years of graft recorded on a single CD. Why? Is it intended to be some sort of get-out-of-jail card? The ultimate bargaining chip? Or just an act of random inculpatory stupidity?

It does explain why the Adonis family is all over his ass. He Googles the rest of the names on the disc. Of the eight names he didn't recognize, he gets hits on all but two.

Some surprising names, including the FBI Supervisory Special Agent in Charge for the Organized Crime Unit for the state, a guy named Michael De La Torre.

He checks the table. For the last four years De La Torre received monthly payments in the amount of $8,000. Before that it was $4,000. Mike must've done something to get himself a raise. Charlie does a quick Google search. De La Torre got his big raise at the same he was promoted to Supervisory Special Agent in Charge of Organized Crime Unit.

Makes sense.

The message is clear, as if there was ever any doubt. He can't trust anybody.

He clicks on copy, thinking he could save it to his email account, but he gets a message that the CD is locked. He'll have to take good care of this CD.

He walks upstairs to the children's section. Amy is sitting on the floor, surrounded by books. She's reading a thick hardcover book. Thoroughly engrossed, she doesn't even realize he's there. Charley always liked to read, although it was never Carol's favorite thing. Perhaps something of him had passed on to Amy. Charlie watches her and for the first time in years, thinks, I have a child.

He's not sure how he feels about that. For a long time he's had nothing to lose. Nothing of value, anyway. He doesn't want that to change. Having nothing to lose gives him freedom and freedom is what he needs right now.

He gets her attention and tells her he's going to the motel room to change into his swimsuit and he'll be right back.

Chapter Twenty-One

Phil surveys the Pink Flamingo Motel. He thinks you couldn't pay him enough to take a crap in a place like this.

He didn't sleep all night, he's hungry, he's got a headache, and he's in a crappy mood. Jerry O'Brien's words from last night still ring in his ears.

Think of it as a test. A chance to prove yourself.

He doesn't have to prove himself. Not to anyone. Least of all the boys from New York. And the idea wasn't his, it was Moe Baker's, so why should he have to take the blame? And where was Big Jerry when this plan was being discussed? If it was so stupid, why didn't he say anything? O'Brien is worthless. His old man only keeps him around because O'Brien got him acquitted a couple of times years ago.

When this is over, he'll be in charge and he'll take care of O'Brien. A bullet behind the ear and then dump the body in the salt marshes. No fuss, no muss. That's how you get rid of a pain in the ass.

Phil's never trusted the bastard.

Still angry, he pushes open the door to the office of the Pink Flamingo. Hard. So hard it slams against the wall.

A middle-aged fat guy is behind the desk.

"Hey watch it!" he shouts.

"Are you Tommy?" Phil asks.

"Yeah, who the hell might you be?"

"Phil Adonis. Glad I got your attention."

Tommy examines the glass in the door.

"It's about time," the guy says. "Wondered when you'd finally get here." He points at the door. In a belligerent voice he says, "This crack wasn't there before."

Phil doesn't like the way Tommy's talking. It's as if Phil isn't somebody he should be worried about. He doesn't like Tommy's tone of voice. He doesn't like Tommy, for that matter. And even though Tommy's ten years older, he should be referring to him as "Mister Adonis." He can have Marco teach him a lesson, lean on him a little, maybe break a bone or two. But Tommy's uncle runs a highly lucrative sports book in Atlantic City and pays protection to the Adonis family. Phil doesn't want to mess up that relationship, as it generates thirty grand a month for the family.

"I hear you have some information for me," Phil says.

"You're looking for a guy," Tommy says. "That's what I heard."

"You heard right. You know where he is?"

"Guy checked in here last night. Real late. White guy. Tall and skinny. Actually, he didn't check in. Not strictly speaking. There's no record he's been here."

"What makes you think this is the guy I'm looking for?"

"He had a broken hand. It was in some sort of cast. That's the guy you want, right?"

"That sounds like him."

"And he had his daughter with him. That's what he said, anyway. I didn't actually see her."

Phil hands him the Xeroxed photo of McCoy.

"That's him," Tommy says, jabbing at the photo.

"So what room is he in?"

Tommy pauses, as if he's waiting for something, like a bellboy does after he's shown you to your room.

"Come on," Phil says. "I don't have all day. What room is he in?"

"He's in number two. But he's not there right now."

"So where is he?"

"He left a couple of hours ago. But he's coming back."

"You didn't stop him?"

"I couldn't stop him. What was I going to do? Throw my body in front of his truck?"

"How do you know he's coming back?"

"I looked in his room. Everything's still there."

"That's good. For everybody concerned. And I'll be wanting a key to room number two."

Tommy passes a plastic key card over the counter.

"I'd appreciate it if nothing happens here," Tommy says. "You understand?"

Phil tucks the card in his shirt pocket.

"Sure, we understand," he says

Phil turns to leave.

"What about the door?" Tommy asks.

Phil says, in angry voice, "What about it?"

"It's broken, man. Do you know what it's gonna cost to get that thing fixed? A small fortune."

Phil starts to speak but Marco pulls him outside.

"Take it easy, boss" Marco whispers. "We need this guy. At least for right now."

Chapter Twenty-two

De La Torre slips through the back door of Luigi's. O'Brien is sitting in his usual spot.

"So what's all this about?" O'Brien asks. "What's so important you have to call me at eight-thirty in the morning?"

"The cops have a witness. She saw McCoy leaving the scene where he dumped a certain Toyota. The Toyota can be linked to the Moe Baker shooting."

He slides a photocopy of the composite across the table.

"I have a question," O'Brien says, looking at the photo. "Do the cops know the suspect is named McCoy, or do they just have this composite drawing?"

"They don't have a name to go with the picture. Yet. But they do have the witness and she could identify McCoy."

O'Brien lowers his head and squints at the composite.

"The cops don't have McCoy's name," he says. "But you have McCoy's name. How did that happen?"

"I read today's paper. A couple of bodies were found, one was tortured to death. Putting two and two together, I thought it sounded like Little Phil's handiwork. I poked around a little and it all added up to a guy called Charlie McCoy."

"And how did you do this poking around?"

De La Torre pauses.

"On my laptop."

"Your FBI laptop?"

De La Torre nods and O'Brien bangs his fist hard on the table.

"You were told not to look into this," he says, his face turning red. "I told you to leave it alone and just monitor the situation. Easy. Just do nothing. Now there's a record of your activity. You should just do what you're told. "

"And then what? Let Little Phil take care of business? He's already left quite a trail."

"That was regrettable. But nobody's going to trace that to us."

De La Torre nods his head.

That's what you think.

In De La Torre's jacket pocket is a copy of the GPS trace information on Marco Delassandro's Mercedes G-class that shows that between 10:15 and 10:34 the previous evening the vehicle was parked outside the residence of Carol McCoy, Charlie McCoy's ex-wife. This is particularly interesting since the coroner put the time of Carol McCoy's death between 9:00 p.m. and 11:00 p.m.

De La Torre doesn't mention what he knows to O'Brien as it would be hard to explain why he hadn't divulged the existence of the tracking device before. It's time to play his cards close to his vest.

"What happened was regrettable," De La Torre says. "That's what you're saying? Who does Little Phil think will be the number one suspect in the death of Charlie McCoy's ex-wife? I'll let you in on a secret. It'll be the ex-husband, a guy by the name of Charlie McCoy. That means the cops are looking for him right now on a double-murder rap. And what happens when they find him? They'll find this stuff that's got you so worried."

"Have the authorities connected the deaths--any of the deaths--to the break-in at Big Phil's?"

"I don't think so. But with this witness it's just a matter of time."

"Tell me, what exactly did this witness see, anyway?"

"She saw a guy getting out of a car, carrying a bag. The license plate of the car matched one that was traced to where Moe Baker's body was found."

O'Brien snorts and shakes his head.

"Jesus. This just gets better and better."

"So you didn't know about this witness," De La Torre says. "Your intelligence network isn't quite perfect, is it?"

O'Brien doesn't say anything.

De La Torre continues, saying, "I'm guessing Detective Jackson was one of your guys. With him out of action because of a badly timed heart attack, you're kind of in the dark. Just stumbling around blind."

"We have other assets. In addition to you, that is."

"I'll tell you something. Without me, you wouldn't have squat. You wouldn't even know about this witness. You'd still be sitting around with your thumb up your ass, if you don't mind me saying."

O'Brien sticks a piece of gum in his mouth.

"Don't get so high and mighty," he says. "You're just doing what you're paid to do. Nothing more." He pauses. "Is that all the cops have to connect McCoy to the Moe Baker shooting? This single witness?"

"As far as I know."

"I need to know for sure. Is that all there is?" O'Brien's voice gets louder, harsher. "Is that all there is? Just this one witness."

"Yeah, the witness. That's all. I'm sure."

O'Brien nods. "You need to do something for me."

"What's that?"

"Get me the name and address of this witness. I'll take it from there."

"What are you going to do after you get the name?"

"Don't worry about that. You don't need to know."

"This isn't going to be like Lisk, is it? I'm just letting you know your time is running out to find McCoy. You gotta step on it. That's all."

O'Brien stares at him. It's the kind of stare a fly might see coming from a hungry frog just before the fly's existence is snuffed out.

"What do you care what happens to her?" O'Brien says. "You tell us about an informant, we're going to take the steps necessary. It's happened before. And if she identifies McCoy, it'll be bad for you. You need to think about that."

"This woman isn't an informant. She was just a civilian who happened to see a guy get out of car. I mean, she hasn't done anything."

O'Brien casts him a baleful glare.

"Just get me the name. We'll take it from there."

Chapter Twenty-Three

Charlie parks down the street from the motel and walks a block and comes up from behind. There was something hinky about the desk clerk. When Charlie drove out of the parking lot, the guy was at the window of the motel office, watching the truck leave. Charlie figures, everything considered, it's better he comes in the back way, gets their stuff, and splits and never comes back.

A six-foot chain link fence runs along the back of the motel. Charlie scales the fence and drops down the other side to the ground, pain shooting through both knees. He walks slowly alongside the back of the swimming pool and around the rear corner of the motel. The black Mercedes SUV with the blacked out windows is parked next to the office.

He scrambles across the parking lot and ducks behind a battered Trans Am and peeks out, hoping nobody saw him.

Two men shamble out of the office. One is pulling on the jacket sleeve of the other. Two other men climb out of the Mercedes. Together, they look up and down the street, looking for him no doubt, thinking he might come back at any moment.

They speak for a minute. A lot of shaking heads, kicking at the dirt, then laughter. Charlie hears relief in their laughter.

They think they have me.

The two men who were in the office walk in Charlie's direction. One is Little Phil Adonis. The other is a giant of a man. He looks like a body builder, his chest, shoulders, and biceps stretching at the thin fabric of his polo shirt. They're talking to each other, not looking around. Still, Charlie has a tight grip on the Beretta. They open the door to his room with a plastic card, look inside, and then enter. The Mercedes drives away.

He waits a couple of minutes. What would've happened if he and Amy returned to find the two animals in his room? He thinks of Carol, half her head blown away. Then he thinks of Amy again. Everything's spiraling out of control.

This is all my fault.

Confident that they're not coming out, he climbs the fence and drops into the street. He runs to his truck, puts it in reverse, and backs down the street for another block, so he doesn't have to drive past the motel.

He pulls away, thinking he has a telephone call to make.

Chapter Twenty-Four

De La Torre is in his office, calling from his cell phone. He doesn't want anybody overhearing the conversation, so he's keeping his voice low.

Polaski answers and asks what he can do for him.

De La Torre says, "You have that eyewitness who saw the suspect leaving the scene where that Toyota was found. I need the witness's name and address."

A long moment of silence.

Then Polaski says, "Can I ask you why you need this information at this particular time?"

Polaski's voice has a hard edge to it.

"That's really confidential," De La Torre says. "It's part of an ongoing investigation and it's at a delicate stage. The Moe Baker murder is part of something much larger."

That last part is certainly true.

More silence.

"What are you going to do with this information?" Polaski asks.

"We need whatever we can get." De La Torre says. "Lives are possibly on the line here. Time is of the essence."

Another true statement.

"We just need to speak with her," De La Torre continues. "Honestly, our case is a lot bigger than just one murder. Look, I am who I say I am. You can check me out."

"I already have. I wouldn't even be talking to you unless I knew who you were."

De La Torre feels a rock of desperation sinking in his gut. There will be a record at the Bureau that Polaski called and checked on him. Who did he talk to? What did they say? What did Polaski say? De La Torre can't ask him, it will just arouse more suspicion on Polaski's part. De La Torre only knows one thing. He has to find McCoy. Soon, people at the bureau will be asking questions, if they weren't already.

"You still there?" Polaski says.

De La Torre closes the door to his office.

"I'm still here," he says.

"Maybe you can wait a few days on this witness," Polaski says. "Doesn't sound like you need the ID right this minute."

"Look, do I need to speak to your superior about this?"

***

De La Torre sits in his car in the parking lot of the 7-11. He lights a cigarette, his hand shaking. It's the first time he's had a smoke in thirteen years. He was shocked at the price of a pack of Camels.

He stares at the burning cigarette. Did he push Polaski too hard such that he became suspicious? As the complications keep arising quicker and quicker, it's becoming more difficult to stay confident. He feels like a juggler. Just one more ball thrown at him and the whole thing comes tumbling down. He tells himself this will work out, but it's hard to see a clear path forward. It's true, the Bureau has no reason to suspect him of anything. And he's not answerable to anybody, at least nobody outside of Washington. Over the years he's managed to cut the local office out of the loop on organized crime issues.

And nobody at FBI Headquarters really knows what he's up to. He sends his reports to DC, where they get filed away, never to be seen again. Nobody reads them and nobody asks questions and nobody's the wiser.

But as soon as the confidence comes back, he feels it ebb away. He's made mistakes. He can't kid himself about that. Using his Bureau laptop to check out McCoy was a mistake, especially since it's been seven hours and he hasn't mentioned McCoy to anybody at the Bureau. He's going to have a hard time explaining the delay now, if he even tried. And there's no way to truly eliminate that search trail--once it's on the hard drive, it's there forever. He's just going to have to lose that laptop. But will the search still show up on the FBI server? And he'll have a hard time explaining why he contacted the local police about the Moe Baker shooting--how was he supposed to even know about the Moe Baker shooting?--but failed to document any of his activities. Or even tell anybody at the Bureau.

He takes another drag of his cigarette. He's violated a whole passel of Bureau policies and procedures, any one of which might be cause for dismissal.

But he's thinking that he's about to make his biggest mistake of all. But what choice does he have? What if the cops find McCoy first? What if his name is in that crap that McCoy stole, whatever it was? And what if they find him guilty as an accessory to the murder of Lisk?

He doesn't even want to think about that. There's only one thing he can do.

He removes a disposable cell phone from his glove compartment and punches in Jerry O'Brien's number.

Chapter Twenty-Five

Marco and Little Phil sit in the darkened motel room. They both have semi-automatic pistols with silencers lying in their laps. Phil is admiring Marco's neck. It's bigger around than one of Phil's thighs.

They've already tossed the place. They rifled through the drawers, looked under the beds, even pulled the mattresses off the beds. Then they checked the HVAC vent.

Nothing.

Now they just have to wait for the guy to return, however long that turns out to be. Then they'll find out where the stuff is, and they'll kill him and his kid and it'll all be over.

"How long do you think he's going to be?" Marco asks.

"No telling. But he's gotta come back some time. They left their stuff here."

"What if he's got his daughter with him?"

"We'll play it by ear."

"I don't want to hurt a kid. I've never done that."

Phil stands and paces the floor.

"It won't be our fault," he says. "It's this mook's fault. Shouldn't have involved his own kid in this."

"But still, a kid. I don't--"

"I haven't made up my mind, okay? I dunno how we'll handle it." Phil stops and stares at Marco. "Hey, I got a question for you. How big is your neck?"

"My neck?"

"Yeah, your neck size. I'm betting eighteen inches."

"Actually, nineteen. It's a pain in the ass. I've gotta get all my shirts tailor-made."

"Nineteen inch neck. You're built like King Kong, dammit. What about your biceps?"

Marco flexes his right bicep. "Twenty inches pumped."

"Jesus, twenty-inch guns. Amazing."

Marco laughs. "Here you want to feel them?"

There's an awkward silence. Then Phil's cell phone rings. It's O'Brien. He says the cops have a witness who might identify McCoy. He gives Phil the name and address of the witness.

Phil calls Tino Scaramucci, an Adonis family capo, and gives him the information and tells him what to do.

"Take care of it and I mean pronto," Phil says.

Suddenly, there's a loud banging on the door.

"You guys gotta get the hell out of there, man. The cops are coming."

Phil opens the door, blinks in the bright sunlight. Tommy stands there, all red-faced and waving his arms.

"What's going on?" Phil says.

"The cops are coming. I got a call from a guy I know in dispatch. Somebody called the cops, said two men were breaking into room number two. You need to get out the hell out of here, like now."

"I can't believe this," Phil says. "How did this happen?"

"Don't ask questions. You've got to go. I can't have the cops snooping around this place. That would be real bad."

Phil trots toward the office, speaking on his cell phone, telling Dutch to get his ass back to the motel.

Inside the office, Phil paces back and forth a few times before kicking a soda machine.

"I was so close," he screams. "I swear I had him. I could feel it."

Tommy steps through the doorway.

"Hey, don't kick the machine, man" he says.

Without thinking, Phil picks a large metal rolodex off the desk and in one whirling motion hits Tommy in the side of the head with it. Index cards flutter in the air and fall like snowflakes. Tommy stumbles backward, holding the side of his head.

"Were you behind this?" Phil screams. "Did you tip McCoy off?"

He slams the rolodex into Tommy's head again. The rolodex has sharp edges and a large cut has opened on Tommy's forehead. Tommy's begging Phil to stop. Phil hits him again and again. Tommy's jaw breaks with an audible crack. The cards continue to float like snowflakes except now they are splattered with blood.

"What are you saying?" Phil says. "Speak up. I can't understand you, man."

Blood's flowing down the side of Tommy's head and onto his shirt collar. He falls to his knees, making incomprehensible noises now, and Phil kicks him twice in the head. Tommy drops to the floor and curls into a ball, trying to protect himself.

"Come on, boss," Marco says, grabbing Phil's arm. "We gotta get out of here. The cops will be here any minute."

Phil turns and gives the machine another kick. It makes a clunking noise and a root beer can falls out.

***

Charlie watched the gangsters go into the office. Then he loped across the parking lot to the room. He shoved open the door and reached inside. Amy's backpack was by the door. It was open and the contents were spread out on the floor. He jammed some of the clothes, a tablet computer, some tampons--tampons?--and a small toiletries bag in the backpack. The rest of the clothes he shoved into the little suitcase. After all the grief he'd received about the fricking teddy bear, he's not going to leave her backpack behind.

There was something else on the floor. It was a small paperback called "The Book Thief." Charlie stared at the cover, wondering what it was about. Who would want to steal a book? Not much money in that. And it would be tough to sell if it's worth anything because it would have to really rare and everybody would know it was stolen. He shoved the book into the backpack, thinking he might ask Amy about it.

He was about to step outside when he heard shouts and screams coming from the office. These went on for several seconds. Then stopped.

He ducked his head out the door and glanced back at the office. All clear. Time to go.

***

He takes a step outside, when the two men come out of the office, walking toward the Mercedes. Charlie steps back, hoping they don't look this way and see the open door. If he tries to close it, that would risk attracting their attention. He waits, listening for the sound of footsteps or voices, his hand gripping the small Beretta. What are the chances that he takes out four of them with the little pistol before they kill him?

Not good.

He's thinking if he didn't return for Amy's stuff he wouldn't be in this situation. He could be somewhere far away from here, somewhere safe. Being a parent is much harder than he imagined.

After a minute, an eternity, he looks out the door. The men are gone, the Mercedes is gone, and the parking lot is empty.

He's over the fence and walking down the street when a police car pulls up next to the office.

Chapter Twenty-Six

Charlie knocks on the door of the ranch-style house. It's immaculately maintained with a neat and tidy yard and freshly painted siding. George Krebs, a small, wiry man with a shaved head and acne-pitted skin, answers. Tattoos snake up both his arms and peek out from the collar of his shirt. Krebs is tight with a local neo-Nazi motorcycle gang that's associated with the Aryan Nations. He supplies them their guns.

"Charlie McCoy," he says. "Long time no see. It's great to see you. It's been so long. What can I do you for, man?"

There's something in Krebs's voice. He's acting as if seeing Charlie is the high point of his life. Charlie's reasonably certain that seeing him was never anybody's high point. And Krebs was never the world's most enthusiastic person. Of course Charlie hasn't seen him in five years. Not since shortly after Charlie got out of the joint. Maybe Krebs has changed.

"You going to invite me in or leave me standing here?" Charlie asks.

Krebs waves him in.

Charlie met Krebs after he came to Charlie with a pharmacy job. Charlie and another guy Krebs knew went through the wall of a video rental store that was next door to the pharmacy. This avoided the pharmacy's state-of-the-art alarm system. The papers later said they got away with $350,000 worth of schedule 2 narcotics, Hydrocodone and Oxycontin mostly. Krebs paid them $50,000 total, split equally. Word was, the drugs were retailed through the Aryan Nations.

Krebs's house is filled with motorcycle and Nazi memorabilia. Lots of photos of Krebs with motorcycle gang members. A huge Nazi flag, red background with a black swastika in a white circle, covers an entire wall.

"I like what you've done with the place," Charlie says.

"You mean the flag? Yeah, it's a real conversation starter. So, to what do I owe the pleasure?"

"I need a weapon."

"Can't you get one the regular way?"

"I've got a felony hit on my rap sheet."

"Really? I always thought you were too smart to allow something like that."

"Yeah, nobody's perfect."

"What happened?"

Charlie looks away.

"I trusted somebody I shouldn't have," he says.

"I hear you," Krebs says. "So, what do you need?"

"I'm looking for a shotgun." Charlie holds up his right arm. "I'll need a semi-automatic, not a pump action."

"What happened to your hand?"

"Accident."

"Sorry to hear that. I think I can help you with the shotgun."

Charlie nods.

"How does a Mossberg 930 with a pistol grip sound to you?" Krebs asks. "Semi-automatic. Eight shots without re-loading. It'll cost you three grand."

"Sounds reasonable. Can you throw in three boxes of shells? Double-ought buckshot should do it."

Krebs rubs his ear. "You plan on using this for self-defense?"

"If I have to."

***

Charlie's back in his truck. It's parked down a sidestreet where he can see the front of Krebs's house. Krebs said he needed a couple of hours to get the shotgun. He explained that he didn't keep any merchandise on the premises, for obvious reasons. They would meet back at Krebs's house at 2:00 P.M. There was something in his voice. Something unnatural. Charlie considers the fact that maybe he's being paranoid, rejects it. Like they used to say back in the Seventies, it's not paranoia when they're out to get you.

Five minutes later the garage door opens and a white Chevy Silverado pickup pulls out. Through the binoculars, he sees Krebs behind the wheel.

Charlie waits until the Chevy is out of sight before he climbs out of his truck. He opens the tool box in the back seat of the truck and removes a metal coat hanger. He slowly unbends the coat hanger as he walks down the street. He looks around as he walks and sees nobody. It's noon on a Wednesday in a family-friendly subdivision.

Everybody's where they're supposed to be, sitting in front of a TV or a computer monitor or a video game console.

He has the coat hanger straightened by the time he gets to Krebs's garage door, where he's betting there's no burglar alarm. Krebs's house is probably wired every which way from Sunday, but nobody ever wires their garage because when you're out there's nothing in it except a lawn mower and box of Christmas ornaments.

He examines the garage door. Along the top are four small square windows, which allow just enough light for Charlie to see inside. It's always been a mystery to him why they put windows in garage doors. The windows aren't good for anything, generally speaking. But they are perfect for what Charlie needs.

He fashions a small hook at the end of the hanger and then slides the wire through the space at the top of the garage door where it meets the lintel. He guides the hook toward the garage door mechanism that's attached to the ceiling. On every electric garage door opener built in the last thirty years there's a quick release mechanism. The government requires it in case a kid gets trapped under the door. A rope with a plastic handle on the end hangs from a lever. The lever's connected to the electric motor that in turn is connected to the chain that opens and closes the door. If a kid is getting crushed under the door, you pull the rope, and the lever disconnects the chain drive from the motor, releasing the pressure on the kid and saving his life.

But Charlie doesn't care about the rope. There's nothing he can do with that. It's the lever he's interested in. Looking through one of the windows, he maneuvers the end of what used to be the coat hanger. He slips the hook through the one-inch circular opening in the lever of the release mechanism where the rope is tied. With a sharp tug, he pulls the lever down and forward. There's a thunk sound, and the chain drive is disconnected from the electric motor.

Charlie pulls up the garage door and steps inside.

All this took less than ten seconds.

He pulls the door down with a sharp jerk, which reconnects the chain drive to the electric motor. He waits as his eyes become accustomed to the dim light. To his left is a cherry red Corvette Stingray, an early 1960s model. Krebs's weekend driver.

He sits in the darkness, on a bag of Scott's lawn fungicide, his back against the cinderblock wall. Siting in the narrow space between the wall and the Stingray, he won't be seen when Krebs drives in. He's hoping Krebs isn't gone too long. And that he doesn't decide to park in the driveway and go in through the front door.

***

Charlie checks his watch. He's been sitting here for an hour, but he figures he doesn't have too much longer to wait. Krebs told him to come back in two hours, and Charlie is sure he'll be back well before then.

At that moment, the electric motor starts whirring and the garage door opens. The Chevy Silverado slides in, stops. Krebs is behind the wheel. Nobody else is in the truck. As the garage door closes, Charlie moves, head down, behind the low-slung Corvette, the Beretta in his left hand. He lays flat on the concrete floor. Dust billows up and gets in his eyes and nose. He has to work hard to suppress a sneeze, his eyes watering.

Krebs walks between the truck and the Corvette, checking something on his cell phone. When Krebs turns toward the side door that leads into the house, Charlie stands and jams the gun into his left ear.

"Don't move, George. You so much as twitch and you're a dead man. I'm a pretty good shot, and I not missing from this distance."

"What the hell, Charlie? What you doing, man"

"Keep your voice down. Tell me something. Is there a black Mercedes SUV parked outside?"

"The hell are you talking about?"

"Is there a black Mercedes SUV parked outside?"

"No, there isn't. Look for yourself."

"I can't see anything through those stupid windows."

"There's nobody there. Really."

Charlie jams the barrel of the Beretta into Krebs's ear canal.

"I don't trust you, George. You're not asking the right question. You should be asking me what this is all about, but you're not asking that question, which tells me you already know what this is all about."

"Take that gun out of my ear. I didn't do anything to you."

"Where you been, George?"

"Taking care of business. Getting that shotgun for you, like we talked about."

"I've got a question. Is there a Mossberg 930 with a pistol grip and three boxes of double-ought buck in that truck of yours? You know, the gun and ammo we talked about. If there isn't, you've got a big problem."

A pause tells Charlie all he needs to know. He slugs Krebs hard with the barrel of the Berretta. A nasty cut opens on the back of Krebs's head, an inch above the ear.

"Jesus Christ," Krebs says, "stop it."

"You've got to have a shotgun," Charlie says. "In your house. Somewhere."

Krebs smirks.

"Yeah, but it's a pump action. That ain't doing you any good, is it?"

"When are they supposed to be here?"

"Why don't you leave right now? Make a run for it. While you have the chance. Before it's too late."

"I asked you when they'd be here."

Krebs shakes his head.

"Half an hour. You can know when they're coming, but it's not going to do you any good. How long do you think you can run from these guys? They'll catch you sooner or later. Probably sooner."

"So you were setting a trap for me. They'd be waiting for me when I got back."

"That's about the size of it."

Krebs is getting too comfortable. Charlie thinks about shooting him in the foot to send a message. But the sound of the gunshot will attract attention.

Charlie says, "We're going to take a little drive, George."

Chapter Twenty-Seven

Phil parks Marco's Mercedes SUV on a side street opposite Kreb's house. He checks his watch. He's a few minutes early.

He's driving because he's frustrated and he needs to do something to work off the tension. Beating the crap out of that guy Tommy hadn't been enough.

"I'll give it a couple more minutes," he says. "Then I'll call Krebs. See what the story is."

Marco nods.

"You know what I think," Marco says. "I think it was that guy McCoy who called the cops on us."

"No kidding," Phil says. "You're a fricking Einstein, you know that?"

It occurs to him that Marco may not know who Einstein was.

"Why did he do that?" Marco asks.

"To screw with us. He also figured if we got taken into custody, we wouldn't be able to chase him. Thing is, I can't figure out how he knew we'd tracked him to that motel. If I find out that guy Tommy told him, I'll slice him into thin strips and use him for bait."

Phil checks his watch again.

"McCoy should be here at any minute. That's what Krebs said."

"Isn't this guy Krebs a motorcycle dude?" Marco asks.

"That's right."

"I don't like motorcycle dudes. They're weird. All that leather and everything."

Dutch says something about leather and Taco laughs.

What a couple of morons.

Phil points at a gray pickup that is parked behind them, further down the street. "Hey, doesn't that scumbag McCoy have a gray pickup?"

"That's right," Marco says.

Phil hands him a copy of the registration information they'd obtained from a clerk at the DMV.

"Go over and check the license plate. See if it's our friend's truck. He isn't supposed to be here yet."

Marco gets out and saunters over. He looks at the plate, then at the paper, then at the plate again. He looks at Phil and shakes his head. He walks back. He's a few steps from the Mercedes when a Chevy Silverado pulls up next to the gray pickup. A man jumps out. He's tall, rangy, and dressed in a T-shirt and jeans. He has a shotgun in his left hand. His right hand is in a splint.

Phil points and screams, "That's him. That's McCoy."

Marco whirls, pulling a pistol from his waistband. He points in the direction of McCoy and fires. Misses. McCoy calmly raises the shotgun and pulls the trigger. There is an explosion and Marco drops like a bag of hammers. McCoy walks in the direction of the Mercedes. He points the shotgun. Phil ducks down behind the dash, praying that it will protect him. Another explosion and shards of glass rain down on Phil. A third explosion and a fourth explosion and the giant Mercedes sags on its haunches like a wounded animal. The rear tires have been shot out. The guy's circling the Mercedes. He's having fun. He's telling them at any moment he can stick the shotgun in the window and turn them all into hamburger. Dutch is screaming in the back seat. A fifth explosion, and Phil hears the hiss of steam escaping from the destroyed radiator.

Then silence except for the sound of Marco moaning for help.

Phil's trying to reach for his pistol but it's stuck in his waistband. He'll have to sit up if he wants to extract it, and there's no way he's sticking his head up where it can be blown off.

He's still under the steering wheel, quivering, when he hears a vehicle drive away.

***

Charlie pulls up outside the library. He sits in the car for five minutes, waiting for his heartbeat to return to normal and for his hands to stop shaking.

Before leaving, he'd blown out the front tires of Krebs's pickup, so nobody could follow him. He went a half-mile before passing a police cruiser with its lights and sirens on coming in the opposite direction.

It passed him without slowing down. He pulled into a parking lot behind a large SUV as two more police cars and an ambulance passed. He waited a couple of minutes before pulling out of the parking lot and driving to the library.

He can't sit here all day. He needs to get far away and quickly. The cops will be out on the streets and looking for a gray pickup. And he still has the shotgun in the duffle bag in the back seat. Forensics could probably match the spent shells at the scene to the shotgun's firing pin and that would mean life in prison for Charlie.

And two run-ins with the Adonis family in two hours is more than enough. He needs to find a safe place for Amy before they catch up with him again. He climbs out of the pickup, looking in all directions.

Inside the library, Amy is laid out on the floor, immersed in a Harry Potter book.

"Come on, sweetie," he says. "It's time for us to go."

Chapter Twenty-Eight

"Dad, what do you do exactly?" Amy asks.

They're travelling north on Highway 9, driving just under the speed limit.

"To make a living? I do a variety of things. Electrical. Mechanical. Mostly stuff involving locks and security systems. I'm good with my hands."

"Do you have an office?"

"Yes, I do."

If you meant by an office a rented warehouse location, the size of a twin-bay garage and filled with key machines, key blanks, bolt cutters, auto opening kits, saws that cut through drywall and saws that cut through metal, padlock shims, slim jims, pick guns, door handle removers, FM oscillators that jam TV cameras, and drawers full of lock picking tools.

"Can I see it sometime?"

"You mean, like take your daughter to work day?"

"Why not?"

"I think we could do that. Sometime."

"Do you work with other people?"

A large sign by the side of the road is flashing red and in big neon letters it's saying CAUTION. There must be an accident up ahead.

"Sometimes I work with other people."

"Do you have a boss?"

The traffic is stopped, and he gently presses the brake pedal until the truck comes to a halt.

"I'm my own boss," he says. "You really like to read, don't you? I noticed that. In the library. What book was it?"

"The Deathly Hallows. I read it in fourth grade, but it's still good. There's nobody who writes like J. K. Rowling."

"Who's that?"

"She wrote the Harry Potter books," Amy says. "You must've heard of those."

"Sure. I think so. They're about a kid who's a magician, right?"

"Wizard. I'm going to be a writer someday."

"No kidding. What kind of books are you going to write?"

"Novels. Short stories. Serious literary fiction mostly. But fun, as well."

They're moving at a snail's pace. This isn't good. There must've been witnesses to his shooting spree. The cops will be looking for an old gray pick-up. He needs to put some space between him and the crime scene.

"I enjoy reading," he says. "I don't remember your mother reading anything except those magazines of hers. Maybe you get it from me."

"Or maybe the mailman liked to read."

"You're a funny kid, you know that? You actually written anything yet?"

"Some poems. And a short story. Mister Adler said it was very good. He said it was very realistic and painfully honest. He thinks I can be a published writer."

"Who is Mister Adler?

"He's my English teacher. He's also the tenth grade creative writing teacher. I'm going to be in his class next year."

"You're going into tenth grade? You just turned fourteen, right?"

"I skipped fourth grade. Didn't you know that?"

He sees the problem--there's a disabled car up ahead that's backing up traffic. Some idiot probably forgot to gas up their car.

"You skipped fourth grade--I think I remember something about that. So this guy Adler, he's your English teacher at that school you go to, right? What's that school called?"

"The Friends School. It's a Quaker school. Quite well-regarded."

"That's right. I knew that. Do you like it?"

"It's all right. Did you know Mom works in the office there?"

"I guess I heard that. What was the story about?"

She shakes her head the way she does when she's embarrassed.

Then, after a moment, she says, "A girl growing up without a father. Mister Adler told us to write about what we know."

Charlie turns off the highway and onto an exit ramp.

"Where are we going?" she asks. "This isn't the way back to the motel."

"There any money in that writing business?"

"Are you lost? This isn't the right way."

Now he's stopped again, in line for a red light.

"That guy Stephen King makes plenty of dough, right? I think I read that somewhere."

"Didn't you hear me?" She says, raising her voice. "This isn't right."

"I heard you. You have a good sense of direction. We're going north. We're going to visit your aunt in Maine for a while. You know, instead of staying at the Shore."

"What about our stuff in the motel room?"

"It's in the back seat. I checked us out early."

Her head swivels around to check the back seat.

"Why did you do that?" she asks.

"I was getting tired of that town. Too many people around."

"But we didn't go to the beach."

"Don't whine. We'll go another time."

"What's going on, really?"

The light turns green and they're moving again. He takes a left onto a county two-lane. It's not the direction he wants to go in, but it's away and that's all that matters.

"Nothing's going on," he says.

"I have a right to know."

"What you don't know can't hurt you. You ever hear that expression?"

"I want to know what you're hiding from me."

Charlie makes a hard right turn onto the narrow shoulder, and then slams on the brakes. The truck skids on the gravel as it slides to a stop.

"It's like this," he says patiently. "We can't go back to the motel room because there are some men looking for me. They'll find me--us--if we go back. And that would be bad for us. Very bad. Do you understand me now?"

"I knew it. It's like Mom said. You owe those men money, that's why they're looking for you."

He shakes his head. "As a matter of fact it's not about money. Well, it is about money because everything is about money, but it's about something else."

"What?"

"I have something that belongs to them."

"You stole it from them?"

"That's right. I stole something that didn't belong to me, and they want it back."

"Just give it back."

"It's not that easy."

Her mouth hardens into a grimace.

"That's what you do, isn't it? For a living. You're a thief."

Crap.

"What did you say?"

"Don't lie to me," she says. "Mom told me all about it. When I was little. You were in prison. Because you got caught stealing stuff."

He's silent, staring out the windshield, trying to think.

"She shouldn't have told you about that," he says.

"It wouldn't have made any difference. I looked you up on Google. I would've known sooner or later, anyway. You can't hide the truth now."

She says this with an attitude of absolute assurance.

"It's true," he says. "That's what I do for a living. I'm a thief. Sad, but true. I steal other people's stuff."

"What kind of stuff?"

"Money. Or whatever I think I can sell for money. What do you think of that?"

"Who do you steal from?"

"Rich people mainly. I don't steal from poor people on account of the fact they never have anything worth taking."

She frowns. "Why can't you just give back the stuff you stole from these men?"

"I've thought of that, believe me. I don't think that'll work. These people I stole from are very bad. Just getting their stuff back won't be enough."

"What is this stuff?"

"I can't tell you that. Really. You're better off not knowing."

"Are they thieves, too?"

"They're worse than thieves."

"Worse than you?"

He shifts into gear and pulls back onto the road.

"Yeah, even worse than me," he says.

Tears form in the corners of her eyes.

"I'm scared. I want to go back to mom. Right now."

"That's not possible at the moment."

"Why not? You shouldn't have dragged me into this. It's not safe being with you. You just said so."

"I can't take you back to your mother. Not right now. If we go back there, it'll put her life in danger. Yours, too if you're with her. It's safer this way. I'm taking you to Maine. You'll be safe with your aunt and uncle. Nobody will look for you there."

She asks when she can go back to her mother. Tears are rolling down her cheeks. He tells her she'll see her mother soon.

Lies. All lies.

But what good would it do to tell her the truth? It is too late for the truth now.

"When will I see her? Just tell me."

"Not long. I promise. This will all be over soon."

"You should go to the police. Tell them what happened."

Charlie squeezes the steering wheel, feeling the little ridges bite into his hand.

"And tell them what?" he says. "That I stole some stuff. I'll get sent to prison. With a previous felony conviction I could get fifteen years. Or more." He turns to her and wags his finger. "I've been in prison and I'm not going back. Not ever. I'd rather die."

Chapter Twenty-Nine

De La Torre is walking toward the front door of his house when his cell rings. It's Polaski.

"That witness came in early this morning," he says. "The one I told you about. I thought you'd like to know."

De La Torre swears under his breath.

"You say something?" Polaski asks.

"No nothing. I thought she wasn't coming in until tomorrow."

"Came in today on account of she decided to leave town for the Fourth. We had to make some quick arrangements."

De La Torre watches some people he doesn't know enter his house. The driveway is already filled. Cars are parked in the street, a block in both directions. Old man Stephens's sixty-fifth birthday is going to be some kind of shindig.

De La Torre says, "Why didn't you let me know about the witness? I wanted to be there when you spoke to her."

"It was kind of last minute, you know. But get this. She did make a positive ID."

"Really? You sure?"

"She was certain as a heart attack. It's a guy named Charles Lawrence McCoy."

"How can you be so sure?"

"She didn't have any doubt. And he fits. I don't have any doubt it's him."

"So, who is this guy McCoy?"

"Strictly a small time punk. I didn't even think he was involved when she first identified him. I thought he was just a guy who happened to be in the neighborhood, passing through. That's what I figured. Or maybe the witness made a mistaken ID. Shooting a guy doesn't seem to be quite McCoy's MO. He's more of a B and E guy, at least from his record."

"But you changed your mind?"

"Sure did. I was checking reports and saw that McCoy's ex-wife turned up murdered this morning along with her boyfriend. That set my radar humming. Now what're the odds on that? He's seen walking from the getaway car, and his wife is killed a few hours later?"

"So, what are you thinking?"

"McCoy's gone off the deep end. First he kills this guy Baker. Now his wife and her boyfriend. Probably walked in on them and something snapped. Or maybe it's drugs."

"What's the plan?"

"We've got an APB out as we speak. Armed and extremely dangerous. This guy McCoy must be some kind of bad actor. I understand he did a real number on his ex-wife."

De La Torre watches as two small boys ride by on bicycles. It's a warm day in the middle of the summer, and they don't have a care in the world. He'd give anything to be one of those boys right now.

"Hey, you still there?" Polaski asks.

De La Torre says, "Yeah, that's good news. We're starting to get somewhere. Please, keep me updated of any additional developments. Especially if you get a lead on McCoy's location."

He gets in his car and hurriedly calls Jerry O'Brien on a disposable cell. He leaves a message on O'Brien's voice mail, not even bothering to disguise his voice because he doesn't want to waste the time with the tape recorder.

Why didn't Polaski tell him before about the witness coming in? He doesn't buy Polaski's explanation. Seems more likely Polaski decided to keep the info from him for some reason. Does Polaski suspect something?

He thinks for a minute, then turns his car back toward the city and, as he does, he asks himself how he got into this mess.

The answer is easy and it goes back more than twenty years--shortly after he became a Newark PD cop and he first met a small-time dealer named Fat Ray Shavers. Fat Ray had a business proposition for him. "Mutually beneficial," he called it.

A few years later, he was a first year detective with Newark PD, the youngest on the force. Late one night, he was standing in the parking garage of his condo, waiting for the elevator. He'd just worked back-to-back shifts, and he was bone-weary.

A black Town Car pulled up next to him.

A voice from inside shouted, "Officer De La Torre, wait up."

De La Torre turned. Whoever's inside knows I'm a cop. His hand slid into his pants pocket, where he kept his off-duty piece.

O'Brien heaved himself from his limo and waddled over.

"Do you know who I am?" he said.

"You're Jerry O'Brien," De La Torre replied. "I've seen you at the courthouse. And, by the way, it's Detective De La Torre, not officer."

"Then you know I'm Phil Adonis's lawyer."

"What I know is you're pretty stupid approaching me like this and all."

De La Torre pointed at CCTV camera in the corner above the elevator. "You shouldn't be here talking to me, especially the day before trial. And now there's a record. Lose your law license for a stunt like this."

O'Brien pulled an eight-ounce can of gray spray paint from his pocket.

"That camera's not recording anything," he said. "My driver sprayed the lens. And the cashier never saw me when we came in because the back seat has a tinted divider and good luck trying to trace that limo to me."

De La Torre chuckled, but deep down he was scared. He couldn't figure O'Brien's angle.

"Sounds like you've gone to a hell of a lot of trouble," he said. "What for?"

"I need you to get all confused tomorrow at trial."

"Confused? This'll be a walk in the park. I won't be all confused about anything."

"Yes, you will. You'll not be able to identify the knife when you're shown it."

De La Torre shook his head and asked why he'd do a fool thing like that.

"Because you'll incur the good will of Phil Adonis, Senior, that's why. He doesn't want his son and namesake going to prison for a stupid prank."

The overhead fluorescent light flickered, causing O'Brien's face to move in and out of darkness.

"Stabbing his girlfriend isn't what I would call a prank," De La Torre said. "Anyway, if I don't identify the knife, the girl will, so what's the difference?"

"She won't be identifying anything. She won't even be in the courtroom tomorrow. As we speak, she's on a plane to Madrid to study art for a couple of years. Don't tell the assistant D.A. We want it to be our little surprise."

"I'm still not doing it. Why should I? The name Phil Adonis don't mean anything to me, except he's a known hoodlum."

"You might want to rethink that. If I have to, I'll cross-examine you regarding your business relationship with a certain individual known as Fat Ray Shavers."

"Fat Ray Shavers?"

"You know, the arrangement you have with him where you take a couple of ounces of heroin or cocaine from the evidence room and sell it to Fat Ray for about half the street value, which he then retails."

"You're crazy."

"I'm guessing the judge allows this line of cross examination since our theory is the evidence in this case was mishandled."

De La Torre pushed the elevator button.

"This is all bullshit," he muttered.

"Even if the judge doesn't allow the cross examination, the assistant D.A. will hear my arguments and report back to your superiors. What happens to your career when Internal Affairs investigates? You know Fat Ray will roll over on you at the slightest touch. You won't be able to stay out of prison. And you know what happens to cops in prison."

The elevator doors opened.

"What happens if I testify the way you say?" De La Torre asked.

"The charges against Phil Adonis go away and everybody's happy."

"And that won't be the end of it. You'll keep coming back, wanting more. Reminding me of Fat Ray every time."

"We're always on the lookout for a bright young cop who knows which way is up. We're in a position to help you. We can let you know when drug buys are going down and where illegal poker games are being held and who're running prostitution rings with illegal immigrants."

"All by your competitors, no doubt."

"The Adonis family has no real competitors. But you do catch on fast."

"You're forgetting. I'm in robbery-homicide. Not vice."

O'Brien chuckled. "Then transfer to vice."

That was sixteen years ago and he's been in the pocket of the Adonis family ever since. He sometimes thinks how differently things would've been if he wasn't assigned to investigate that particular aggravated assault involving Little Phil. He would never have been a target for the Adonis family. It wasn't until years later he learned that he received the case assignment because no other Newark PD detective would come near it.

Chapter Thirty

"Why were you put in prison?" she asks. "Mom would never tell me. But I overheard her talking to Aunt Louise. It had something to do with a robbery."

This has been going on for over an hour. He's tired of the questions, but there's nothing he can do. He's stuck in the car with her until they get to Maine. He can't get away and he can't get her to shut up.

And if they stay on the back roads, they'll still have fourteen hours of drive time.

He's thinking they can stop at a restaurant and while she's in the restroom he can stuff a couple of grand in her backpack and then drive off. He tells himself she'd be safer without him around. What will happen to her if he abandons her? Will the Adonis family come looking for her to find out what she knows? Who will protect her then? Will she end up like Carol?

So, is she safer with him or without him? Now, that's a hell of a question.

His mind is just going around in circles now.

He isn't going to dump her, that's all there is to it. This may be the last time she ever sees him. He doesn't want her last memory of him to be that he dropped her at a Howard Johnson's and drove away when she wasn't looking.

"My past isn't something I want to talk about," he says. "It's in the past."

"Are you a jugger?" She asks in an excited tone.

"A what?"

"A safe cracker."

"Jesus. A jugger. I haven't heard that in twenty years. Where did you hear it?"

"I read about it online in the library. Jugger. Wheel man. Button man. I read about all of it. Thieving, that is. Except you call yourselves heisters."

"I thought you were reading Harry Potter books."

"Nah, that's for kids. I was just pretending to read it when I saw you pull up. How come you sat in the car for so long after you parked at the library?"

"I wasn't feeling too great."

She gives him that inquisitive stare of hers.

"You know what I want to know?'

There's an officious tone in her voice that he doesn't like.

"What's that?"

"Why did you go to prison?"

He gives her a look but she continues to stare.

"For committing the worst crime there is," he says. "The crime of being stupid."

She continues to look at him, evidently expecting more.

"Did you steal something?" she asks.

"Tried to. Thirty-five inch TV sets. Sonys. Top of the line. One hundred of them to be exact. We had a fence who'd pay us two hundred per TV. Twenty grand altogether, to be split four ways. The TVs were in a warehouse. There wasn't supposed to be any guards, only an alarm system. It was my job to take care of that and the locks. I arrived with a couple of other guys and took care of what I was supposed to do, but the guy with the truck was late and that delayed everything. I should've backed out right then, but I needed the money. A lousy five grand."

"So what happened?"

"While we were waiting, two armed security guards drove up. Me and another guy got away clean another guy got shot in the gut and was bleeding pretty bad. We talked about dumping him in the salt marshes. He said--"

"But he'd die!"

"If we took the guy to the ER, they'd call the police. They always call the police when somebody comes in with a gunshot wound, figuring there's a good chance he was up to no good, otherwise he wouldn't have gotten shot."

"What did you do?" she asked.

"The guy begged us to take him to the ER. He promised he wouldn't give us up. He pleaded. He wept. He said he had two kids and a wife to support. He swore on his sainted mother's grave that he wouldn't rat us out. All the while, he's bleeding in the backseat of my truck. So I dropped him outside a hospital emergency room and then we took off."

"What happened?"

Charlie sighs. "He gave us up in record time. Sang like a choir girl. The next day, a Sunday, the cops broke down the front door and took me into custody. It was embarrassing. Your mother was in the shower. You were at a friend's house. It had been your birthday the day before and you were having a sleep over. The DA told me he'd recommend two years if I told them who the fence was. I'd get out in one year with good behavior. I didn't squeal, so I ended up getting nine years and serving six."

"But you did the right thing. You didn't let the man die."

"Yeah, I did the right thing."

"So why do you think you were stupid?"

The traffic has come to an abrupt halt. He went twenty miles out of his way to avoid the Philadelphia traffic, and still he's still stuck in a gridlock. He can't win for losing.

"I was stupid because I didn't have a backup plan," he says. "I've got three rules in life. The most important is to always have a backup plan."

"What's a backup plan?"

"An exit strategy. A way out."

"So you go into everything looking for a way out?"

"Right, and that time I had no backup plan, and I paid the price with six years of my life."

There must've been something in his voice, or the expression on his face, because she suddenly looks shocked, afraid. He doesn't know how to act around her or what to say to her.

She says, quietly now, "I was three when you went to prison, but I don't remember you from then."

"You were too young, I guess. I don't think people start forming memories until they're about four. I read that somewhere."

"I had a picture of you and Mom together. I found it in the trash after she cleaned out the attic. I used to stare at it, wondering what you were like. Sometimes I dreamed about you . . ."

"Look, I'm sorry--"

"I wondered if you were framed for a crime you didn't commit. When I was seven, a man moved in across the street. He looked kind of like you. I was sure he was you, released from prison. I watched him for two weeks, and then I went to his house and rang the doorbell. When he answered, I told him that I knew that he was my father. He denied it, but I was sure he was lying. He wasn't, of course."

"What happened?"

"He told mom, and she said the man wasn't my father and I should leave him alone. Then he moved away a couple of months later."

"This happened when you were seven? Yeah, I would've still been in the joint then."

"I have a question," she says. "Why didn't you tell them who the fence was? You would've gotten out of prison much sooner. Was he your friend? That's why you protected him?"

"No. Actually he's a real asshole. His name's Billie Joe Fish. He owns a pawnshop and he's a first-rate jerk."

She tosses him a glance that suggests she doesn't believe him.

"So you went to prison to protect a person you don't even like?"

"I'm not a squealer. It's not about friendship. It's just not good business to squeal. You don't want a reputation as a rat, especially if you're in prison."

She nods, as if she understands. Then she asks what it was like in prison.

"You keep your mouth shut. Mind your own business. Keep looking over your shoulder. It's not too different than real life."

Chapter Thirty-One

De La Torre tries to open the back door to Luigi's but finds it locked.

Weird.

There's no way that O'Brien would ignore his call. He made it clear he had to speak with him immediately.

He thinks for a moment and then walks around to the front. It's after the lunch hour and the restaurant is almost empty. Luigi is standing near a table, some menus in his hand. He sees De La Torre and turns abruptly toward the bar.

De La Torre heads him off saying, "Hey, wait up a minute, Luigi. We need to talk."

"What do you want?" Luigi asks. He sounds upset.

"I'm here to see the big man. You know, that guy."

"I know who you mean. I haven't seen him."

"Shit, that's bad. There's something I have to tell him. It's really important. He's supposed to meet me here."

"That's your problem. Listen, I don't want you here. You're being disruptive. Your swearing is bothering my customers."

De La Torre looks around.

"There's nobody here," he says.

"Go. Now."

Luigi points toward the door.

De La Torre steps outside and looks up and down the street. He has to talk to O'Brien before something happens to that witness.

He gets in his car and drives toward center city, thinking how different Luigi was from all the other times. No charming, laughing Luigi this time. Why? Because there's no O'Brien here this time, that's the difference. Without O'Brien, he is just another Negro disturbing the customers.

O'Brien's offices are in a renovated two-story brick building on a corner, a block from the federal courthouse. De La Torre drives by without slowing. One of the other federal agencies has surveillance on the building. DEA? ATF? Justice Department? He can't remember.

It doesn't make any difference. He can't be seen going into that building. He stops for a red light. A slender young woman comes out of O'Brien's building, crosses the street in front of De La Torre's car, and steps inside a deli that's on the opposite corner.

As soon as the light changes, De La Torre makes a quick right turn and pulls up next to a NO PARKING sign.

Inside the deli, he sidles up behind the woman, who is waiting at the counter. He leans over, whispers in her ear.

"You work for Jerry O'Brien, right?"

The woman turns. She looks scared. A strange black man approaching a white woman in public will do that.

He flashes his FBI ID. "I'm with the FBI. I need to talk with him. Right now. Tell him it's Mike De La Torre. It's very important I speak with him."

The guy behind the cash register says to her, "This guy bothering you?"

"Butt out, pal," De La Torre says. "This is FBI business."

She grabs her bag of food and slaps a ten-dollar bill on the counter. Without even waiting for her change, she hurries out of the deli, looking back over her shoulder at De La Torre.

De La Torre takes a seat in a booth at the back, with the cashier keeping a close eye on him. Five minutes later, O'Brien bursts through the door and strides straight back to the men's restroom without even looking at De La Torre. De La Torre follows.

In the restroom, O'Brien checks the stalls, sees they're empty, and then turns. His face is blood red. He looks away and then back at De La Torre. Without any warning he swings a massive right fist into the side of De La Torre's head. De La Torre's head snaps backward into a metal paper towel dispenser, and he slides to the dirty floor.

O'Brien tells him to get up. De La Torre staggers to his feet, his ears ringing. O'Brien pats him down roughly, pulling and grabbing at his clothes.

"I'm not wearing a wire," De La Torre says. "What the hell are you doing?"

"What the hell are you doing?" O'Brien shouts in his ear, his lips just an inch away. "You could've been seen. You've already been compromised for all I know."

"I needed--"

"You needed nothing. You needed to do nothing. You needed to say nothing. You just had to stay the hell out of the way. But you couldn't even do that. I can't believe your stupidity. I can't stand this crap. I can't stand it anymore. Everything's falling apart."

De La Torre thinks, he's scared. Big Jerry O'Brien is scared.

"I needed to talk to you," De La Torre says. "I called and left a message. You weren't at Luigi's."

"That should've given you a clue. I don't need to talk to you. Not right now. Maybe not ever again. Ever. Understand?"

"I needed to tell you the witness had already spoken to the police. She's already identified McCoy."

O'Brien stares into space for a moment.

"You're saying this like it's a good thing that the cops have identified McCoy. I don't see it that way."

"I'm saying call off the dogs. It's too late, now."

O'Brien rubs his chin.

"Thanks for the update. Now get the hell out of here. I don't want to be seen with you."

Chapter Thirty-Two

Charlie's standing next to a pay phone located on the exterior wall of a small supermarket, a few feet from the doors. He glances at Amy, who is sitting in the truck. She nods her head twice. He calls the operator and gets the number for the FBI. A woman answers, and he tells her he wants the assistant director.

"What is the nature of your business?" the receptionist asks.

"I've got something the FBI will want to hear."

He gets put on hold. Classical music comes on. He waits. They're taking too long. Finally a man's voice comes on the line.

"What can I do for you?" he says. He sounds young. Probably a small cog in the vast FBI machine.

"I've got some information," Charlie says. "It concerns the Adonis crime family."

"What kind of information?"

He doesn't sound interested, bored really.

"The kind that'll blow your socks off. Really. I'm not kidding here. Pay attention."

"Can you be a little more specific?"

A woman comes out of the store, pushing a full shopping cart. Charlie waits until she's out of earshot.

"This involves bribes to public officials," he says. "Money laundering. The financial operations of the Adonis crime family, going back many years. What they do with their illegal money. That sort of thing. It's all recorded on discs. And I have the discs. "

"How did you come by this information?"

The kid sounds amused, as if Charlie has offered to sell him the complete library of Glen Miller recordings on vinyl.

"You're not listening," Charlie says. "This could put dozens of people away for a long time. Some serious people. That's what's important here."

"May I have your name?"

"What's yours?"

"James."

"Listen up, James. You'll want to report this to your boss. Right away. Understand. I'll call you back."

"We need some confirmation that you're not . . ."

"A nut? Look, I know you get calls from crazy people all day long. It's probably your job to field those calls. But I'm not a nut. Really."

Charlie realizes that's the sort of thing a nut would say.

"I still need your name," the kid says.

"Not right now."

"Can you come in? Show us what you have?"

"I'll have to think about that."

"How can we get in touch with you?"

Charlie waits as an elderly man walks by him and into the store.

"Don't worry about getting in touch with me," Charlie says. "I'll get in touch with you. In the meantime, run this name. Moe Baker. See what turns up. By the way, this is a public phone, so your trace won't do you much good. Five minutes from now, I'll be a couple of miles away. And I'm wearing gloves, so you can save some time by not dusting for prints. And I'm hanging up now."

Chapter Thirty-Three

De La Torre walks into his house. With so many folding chairs and tables set up, it's as if he's navigating a minefield. The dining room table and the buffet are covered in plates overflowing with food. A guy in a waiter's outfit is slicing a ham and putting the slices on a tray next to slices of rare roast beef. There are a couple of large platters of asparagus with hollandaise sauce, another of devilled eggs, another with rumaki, and a couple of others of prosciutto and melon. A huge fat woman whom De La Torre doesn't recognize is fishing boiled shrimp out of a large silver bucket. He steps into the kitchen, where oysters of the half shell are being prepared. The kitchen table is occupied by a huge three-tiered birthday cake that reads HAPPY BIRTHDAY THAD! In the back yard, a bar has been set up next to the pool.

It's like a dream. Or, rather, a nightmare. He walks through what is his home and nobody says a word to him. His two sisters-in-law float past as if he doesn't exist. It's as if he's a ghost.

And that's not the worst part. The budget for this event is supposed to be $4,000. His eyeball estimate tells him it's been exceeded by at least twice that much, and all for the birthday of a man who can't stand him.

He secures a Chivas and water from the barkeep, quickly downs it and asks for another.

He surveys the scene. Two dozen of his wife's family are already prowling around. De La Torre has never been able to talk to those people. Mostly because they never wanted to talk to him. They've always taken their cues from the judge in that regard. Still, it made him feel good that they were eating his food and drinking his liquor at a house that is better than any of theirs. And none of them has the best part of $200,000 in a Bahamas Island bank account.

He sees his daughter chatting with a couple of her cousins. He waves, but she ignores him. This irritates him even more. He asks for a third Chivas and water.

The bitter taste of bile creeps up his throat and he pushes his drink away. He heads toward the house, thinking he'll go for a long drive, when he hears a booming voice, like a clap of thunder, from behind him.

"There's the man I want to see."

De La Torre turns to see a heavy-set black man in plaid Bermuda shorts bearing down on him. It's his father-in-law, Federal District Judge Thaddeus Stevens.

Chapter Thirty-Four

Phil is in the waiting room of a hospital, handcuffed to a chair, sitting between two uniformed cops. Dutch and Taco sit on the other side of the room. Both are handcuffed to their chairs.

He's been held for two hours. Two hours that McCoy has had to make his escape. He has an idea how to find McCoy, but he has to be sprung from police custody first.

Jerry O'Brien walks in with that mincing gait of his.

"Jesus," O'Brien says, looking around. "What's this all about?"

The older of the two cops, the one with sergeant's stripes, looks at O'Brien.

"Who're you?"

"I'm Phillip Adonis's attorney. I'm also Robert Bell's attorney and I'm Rutger Aalbers's attorney. Now, you want to answer my question?"

"They're being held as suspects in the shooting of a Marco Delassandro."

"I'm Marco Delassandro's attorney as well. My information, limited though it may be, says this was a random drive-by shooting and that my clients weren't involved. What evidence do you have to warrant holding them regarding this tragic incident?"

"They've been less than forthcoming, let's put it that way. I've got reasonable suspicion to hold them in Delassandro's shooting. We're figuring their memories will improve after a night or two in jail."

"It all happened so fast," Phil says, piping up. "This guy comes out of nowhere. Shoots Marco. Then he drives off. I was just trying to avoid getting shot myself."

"Same with me," Taco says.

"Me, too," Dutch says.

O'Brien says, "There. You have all the information you need. Like I said. A random drive-by incident. Tragic in its consequences. You have no basis for a reasonable suspicion that my clients committed a crime. Now let them go."

The sergeant says, "So I'm supposed to believe some unknown person drives up, shoots a capo of the Adonis crime family, and shoots up a vehicle with Little Phil Adonis in it. And then drives off and none of your clients have any clue who it was?"

O'Brien's face settles into a frown.

"That's about the size of it. And by the way, my clients don't like the term Adonis crime family. It has certain negative connotations, as well as being inaccurate. Also, please don't use the term Little Phil when referring to Mister Adonis. It shows a lack of proper respect."

The sergeant laughs derisively.

"Lack of respect. I'll show you some lack of respect--"

His partner grabs him by the arm and shakes his head. The sergeant purses his lips. You can practically see him counting to ten.

The sergeant takes out a little spiral-bound notebook from his breast pocket and turns to Phil.

"What did the shooter's vehicle look like?"

"A gray pickup truck," Phil says.

"Did you get the license?"

"No way."

"What about the shooter?"

"He was a white guy."

"Young or old?"

"Middle aged."

"Tall or short?"

"About medium. That's all I remember. It happened so fast."

"That's all I remember," Taco says.

"Me, too," Dutch says.

"Any idea why this unknown middle-aged white man would've wanted to shoot up your vehicle?"

Phil squints and cocks his head to the side.

"Can't think of any."

"What were you doing before the shooting started?"

"Trying to decide whether to go to the amusement park or the beach."

The sergeant gives Phil piercing look.

"How do you know George Krebs?"

"Who's that?"

"Your little firefight occurred outside his house and he was a witness, although he says he didn't see anything either."

"Still drawing a blank on this Mr. Krebs."

"He's heavily involved with an outlaw motorcycle gang which is associated with the Aryan Nations. Does that jog your memory?

"No, can't help you. But he does certainly does sound like a bad man. And it seemed like such a nice neighborhood."

The sergeant looks at O'Brien.

"That's all your clients have to say?"

"Apparently so."

"I just let them go based on your say-so?"

"That's about the size of it."

The sergeant tucks away his notebook in his shirt pocket.

"Listen, mister, I take it you're old school, looking at you and all. Things may have been handled that way in your day, but it's a different world now." He points a finger at O'Brien. "Get it? Nine-eleven changed everything. If we think somebody has information related to a crime, we're authorized to take them in. Even if they are Little Phil Adonis."

O'Brien clears his throat and says, "For your information, the Fourth Amendment to the United States Constitution has yet to be repealed."

"We can hold them for up to forty-eight hours without charging them. You should know that. To facilitate our investigation. And I don't care what some smart-ass lawyer says."

O'Brien leans forward, toward the sergeant, getting in his face.

"Be reasonable. Mister Adonis and his associates are busy men. There are important matters he has to attend to."

The cop snickers.

"I'm familiar with Little Phil's line of work. And his friends. We all are. Keeping them off the streets for forty-eight hours won't hurt anybody."

O'Brien looks around, a quizzical expression on his face.

"Does anybody know where I can get a cup of coffee around here?" he asks.

"There's a cafeteria down the hallway," the young cop says, pointing. "There's a coffee machine in there."

O'Brien nods, and he shuffles into the hallway, disappearing around the corner.

After a few minutes, the young cop nods toward the window.

"The other squad cars are here," he says.

"Good, it's about time," the sergeant says. "I want each of these bastards in a different car. So they can't get their stories together."

The younger cop unlocks Phil's handcuffs from the chair and tells him to stand.

"You don't look so smart now, do you?" the cop whispers in Phil's ear.

Phil shakes his head.

"I'm not going anywhere until my lawyer gets back."

"We're doing this on our schedule, not yours. You'll be on your way to the station before he gets back. Great lawyer you got there. Walks off to get some coffee and leaves you hanging. What a dumbass."

The young cop is handcuffing Phil's hands behind his back when the sergeant's cell phone rings. He answers it, nods his head twice and then listens. The corners of his mouth pull down.

"We've got them right here," he says. "We can hold them. If nothing else, they're material witnesses to an attempted homicide."

He nods again and the frown deepens.

"You're the boss," he says tersely.

He slips the phone back in his shirt pocket and turns to the young cop.

"Take the cuffs off them. We're letting them go. All of them. The captain says so." He shakes his head. "Screw this."

Phil smiles at the young cop.

"What a dumbass," he says.

A couple of seconds later, O'Brien wanders in, blowing on a cup of coffee.

"Anything happen while I was gone?" he asks.

***

Outside, they're in O'Brien's Escalade. Dutch and Taco are standing next to the front doors of the hospital, whispering. O'Brien doesn't like hospitals. Nobody likes hospitals, but O'Brien is terrified of hospitals. They remind him of the doctors who are always urging him to lose weight before he has a heart attack or a stroke or lapses into a diabetic coma.

"I had to call in some favors to get this taken care of," O'Brien says. "A lot of favors."

"A police captain," Phil says. "So what? Couldn't have cost much."

"I had to go higher than a captain."

"What? Chief of police? Commissioner?"

"Mayor. And it cost plenty. Word on the street is that the Adonis family is a wounded beast. Everybody's going to try to tear off a chunk while they have the opportunity. People are suddenly emboldened. I can feel the fear ebbing away. Everything considered, it's a damned lucky thing you're out of police custody."

"That's what we pay you for."

The late afternoon sun is directly in O'Brien's eyes and it's aggravating an already intolerable headache. The meeting with Joey Bats caused him to skip lunch and his blood sugar is low and he's cranky and he feels like hitting somebody.

"What did you do with your guns?" O'Brien asks.

"We gave them to a guy."

O'Brien tries to shield his eyes but it doesn't help. He flips the sun visor down, but it doesn't help either, so he puts it back up.

"Can you trust this guy you gave the guns to?" he asks.

"Sure. Guns are his business. And he's the one who gave us the tip on McCoy. How come you haven't even asked about Marco? You know, the guy who's your client."

Phil shoots him a malicious grin. Phil has a large wide mouth with too many teeth. It's the kind of mouth an apex predator would have.

"Tell me," O'Brien says. "How is dear Marco?"

"They say he'll probably live. But he's going to lose his right arm. That's what I heard."

"That's terrible."

"Terrible? Are you kidding? It's a tragedy. Marco loses his arm because of a two-bit punk like this guy McCoy. What kind of justice is that?"

"Let me remind you of something that's far worse than Marco losing his arm. McCoy is still running around. With our information. And you haven't accomplished a damn thing except draw attention to yourself. The FBI's going to be wondering what's going on with all this gunplay. Combine that with the locals looking for McCoy and we're up shit creek in a chicken wire boat."

"Don't worry yourself. I have an idea how to find McCoy."

O'Brien rubs his temples, trying to make the headache go away.

"We have a couple of additional problems that you're not aware of," he says. "The first is that the cops have already figured out who McCoy is."

"How did that happen? Tino took care of that witness this morning."

"Too late. She already visited with the cops and identified McCoy."

"She wasn't coming in until tomorrow. It wasn't supposed to happen like that."

O'Brien glances at Taco and Dutch. What are they whispering about? O'Brien's feeling as if he can't trust anybody. He's relying on a sociopath with anger management issues to take care of their problems. For the first time he's thinking he's not coming out of this alive.

"She's not testifying," Phil continues. "That's for sure. And that's a good thing."

"It doesn't matter. The cops know it's McCoy they're looking for. And our other problem's worse."

"What's that?"

"You're almost out of time."

"We had him twice today. We'll get him soon. I have a plan."

O'Brien thinks, Christ, they had him twice and he got away both times. His chest tightens, as if somebody has a death grip on his heart. O'Brien assumed that McCoy was just another ignorant street felon. That was a mistake.

"You need to know," O'Brien says. "I had a visit from Joey Bats today."

Phil grins again. "Uh-oh, they let Joey Bats out of his cage. Am I supposed to be impressed or something?"

O'Brien clears his throat.

"It wasn't a pleasant meeting. New York has put us on notice. They're an inch away from taking care of this business themselves."

"What the hell does that mean?"

"It means you're almost out of time. And I take that to mean permanently. Get it? He brought a hitter with him just to make the point."

"They can't pull the plug on us."

"Yes, they can. And they will. And they're going to pull the plug on everything. And I mean everything and everybody. Do you understand what I'm trying to tell you?"

Chapter Thirty-Five

De La Torre has been trying to escape from his father-in-law for a half hour, but to no avail. He's been getting the official life story. Again. Poor boy makes good, goes to Princeton. Then Berkeley Law School. Then Arnold & Porter, a big-time law firm in Washington DC. And before you know it, a position on the federal bench. It's the judge's origin story.

De La Torre's heard it a half-dozen times. He's not sure whether his history is the only thing the judge is comfortable taking about with him or whether it's a sign of early onset Alzheimer's. What's always left out--De La Torre learned from other sources--is that the judge's grades were never that good, but he applied to law school pre-Bakke, when simply being a black with a college degree from an Ivy League school and the ability to fog a mirror was sufficient to get admitted to a prestigious law school. Arnold & Porter hired him for diversity purposes and shunted him from one relatively insignificant task to another. After eight years, the firm imposed upon its friends in the Reagan Administration to make Thaddeus a federal district judge so that they wouldn't have to make him a partner.

How to fail upwards. With style.

"You know," the judge says, "I remember when I was a young lawyer. Leticia and I barely had two nickels to rub together." He lets his eyes wander around the outside of the house and across the pool. "But look at all this. And on an FBI agent's salary."

"That's supervising special-agent-in-charge. And when it comes to money, Cynthia I are quite frugal."

The judge let loose with a raucous laugh. "I know my daughter, and the one thing she ain't is frugal."

"What is this you are saying about me?"

It's Cynthia. She has a phone in her hand and the way she's holding it--as if she's about to throw it at him-- suggests she's not happy.

"Here," she says to De La Torre. "It's your office calling. Big surprise."

Prescott's on the phone and he sounds excited. De La Torre ambles over to a corner of the yard behind the pool.

"There have been some big developments in the Adonis case," Prescott says.

"What kind of developments?"

"Why don't you come in so we can talk about this?"

"There's a party at the house. For my father-in-law. You know, the federal judge. It's his sixty-fifth birthday."

"Mike, you need to come in. Now."

Chapter Thirty-Six

It's twilight now and the highway is poorly lit. They're in Northeastern Pennsylvania, the coal region, that area of Pennsylvania that once produced the coal that fired the steel furnaces--now shuttered--for Bethlehem Steel and US Steel, who produced the steel that made the trains, the cars, the planes, and the sky scrapers that once made America great.

Charlie's not hungry, but Amy must be. They haven't eaten since breakfast and that was eleven hours ago.

A large green sign says COAL CITY. A hundred yards further on another sign says FOOD. Some marksman put a bullet right through the D. Welcome to Coal City.

He pulls off the highway and onto a two lane asphalt road, which is strewn with potholes and gravel. The old truck bumps and shimmies.

"Where are we going?" she asks.

"To get something to eat."

"I meant after that."

"Like I said, I'm taking you to your aunt's house."

"I didn't think you really meant it. She lives in Maine, which is pretty far away. From everything. And her house is way too cold."

"It's an old farmhouse. Those places are tough to keep warm. Anyway, it's summertime. How cold can it get?"

"That house is spooky and dark. I don't like it. And there's nothing to do up there. They don't even have cable."

"You'll find something to do."

"And I don't like Aunt Louise. She's mean."

Charlie thinks about the time Louise called him a force for evil and chaos in their lives. And she wasn't kidding.

"I'm not going to disagree about Aunt Louise," he says. "But you can't stay with me."

"Why not?"

"It's too dangerous."

"What about going to the police?"

They drive by a few run-down ranch-style houses. They must be approaching Coal City.

"I'm still thinking about the police."

He definitely made the right decision when he didn't tell her about her mother. She'd insist they go to the police if she knew Carol is dead, that is for damned sure.

"What happened when you made that call?" she asks.

He slows down as they reach the city limits.

"They asked too many questions, so I hung up."

"You were supposed to talk to them about giving yourself up."

"Right now, I'm thinking about getting some food."

"You've got to go to the police. You can't keep putting this off."

"Yes I can. Just watch me."

They drive through town. The streets are poorly lit. Half the stores are boarded up. The other half look as if they should be. They're on their way out of town when he spots an aluminum-sided diner up ahead. The neon sign on top says NIGHTHA KS. The "W" is burned out.

"Let's try that place," he says.

"It looks kind of creepy," she says.

"Yeah, but maybe the food's good. Appearances can be deceiving. Sometimes."

He parks across the street. As they walk to the diner, she extracts a cell phone from her backpack and starts tapping on it.

"What the holy hell is that?" he says.

"It's a cell phone," she says with a funny look on her face. "I'm texting mom. I haven't heard from her. I don't know what's going on with her."

"That cell phone wasn't in there before. Not when you were at the library."

"Of course not. I had it with me in the library in case I needed to make a call." She pauses. "Wait a minute. Are you saying you went through my backpack?"

"Never mind that. What are you doing with a fricking cell phone?"

"You went through my backpack? Without telling me? That's an invasion of my privacy!"

"I don't care about your privacy. Why do you even have a cell phone?"

"Everybody has one nowadays. Except you, that is. Mom tells me to keep it with me all the time. Just in case she needs to call me. Or I need to call her. Or there's an emergency."

"You can't have that thing. We need to get rid of it. Right now."

She scowls. "Get rid of it? No way."

"They can track us by using that cell phone."

"Who can? The bad men you're running from? Whose stuff you stole?"

He looks around, scared that somebody might've overheard her, but the parking lot is empty.

"This isn't my fault you're in trouble," she says. "Call the police, like you promised. Give yourself up. Then you'll be safe."

He laughs.

"You think I'd be safe in jail? Really? That's the least safe place I could be. In the meantime, you've got to get rid of that damned phone."

"I can't. Mom got it for me. What if she calls? It's the only way she can get in touch with me. And it's got all my friends' numbers on it. It's got all my pictures. I can't just get rid of it."

He grabs it out of her hand and holds it up.

"Give it back," she cried.

"Those men could be tracking us with this thing. Aren't you listening?"

"You're being paranoid. How would they track us? They don't even know my number."

They could've gotten it out of your mother.

"I don't know how they could get your number, but they probably have ways. These are very powerful people." He tosses the phone in a large trash can by the front door of the diner. "I'll buy you a new one tomorrow. Now, let's get something to eat."

Inside, there are a couple of old people sitting at the counter and, near the front door, sitting at a table, a guy in a brown uniform. He watches them as they come in. It's a moment before Charlie realizes he's just an unarmed private security guard. Relieved, he directs Amy to a booth in the back corner.

The diner has large windows on the front and sides and this makes Charlie uneasy. It's as if he's in a fish bowl. He can be seen by any passerby.

An elderly waitress shuffles up with a couple of menus. He orders a cheeseburger, fries, and coffee. Amy orders a salad and a bottled water.

"You always sit in a corner," she says. "I've noticed that."

"Really? I wasn't aware."

"Why do you always sit with your back to the wall? Are you scared somebody will sneak up from behind?"

"Always."

She has a strange look on her face.

"That's a joke," he says.

"I'm not so sure. I think you don't trust anybody very much. Your life must be very lonely."

"That's the second time you said that. I'm not lonely. I'm alone and I recognize that fact. There's a difference between being lonely and being alone."

"So you choose to be alone, is that it?"

"Not really. Everybody's alone, whether they choose to be or not. When you get older, you'll realize that."

"My English teacher says nobody is an island."

"That's Mister Adler, right? Mister Adler, with all due respect, is wrong. Everyone is an island. Some people just don't know it."

"You'll be alone when you die. No one to comfort you. All alone."

She spits the words at him. She wants to hurt him. It's all about that stupid cell phone.

"Of course I'll be alone when I die," he says. "It's not a group thing. You don't get to take somebody with you. You've got to do it yourself. Like taking the driver's license test."

She glowers and makes a show of looking at the menu.

The door opens and couple of middle-aged state troopers in black uniforms and black leather knee-high riding boots come in and sit at the counter. They've got the hard faces of experienced cops, the kind who've seen it all and who can smell an ex-con from a mile off.

One of the troopers glances over his shoulder at Charlie and says something to the other trooper. They're interested in the stranger. It's a good thing Amy's with him, or they'd be over asking questions. They figure he must be okay if he has a kid with him.

Amy gives him a questioning look, and Charlie goes back to examining his menu. He glances at her. She's staring at the troopers. Is she going to do something stupid because she's still mad? Maybe she'll tell the troopers, "My Dad's a thief and he has some stuff that doesn't belong to him."

It's possible.

Just because of the damned cell phone.

Truth be told, Charlie has no idea what to do.

He can't tell her to keep quiet because somebody might overhear them. And in this small diner there's no way he'd escape from the cops.

"I need to go to the restroom," she says abruptly.

She walks up the counter, next to where the troopers are standing. She looks up at one of the troopers, expectantly. The trooper looks down at her, smiles. Charlie gets to his feet and turns in the direction of the door. Amy says something to the waitress. The waitress points and Amy walks around the counter to an area in the back. Charlie sees the RESTROOMS sign.

He starts breathing again.

The troopers' food comes quickly--they must've called ahead. The waitress hands each a white paper bag. One of the troopers tries to pay, but the waitress waves him off. They all laugh. Charlie figures they've gone through this charade many times before.

He watches the cops go out the door. One of them gives him a strange look, as if he's trying to memorize Charlie's face. In the parking lot they stop behind his pickup. The trooper who gave him the look writes the license plate number down, then they get in their patrol car and drive off.

Amy returns at the same time their food arrives.

"I'll be right back," Charlie says, standing. "I've got to get something out of the truck."

Outside, he opens the tool box and takes a "slim jim," wire strippers, a small flashlight, a flat-head screw driver, a hammer, and a Phillips-head screw driver. He walks hurriedly toward some houses that line a side road fifty yards ahead.

He trots up the road. I don't have much time.

The houses are split-level and look to have been built in the Fifties for the Greatest Generation to raise their families in. The houses are run down now, tired looking, not much life left in them, much like the people inside, Charlie imagines.

Some cars are parked along the side of the street. At the end of the block he finds an early Seventies-model Olds Cutlass.

It's perfect.

Only one house is nearby and it's dark.

He watches the house, looking for signs of life, until he can wait no more. Since the license plate on his pickup truck is from out of state, it'll take the cops a while to trace. But still he needs to hurry.

He takes another look at the house. After surviving a couple of attempts on his life by the mob, it would be unfortunate to die at the hands of an enraged car owner with a deer rifle.

He slides the "slim jim" between the window and the door panel on the driver's side door. A little bit of delicate probing and he finds the latch. He pulls up. A moment of resistance, a click and the door is unlocked.

Then, off in the distance, a police siren. But it's too far away. They're not coming for him, yet.

Inside, the car is clean and smells of pine. The leather seats are like new. It's somebody's baby.

Charlie unwraps the ace bandage and takes off the splint. This is going to hurt but he needs two hands for what he is going to do.

He sticks the flat-head screwdriver in the ignition and pounds the end with the hammer. The pain in his hand is intense, he grunts in reaction, and tears come to his eyes.

He waits a moment for the pain to subside, then turns the screw driver.

The car doesn't start. He's going to have to do this the hard way.

Holding the flashlight in his mouth, he unscrews two screws that hold the steering column shroud together. He pries open the shroud and locates the three wires that lead to the ignition switch. He cuts the wire that leads from the switch to the battery and the wire coming from the battery back to the switch. He holds each wire between the index finger and thumb of his right hand. There's pain again but not too much. He strips the insulation from the ends of the wires and touches the naked wires, and the interior lights come on. He has power, which means there is an operating battery under that hood. Now the tricky part. He cuts the wire from the ignition switch to the starter and strips off a half inch of insulation.

The moment of truth. What if it doesn't start? He doesn't want to even think about that.

Carefully, he touches the wire to the battery wires. The engine sputters, then roars to life. It sounds strong and smooth. Definitely somebody's baby.

Taking a moment, he places the splint back on his hand and wraps the ace bandage around it.

He removes the flashlight from his mouth and wiggles his jaw side-to-side to relieve the muscle tension. No lights have come on in the house. The front door hasn't opened. Nobody's coming at him with a deer rifle. He checks the gas gauge. Three-quarters full. Life is good. He puts on the seat belt and shifts the car into drive.

Thirty seconds later, he pulls into the diner parking lot and gets out, leaving the engine running. He walks to his truck and removes his tool box, the two duffel bags, and Amy's suitcase. He places these in the back seat of the Olds. Then he walks to the pickup and gives it a pat. It's as if he's burying an old friend.

Amy is just finishing her salad. He drops a twenty and a five on the table.

"Where did you go?" she asks.

"Come on," he says. "We're leaving."

"What about your food?"

"I'm not hungry. Come on."

Outside, they walk to the Oldsmobile.

"What's this?" she asks.

"A Seventy-Two Olds Cutlass," he says. "An example of Detroit iron at its finest. The last of its kind before America started building crap."

"What about the truck?"

"We're using this now."

"It's somebody else's car, isn't it? You stole it."

"It's more like we're borrowing it for a little while," he says. "We can't stay in the truck. People are probably looking for it."

"How's the owner of this car going to feel when he goes out tomorrow and it's missing?"

Charlie thinks, who gives a crap?

He says, "It won't be missing for long. And think how great he'll feel when he gets it back."

"What if there's an emergency tonight and somebody has to go to the hospital and they find the car gone? Or they need it in the morning to get to work?"

"We'll compensate them for their inconvenience."

"I'm not going anywhere in a stolen car."

Charlie looks around, figuring the troopers could be back at any moment.

"And I'm not leaving you here in the dark in a strange town in the middle of nowhere. Now stop arguing with me and get in."

"It's wrong. I won't do it."

"You don't have a choice. Be reasonable."

"I won't. I'll just stay here."

He's struck by how much she sounds like her mother when she's angry. She even purses her lips the same way.

"Tell you what. If you get in now, I'll call the police in the morning. That's what you want me to do, right? Call the police."

"You'll give yourself up?"

"I don't know about that. But I'll try to make a deal with them. I promise."

"You have to promise to give yourself up or I'm staying here."

He pauses.

"Okay. I promise. I'll give myself up. Tomorrow morning. First thing."

She opens the passenger door and gets in while throwing him a suspicious glance.

Chapter Thirty-Seven

They're about ten miles out of Coal City, headed west by northwest, when she asks him how he ended up being a thief.

"I worked as a locksmith for several years," he says. "It wasn't all it was cracked up to be. It was hard to get any regular business. A guy I knew offered me this job to help him and some guys break into a Circuit City warehouse. They needed somebody to take care of the security system and the locks, which I did. They took a bunch of computers, TV sets, and other electronics stuff. I made as much in two hours as I did in two months at my regular job, and it was exciting, too. It was as if a light came on. I thought I'd been playing by the rules all those years. But the fact was I didn't even understand the game. I'd made sacrifices and never gotten anything out of it."

"What kind of sacrifices?"

He shakes his head.

"Stuff I don't want to talk about. That robbery was it, I guess. After that it was just one job after another."

"Did you think about going back?"

He slows down. The highway has narrowed to a two-lane blacktop with no shoulder. It's so dark that it's hard to see the road fifty feet ahead even with the high beams on.

"You mean go square again?" he asks. "I can't do it now. Nobody would hire me. I've got a record and all. And how would I explain what I've been doing for the past twenty years?"

"How do you know nobody will hire you? Have you tried?"

The road bends sharply to the left--something he doesn't realize until it's too late--and he almost collides with the guardrail. He twists the wheel to the left and the back end of ancient Oldsmobile slides around and goes off the road and into some high grass.

The engine has stalled. His hands shaking, he gently touches the ignition wire to the battery wires and, thankfully, the engine roars back to life.

"So, that's how you do it," Amy says.

He gently gooses the accelerator, hoping the rear wheels aren't stuck. The engine whines and for a brief moment the wheels spin before catching, and the car jerks forward and they're back on the road.

"Good thing we didn't get stranded out here in a stolen car," Amy says. "We were lucky."

He doesn't say anything. His heart is beating so hard it feels like a locomotive is jammed inside his chest. Running off the road in the middle of the night will do that to you.

"It's so dark out here," he says, gasping a little. "You can hardly see a damned thing."

"Maybe you should get your eyes checked."

"I can see just fine. It's just this part of the state. There are no towns or cities anywhere. Hardly any houses, even. You forget how dark things can really get."

"Sooner or later you'll end up in prison again," she says. "Or dead."

"Not if I can help it. Anyway, I like working for myself. I pick my own hours. I don't have to worry about getting fired. I'm my own boss."

"That's one way to look at it." She pauses. "Have you ever killed anybody?"

"Have I ever--Jesus, what kind of question is that?"

"You're a criminal. Don't criminals kill people?"

He grits his teeth. She's still pissed off about that cell phone.

"I'm not that kind of criminal."

"Why not? What's the difference? Burglary or murder. They're both breaking the law."

"Don't be stupid. There's a difference. Taking a life is different than robbing a house."

A car comes fast from the opposite direction. It too has its high beams on and for a second Charlie is blinded. The Oldsmobile swerves right and left before he straightens it out, missing the other car by a few inches.

"This road's not very safe," she says. "Maybe we should go back and try a different way."

Where the police may be waiting for me?

"Too late to go back. We've come this far. We'll be fine."

"Are we lost?"

He ignores her question while he fiddles with the radio, trying to find a station, but there's nothing. They really are in the middle of nowhere.

"I've been wondering about something. That money you gave me at Christmas. Was it stolen?"

"Yeah. I did a job in Boston just before last Christmas. We broke into this big house, took some jewelry and about forty grand in cash that was in a safe. The fence gave us sixty grand for the jewelry. Thirty was my share plus half the cash. It was a good pay day."

"Where were the people that lived there?"

"They were in Aspen. Skiing. They'd already left for Christmas vacation."

"Who were they?"

"Hell if I know. The guy was some sort of investment banker type, I think. Made his money the old fashioned way, screwing the little guy. Sub-prime mortgages, insider trading, foreclosing on people's houses, that kind of crap."

She gives him an inquiring look.

"Did that make it okay to steal his stuff?"

"It made it easier. Why? Do you want to give the money back?"

"Yes. It was stolen."

"The guy stole the money from other people. You should give the money to them. If you could find them."

She nods twice.

"So you're like a half-way Robin Hood. You steal from the rich. But you keep it for yourself."

He chuckles. "That's the way the world works. You see somebody with a lot of money, he probably stole it from somebody else."

"What about a great singer or great artist? They didn't steal from anybody. Don't they deserve their money?"

"Not really. They were born with a great talent. That's not something they worked for. It was a gift. What did they do to deserve a gift like that?"

"So they don't deserve their money, either."

"Right."

"You have an excuse for everything."

"I've been at this a long time. I've given it a lot of thought."

Chapter Thirty-Eight

De La Torre sits in the eleventh floor FBI conference room. At night, the room is dim, almost like a cave. A few months ago, as a cost saving measure, the 100 Watt bulbs were replaced with 60 Watt.

De La Torre is at one end of the table. Prescott and Robert Winston, the Section Chief of the Organized Crime Section and De La Torre's boss, are sitting at the other end. All the files have been cleared off the table and placed on the floor.

The importance of a DC Section Chief travelling to a meeting on the eve of a holiday weekend is not lost on De La Torre.

"It's been a busy afternoon," Prescott says. "It seems there was a shootout today involving the Adonis Family."

De La Torre looks up.

"No kidding. Where?"

"Down at the Shore. One of Phil Adonis's knee breakers got it with a shot gun. One Marco Delassandro was the victim, and I use the word victim advisedly since he probably had it coming. He's still alive, which may be fortunate or not, depending on your point of view."

"So you figure this shoot out is connected to the break-in?"

"Obviously. It can't just be a coincidence. I figure one of the burglars has gone rogue. The original plan was to fake a burglary. But then our friend goes into business for himself. Now he's blackmailing Phil Adonis with the stuff he took. They had a meeting, things went south. Bing, bang, boom."

"Definitely a theory," De La Torre says. "Any lead on who this shooter might be?"

"Only that he drives a gray pickup. And maybe his name's Charlie, if we believe those tapes. Or he could be the other guy."

"If it even was one of the guys involved in the robbery. We don't know that. We still don't have anything to go on."

There's a knock at the door and a young, pretty blonde woman sticks her head in. De La Torre has never seen her before, but she has a laminated FBI identification card attached to a plastic lanyard around her neck.

"Sorry I'm late," she says in a perky, high pitched voice. "The plane was delayed leaving Reagan National."

Winston stands. "Come in, Cathy. You're not late at all. We were just getting started."

He waves at Prescott and De La Torre.

"This is Cathy Hunt. She's our brand-new Assistant Section Chief for Organized Crime. This is Agent De La Torre and Assistant AG Prescott."

De La Torre says, "She's the new Assistant Section Chief? It's the first I've heard."

Winston says, "We're going to announce it officially next week, but she's already been approved by the director."

"That's great," De La Torre says. "Just great."

She sits at the end of the table next to Winston and takes an Apple laptop from her bag, opens it, switches it on, and starts tapping at the keys.

Winston leans forward. He's a big man who played tackle at Brown and is now fifty pounds over his playing weight.

"Now, I'm not going to sugarcoat this. I'm very unhappy. First Lisk. Now this. I'm very disappointed by the inaction on this case. We are now more than twenty-four hours into this and we have nothing. You know the twenty-four hour rule."

De La Torre thinks, if you don't have a good lead in twenty-four hours, you're probably not going to solve the crime. He has to fight back a smile.

De La Torre says, "This shooting took place at the Shore, right? Maybe we should be concentrating our efforts down there."

"That's an idea," Prescott says. "There's a reason they decided to meet down there. We need to find out what it was."

"I don't know," Hunt says, without looking up from her laptop. "I read the police report on the flight up here. This shooting happened out in the street. In a residential neighborhood. In the middle of the day."

Prescott says, "What's your point?"

"Nobody has a criminal meeting out in the street in the middle of the day. This looks more like an ambush."

"Who was ambushing whom?" Prescott asks.

"Good question. I'm guessing the Adonis family is pursuing this shooter, he was hiding out down there and they caught up with him. That's the only scenario that makes any sense."

"So where is he now?"

"Probably not there. The first thing we need to do is find out who he is. We have any intelligence on this? Anything from any informants?"

"I understand we have an informant inside the Adonis family," De La Torre says. "What's he saying?"

"Haven't a clue," Hunt says. "He's gone dark. One thing I want to know." She pauses, looks at her laptop. "Do we have trackers on any of the Adonis family vehicles? I'd like to see where they've been for the last thirty-six hours. If we can see where they've been, it may give us a lead on this shooter."

Winston says, "Good idea, Cathy. Agent De La Torre, please get on that right away."

Winston stands, signaling that the meeting is over.

Hunt says, "Excuse me, but I have one more question."

"What's that?" Prescott asks.

"What happened to the other guy?"

"Other guy?"

"There were two burglars, right? Where's the other one?"

***

It's just De La Torre, Hunt, and Winston now. Winston told Prescott he needed to speak with the two agents alone.

"I didn't want to say any more in front of Prescott," Winston says. "He's our main suspect right now."

"Suspect?"

"For the leak."

De La Torre scoffs. "Prescott? You must be kidding me. He's a straight arrow."

"We've traced some suspicious activity to his computer. He's been using his computer for purposes that appear to be unrelated to any ongoing cases. It's been happening for a while. We can't think of any good explanations for this activity."

"Are you going to seek an indictment?"

"Not right now. He's only a person of interest. But we definitely think he may be related to the Lisk matter."

De La Torre says, "Can I ask you about something else? If you have this inside source, why not go ahead and get indictments against the Adonis family right now?"

"He's just one guy," Winston says. "And he's a hoodlum. We need corroborating proof. We were on the verge of getting what we needed from Lisk when everything blew up on us."

"What do you want me to do about Prescott?" De La Torre asks.

"Nothing for right now. Just keep an eye on him, watch to see if he does anything suspicious. Another thing. Agent Hunt will be working out of this office until this situation is wrapped up. She'll be heading up this investigation from now on. I want to make sure nothing gets screwed up this time."

De La Torre smiles even though he knows that the comment is directed partly at him. Better to be thought incompetent than crooked.

"Sounds good," he says. "We need all the help we can get. One thing. You know, now that you mention it, it's strange how Prescott was on vacation when this whole thing came down."

"How do you mean?"

"His unavailability delayed getting the search warrant for Adonis's house. And--"

"Everything disappeared in the meantime. See what you're saying." Winston pauses. "I've got a question. How long has Prescott had that thing going on under his eye? It's kind of creepy."

Chapter Thirty-Nine

The yellow sodium halide streetlights flash past as they travel north on the Parkway. Dutch is driving and Taco is riding shotgun. Phil is in the back by himself.

Taco goes, "Hey, Phil, what're you going to do to this guy McCoy when you catch up to him?"

Dutch says, "I been wondering about that myself. You figure you'll use the blowtorch first or the power drill?"

Taco says, "Maybe both at the same time."

"It won't be good for his health, whatever Phil does."

The cretins laugh. They're thinking about what happened to Marco. Talking about revenge makes them feel better. But there's more to it than that--they're trying to curry favor with him. They figure that he's some sort of sociopath that enjoys inflicting pain, so they say this crap to suck up to him, figuring he'll enjoy it in some sick way.

But he's certain that he's not a sociopath. Sure, there were some episodes over the years. There was those incidents with the neighbor's cats. And that guy with glasses who used to bug him a lot in sixth grade. And that prostitute when he was in high school. And that chick who was going to Rutgers. Everybody has a few blemishes in their past. Everybody makes some mistakes. That doesn't make him abnormal.

Phil has thought about this and he figures he's not a sociopath because sociopaths never wonder about whether they're sociopaths. They lack the insight. And sociopaths are impulsive and never plan ahead, and nobody can accuse him of being impulsive--he's very good at making plans. He once read an article about sociopaths, and it said that when they're little, they torture animals, start fires, and wet the bed. Phil never wet the bed.

Dutch says, "Phil, you remember that Chink, the one that wouldn't pay protection?"

Taco says, "He thought he had friends in high places."

"But not enough friends."

"And the ones he had weren't in very high places."

They both laugh. The fact they think he's a sadistic weirdo isn't entirely a bad thing. It invokes fear and the underworld runs on fear. It's the coin of the realm. The whole world runs on fear, really, when you get right down to it. Fear of being fired, fear of being found out, fear of being alone. The power of fear is merely more obvious among criminals because it's not disguised by pretense.

Yes, Phil has thought about it, and he is convinced that he's not a sick fuck. He is interested in the nature of pain, but that comes with the territory. Over the years he's educated himself about the meaning of pain and he's concluded that pain is truth. Truth causes pain. What's more painful than learning the truth about something or someone? And what is the ultimate truth? Death. The only unambiguous event in a person's life and the event that brings the greatest pain.

Phil has watched closely as people died, usually because of what he's done to them. The first was a small-time crack dealer named Armando who decided it would be a smart move to infringe on Adonis family turf. Phil proposed they meet mano a mano at a crack house located on neutral territory to work out their differences. Armando-- apparently thinking there is honor among crooks--showed up alone but Phil brought Taco and Dutch with him. They stripped Armando naked and Phil applied a blow torch to his genitals, so as to discourage anybody else who might get ideas similar to Armando's. When Phil had enough, he put a bullet in the back of Armando's head as Taco and Dutch held him down. They were walking away when-- son of a bitch!--Armando gets up and staggers toward an open window. Phil put two more rounds in the guy's back and then went over to check that Armando was finally dead. He put his thumb on his carotid artery, trying to detect a heartbeat, and as he leaned over, the guy's eyes suddenly opened wide and for a brief moment he felt what Armando the crack dealer felt – fear, no absolute terror. A terror seemingly not of this world. Then he died.

Maybe it was a dread of what additional pain Phil would inflict, but Phil always thought it was something else, a terror of what was coming next.

Phil found the experience exhilarating because for the first time he had some idea what fear felt like.

He tried to relive this moment. He put his arm around his dying victims and stared into their frightened eyes, trying to perceive some glimmer of what they saw at the ultimate moment of truth. Were they experiencing peace? Or fear? Were they ascending a tunnel? Was there a light at the end? Or something else? But no matter how hard he concentrated he never felt anything again.

Phil says, "I remember the Chink. Who could forget a Chinaman running down the street with his head on fire?"

Chapter Forty

"We can get something to eat here," De La Torre says to Cathy Hunt as they step inside the all-night diner.

"You don't mind that I'm taking over this Adonis investigation, do you?" she says after they grab a booth in the back. "I know you've been at it a long time."

And never gotten anywhere.

That's the implication.

"No, like I said. I need all the help I can get."

He's trying to figure her out. Now he's up close and the light is better, he can see the fine lines around her eyes. More like late thirties than early thirties, as he first thought. Dark pants suit, short cut jacket that shows off the Glock 22 that she wears high on her hip, sensible shoes, the absence of a wedding ring or engagement ring, the minimal make-up, and the close-cropped hair all suggest lesbo. There were plenty in the Bureau, some in decision making positions.

He's trying to figure if that gives him an advantage.

Most men have problems picking up on women's facial expressions. But that has never been a problem for him. De La Torre considers himself an expert at recognizing the little cues women put out.

But not this time. He can't figure her angle. The woman has quite a poker face.

"So, where're you from?" he asks.

"I was in Miami."

"A lot of action down there."

"Not like up here. This is ground zero for organized crime worldwide. The big time. I once requested to transfer up here, but Bob wouldn't approve it. He said I was too valuable in Miami."

"Bob?"

"Section Chief Winston. I was supervisory agent when he was assistant director in the South Florida Field Office. That's where I know Bob from."

So she's Winston's protégé. And perhaps something else of a more intimate nature. Now he's starting to get a feel for the situation.

"So bring me up to speed," she says. "I understand you're interfacing with local law enforcement. Any info from that end?"

"They've got an eyewitness they're supposed to talk to tomorrow. She might help."

Everything considered this is the best way to go. It meant having to deny only one of his phone calls with Polaski. Not a perfect solution, but the best lie he can manage.

She sips her coffee. "An eyewitness. Interesting. What did this witness happen to see?"

"A guy near the scene where a getaway vehicle was found abandoned."

"Could be something. Could be nothing. Does this witness have a name?"

Time for another lie.

"I'm not sure yet. They've been pretty tight with information. I'm not sure what the local cops have exactly. What do you know about this mole in the Adonis organization?"

"He's got a big mouth, that's for sure. He likes to talk." She pauses. "He doesn't just tell us what's happening inside the Adonis family, he tells the New York mob as well. He's an all-purpose snitch. Other than that, I'm not at liberty to say anything about him."

He looks at his watch.

"Jesus, look at the time. I'll be in some kind of trouble when I get home."

He digs in his pocket for some cash.

"I'll get it," she says with a broad toothy smile. "You're free to go."

Chapter Forty-One

Niko Falcone sits behind Marco's desk in the office of the Pink Pussycat. The walls are covered by centerfolds, some dating back to when Hugh Hefner could still get a hard on without the assistance of Viagra. Niko's right hand man, Ralph Tocco, an Adonis family capo sits outside.

Four guns are on the desk. Phil recognizes his .40 caliber Smith and Wesson, Taco's Walther PPK, Marco's Colt .45, and Dutch's snub nose .38.

"I just swept this place for bugs," Niko says, looking around. "Didn't find anything."

He points at the desk.

"Here are your guns. I got them back from that motorcycle guy. Figured you'd want them."

Niko sits back in his chair. He's thin as an iron rail with a face pock-marked by acne scars. He's wearing navy blue polyester pants and a floral patterned polyester shirt. Guy makes 700 large a year and still dresses like a street dago from South Trenton.

Niko's the underboss of the Adonis family and in theory he's equal in rank with Phil. Blood is supposed to be thicker than water, and it should be the deciding factor in this relationship, but here is Niko sitting behind Marco's desk, all full of himself.

"What happened this morning with Marco?" Niko asks.

"The situation went sideways. Unexpectedly."

"Worse than sideways, from what I hear. Went freaking backwards in a hurry."

"These things happen, you know that. It's the nature of the business."

"And what about this guy Tommy Russo? What's the story with that?"

"Now I'm lost. Who the hell is Tommy Russo?"

"He's the guy you put in the ICU with a broken jaw, concussion, fractured skull, multiple lacerations, and facial fractures. The guy whose medical bills we're paying. To keep him happy."

"The manager at that motel? That guy's an asshole. He deserved it. Why do we care if he's happy?"

Niko throws his arms up.

"The guy's family knows people who are connected. Why did you do it?"

"Everybody knows somebody who's connected, so what? And I'm pretty sure he gave McCoy a heads up. That's how McCoy got away. It's the only explanation. Tommy was the only one who knew we were there."

Niko's mouth curls in disgust.

"Listen to yourself. You don't make any sense. Why would Tommy Russo want to help McCoy?"

"I don't know. Maybe McCoy paid him off. It's just a feeling I have."

Niko shakes his head.

"You're out of control," he says. "Can't you see that?"

"I can handle this situation if everybody else will stop interfering and let me take care of business."

"I don't think so. That's why I'm gonna be in charge of this search for McCoy. As of right now."

Phil sits up straight. What the fuck? Now Niko's in charge? This is nothing but a power grab. He's putting himself in position for when the old man dies. Phil is getting the crown of thorns feeling now, real bad. He can feel the thorns biting into his flesh. He squeezes the keys in his pocket to stop from rubbing his forehead.

"I don't see you taking charge, Niko" Phil says, trying to keep his voice under control. "Not seeing it."

"Don't fight it, Phil. The decision's been made."

"Is this O'Brien's bright idea? Because he doesn't know how this business really works. He's just a lawyer."

Niko leans forward.

"No, it's your father's idea. He's been speaking with New York. They told him he needed to do things differently."

This hits Phil like a punch to the gut. It's Dad's idea. He grips the keys even harder.

"My father's not a well man," Phil says. "He shouldn't be making important decisions."

"He didn't have much choice." Niko says. "New York's not happy. But your Dad maybe bought us a little more time by agreeing to their suggestion. As part of the deal, they wanted me to take over this operation. Your Dad agreed."

"What is this? Since when did the New York mob tell us how to run things?"

Niko shakes his head.

"Do you think I like being involved in this mess? It's so screwed up now, it's like trying to pick up a turd by the clean end." Niko leans back in his chair. "So, tell me. What can we do to find McCoy? Guy could be anywhere by now. He may have left the damned country. With all that stuff of ours."

Phil eyes his gun, which is still lying on the desk. He can stand, grab the gun, put a bullet between Niko's eyes before he could move and splatter his brains all over Miss July 1986. That will settle this succession bullshit.

But he's not sure there's even a bullet in that gun. Maybe Niko did the smart thing and unloaded it.

"Now you're wanting my input?" Phil says. "Is that what you're saying?"

"I'm looking for anything I can get. This is a dangerous situation."

"Don't get your panties in a wad. I've got an idea on how to find McCoy."

"Care to fill me in on your idea?" Niko asks.

"It involves the guy's daughter."

Chapter Forty-Two

The house is a mess. A half-dozen overflowing garbage bags are outside the front door, drawing flies. Inside, there are a couple of new stains on the rugs and a mark on a wall. A crystal vase in pieces. The sink is full of dirty dishes, which overflow onto the counters.

But the house isn't his main concern. De La Torre's thinking about what Carol Hunt said. You're free to go.

What did she mean by that?

Probably nothing. But she said it with a little smirk, as if she knew something. Was she trying to get inside his head? If so, why?

But he's not too worried. If the DC office suspected something it would be a whole team from the Inspector General's Office looking over his shoulder. Instead, it's just one woman.

Footsteps come from behind. He turns. Cynthia steps into the kitchen.

"Where have you been?" she says.

Her nostrils flare, her jaw sets. She's angry.

She's angry!

"Your relatives certainly did a job on my house," he says.

"Our house."

"I'm the one who pays for it."

"And there's nothing that the maid service can't clean up."

"Great, another expense. How about you get your sisters over here since they're in town, and the three of you clean it up?"

"I simply can't believe you. You bug out in the middle of my father's birthday party, with no explanation. He'll never be sixty-five again, by the way. And now you're trying to ruin what was a great occasion."

"A great occasion? What the--"

"And then you show up at three in the morning and where you've been, I have no idea."

"I was working. I have a job."

"Can't you give work a rest for one day a year? Are you that important to the FBI?"

"The FBI is what pays for all this."

"Really? Sometimes I wonder what really pays for all this."

He pauses. Might be best to let this one alone. But he can't stop himself.

"What do you mean by that?" he asks, his anger getting the better of him.

"There are things you're not telling me. Important things."

"Whatever I do, I do for this family? Understand? Nothing's more important than family. That's all you need to know."

"That's what I mean. You're keeping secrets. The most important thing you can do for this family is be honest with me. My father asked me how we could afford--"

"I'll be sleeping in the guest room," he says, with finality. "We can talk about this some other time."

"Both the guest rooms are taken by guests. You'll have to find somewhere else to sleep."

Chapter Forty-Three

O'Brien stands next to an olive green-colored garbage dumpster and waits. Five-thirty a.m. and nobody's around. He got the call an hour ago. He could tell by the tone of Bernays's voice that it was bad news, and at this point, bad news could mean only one thing.

His cell rings. He pulls it from his coat pocket. It's De La Torre. He thinks about letting it go to voice mail, but hits TALK instead.

"What do you want?"

"I have some information about the rat."

De La Torre says this in an excited tone, as if he expects to be congratulated.

"What's the information?"

"Here's a clue. He's also an informer for the New York mob. That should help. Now you owe me. Big time."

Click.

A late-model convertible Jaguar pulls up and Lenny Bernays gets out. He's short and slender and resembles a brand-new high school math teacher, not the lead attorney for the New York mob. He and O'Brien tried three mobster cases together, all wins for the defense. The New York Post referred to them as the Laurel and Hardy of the organized crime bar.

Bernays, his head swiveling right and left, walks to O'Brien's Cadillac.

"Good to see you," Bernays says without a smile. "Jerry, can you turn around?"

"What is it?"

"I need to see if you're wearing a wire."

O'Brien sputters. "What the hell?"

"Don't take this the wrong way, but you can never be too cautious. You know?"

After finishing his pat down, Bernays says, "You need to know some things. The boys in New York are very unhappy about everything that's going on."

"That's not exactly news. I already had a meet with Joey Bats."

"Joey didn't like your attitude."

"My attitude?"

"They're going to take action. The decision's been made. At the highest levels."

"That's not what I heard. I heard Big Phil talked them out of doing anything."

Bernays takes a small leather cigar case from his inside jacket pocket, removes a small black cigar, and lights it.

"They were leading him on," he says. "They think he's a crazy old coot who can't be trusted to take care of business. None of you can." He looks away. "You know what that means."

"I know this is bad, but it can be fixed with just a little more time."

Bernays shakes his head. "This is only the most recent screw up. That guy Lisk left a bad smell in everybody's nose. You're lucky they didn't take action then. Now this."

"Can I talk to them?" O'Brien asks. "Reason with them?"

"Won't do any good. They've done the risk and reward analysis. You lost."

O'Brien shakes his head.

"It's like that it is it?" he says. "The only considerations are risk and reward. Nothing about honor. Or integrity. It's a different world than the one I knew."

Bernays blows a perfect smoke ring.

"It's worse than that," he says. "They're going to shut you guys down completely. They're coming after everybody. Big Phil. Little Phil. You."

"Me? I'm just a lawyer." O'Brien realizes that his voice is quivering. "Since when did lawyers ever get whacked? Listen, I'm buddies with half those guys."

"That's what's got them so scared. Even the civilians aren't going to survive this time." Bernays points his cigar at O'Brien. "Listen, you've been at this a long time. You've got to have three or four million stashed somewhere. A couple of false identities. Phony passports. Now's the time to use them. Take off for Ecuador or wherever. Shack up with some cute senorita. Drink pina coladas on the beach. You've had a good run. Call it a day while you still can."

"Can I talk to them? This just isn't right. If they start whacking the lawyers, who's going to represent them when they get in trouble? It sets a bad precedent. It's bad business all around."

"Maybe they heard about the surplus of lawyers. They figure it doesn't hurt to whack a few because there're plenty more where they came from. It sends a message, you know. Anyway, they can't afford to be distracted by all this crap. They've got much bigger fish to fry."

"Yeah, this off-shore gambling thing. So, you're saying I should beat it."

Bernays takes a puff on his little cigar.

"That's right. Get out while the going's good. Which is now. You ask me, you shouldn't have ever gotten involved in an outfit run by a sicko like Little Phil."

"When I started with his father, Phil was a little shvanz who was still lighting dogs and cats on fire. I had no way of knowing he'd end up consigliore."

O'Brien turns to go and then stops.

"Hey, I got a question for you," he says. "Who was your mole?"

"Mole?"

"You had a guy on the inside of the Adonis organization. Somebody who was passing you information. I always wondered who it was."

Bernays drops his little cigar, rubs it out. "Niko. He was our man. The fact you guys never copped to him was part of the problem. It suggested you were out of touch."

We're not the only ones out of touch when it comes to Niko.

"What do you know?" O'Brien says. "I always figured it was Marco."

"We tried to buy Marco. A couple of times. He couldn't be bought. An honest man. Sort of. You know. For this line of work."

"Did you get your money's worth out of Niko?"

"Not really. He was always telling us he didn't know anything. Or if he did tell us something, we already knew it. He always seemed to be trying to get more info out of us than he was willing to give. I got some strange vibes from that dude." He points his cigar at O'Brien. "Now get the hell out of Dodge, my friend."

Bernays strides over to his Jaguar, gets in. O'Brien watches as the taillights fade into the gray light of dawn.

He pulls the Escalade into the street. The truth is he doesn't have three or four million stashed away. He doesn't even have a twentieth of that, not in cash. Big Phil always was a cheap bastard. Getting a bill paid was like getting blood from a stone. A couple of divorces and some bad investments and a kid with autism who needed special education hadn't helped. Christ, the bills for that school in Connecticut just about crushed him.

So, running is out of the question. He needs an alternative. He does have a few cards to play. Valuable cards. He just has to play them in the right order.

He takes a left, goes down three blocks. There it is. The federal building, a hulking, gray concrete structure. He slows down, and then accelerates. It's far too early in the morning for anybody important to be in the office.

An upscale Louisiana-style diner is a few blocks away. O'Brien has met with US attorneys there any number of times. They do a pretty good eggs Sardou. And the coffee is strong and flavored with chicory, the way he likes it.

He figures he'll have one last decent meal before he enters witness protection. Who knows where they'd send him. Not New Orleans--too many wise guys there, for sure. Probably a boring suburb of Dallas or Tucson, or some other Sunbelt hellhole where the tomatoes taste like mush and the coffee is weak, but where he's unlikely to cross paths with anybody who would want to kill him.

It's best he enjoy his freedom while he still has it.

Chapter Forty-Four

They check out of the Motel Six at eight. They're in a small depressed city--Charlie can't remember the name--in Western New York State. One of many they've passed through. He's still sticking to the back roads, figuring it's safer that way, although slower.

A waffle house is across the street and they walk in that direction, the grit from the highway crunching under their feet. In his left hand he's carrying Moe's duffle with the shotgun and the discs inside. His right hand is aching so bad he wants to rip the splint off, but he can't do that because he has the little Beretta hidden under the splint. He looks off to the west, where the sky is dark and foreboding. A storm is coming.

He's feeling the weather in his bones. I really am getting old.

Amy wrinkles her nose, points at the waffle house.

"I don't want to eat there. It looks dirty. Sorry."

"You say sorry too much. You know that? You say it all the time. It doesn't sound sincere."

"Sorry. I just don't want to eat there."

"I'm hungry. I didn't eat last night. And I don't want to get on the road and then have to stop again. Not until we need gas, anyway."

"Is that one of your little rules?"

"Yeah, that's one of my little rules."

"You have a lot of rules."

"You need to have rules to keep your life straight. You can't just go with your instincts. If you don't have any rules, there's no telling where you might end up."

"Do any of those rules involve being a thief?"

"Yeah. Don't try to rob a gun store with a baseball bat. For a thief, that's an important rule. Listen, everybody has rules. Most people don't know they have them, but they do."

She nods.

"You say stuff like that because it makes you sound like you know yourself, but I'm not sure you do."

* * *

Amy's examining the menu and frowning.

"There's nothing I can eat here. It's all bacon and eggs and stuff like that."

"I thought the bacon and eggs with hash browns sounded pretty good. How about an omelet? That's healthy."

"Gross. It'll be all greasy. It'll probably give me diarrhea."

"How about pancakes?"

"They're fattening."

"Look, you can't weigh more than eighty pounds soaking wet. What's the difference?"

She puts the menu down and asks him when her mother discovered he was a thief.

Jesus, only eight more hours of this.

When did Carol first figure out he was a thief? This is something he's never been sure of. Carol was a lot of things, but she wasn't an idiot. Did she suspect something but keep her mouth shut? She got a pretty good life out of his criminal activity until he was arrested and convicted. Then she divorced him and took everything.

Charlie's view is that humans have been adapting to hostile environments for millions of years. Civilization has only been around for a few thousand years and hasn't really taken hold yet. When push comes to shove most people will revert to those instincts for self-preservation that allowed mankind to survive for so long. That means getting the most out of your environment, which is what Carol did.

He tries to decide whether he's bitter. He concludes that he isn't. Carol just did what she had to do. For a moment he gets a feeling that perhaps there was more going on with Carol than he realizes, but the feeling is fleeting and then it's gone.

The waitress comes. He orders the bacon and eggs over easy, hash browns, and coffee. Amy asks for bottled water and toast.

"You didn't answer my question," she says. "Did Mom know?"

"About me being a thief? Nah, your mother never knew anything."

"Past tense. You referred to her in the past tense."

"I was talking about back then. You know, when we were married. She didn't know anything."

Jesus, that was close.

The waitress comes with his coffee and Amy's bottled water. He dumps some cream and two sugars into the dark brown liquid, takes a sip, and feels the warm glow spread inside him. God, there's nothing on earth like that first sip of coffee.

Amy opens her bottled water.

"What is this stuff you stole? The stuff in that bag you keep carrying around?"

"I told you. You don't need to know that."

"Why did you steal this stuff if it was going to get you in so much trouble?"

"I didn't know it was going to get me into so much trouble. What I ended up stealing was different from what I thought I was stealing. Completely different."

His food comes. He asks her if she'd like some of his meal, and she shakes her head.

"What did you think you were going to steal?" she asks.

"Money. Cash. A lot of it."

"What did you take?"

He picks up a piece of bacon and pops it in his mouth.

"I told you. You can't know about that," he says while chewing.

"Whose stuff is this?"

He wipes a spot of grease from his chin.

"They go by different names. The Outfit. The Organization. The Syndicate."

"Is this like the Mafia?"

"That's another name for them."

"Seriously?"

"Yes."

"You stole stuff from the Mafia? Why would you do that?"

He takes another sip of coffee.

"I told you. I thought I was stealing money. Everything ended up being different than what I thought it was. It was a set up."

"Why did you need to steal money from the Mafia? Fix up your apartment?"

She says this last bit sarcastically.

"I had a pressing obligation. A bill that needed to be paid right away."

"What kind of bill?"

He shoves some more food in his mouth.

"I owed a guy some money," he says, his mouth full. "Let's just change the subject."

"I want to know why you owed somebody money."

He waves his fork at her.

"Look," he says, "you're gonna learn that in life there are a lot of things you're better off not knowing. Not knowing certain stuff doesn't cause any problems but knowing it just causes a lot of grief."

Her eyes narrow.

"Tell me. It was probably something crooked."

"No, it didn't involve any kind of crime. I had to pay back some money I borrowed. That's all."

"So you had to steal some money to pay back some other money you borrowed?"

He nodded.

"What did you have to borrow money for? That doesn't sound like good planning."

He remains silent as she continues to stare.

"If you've got to know, it was for your private school tuition," he says. "That's why I borrowed the money."

"No!"

"That's what the money was for. I said you wouldn't want to know but you wouldn't listen."

"I don't believe you."

He shrugs. Her face turns red, her lip quivers, then she chokes back something that sounds like a sob.

"You're lying. Mom gets free tuition because she works there. She told me."

"No, I'm not lying. Your mother gets a twenty-five percent discount from the school. I pay the rest. I've been paying your school tuition for years, ever since I got out. I was just unexpectedly short of cash this time and the school wouldn't give me an extension like they usually do. I didn't want you to get kicked out of that fancy school of yours, so I borrowed some money from a guy. I did this other job so I could pay the guy back. But things didn't work out as planned. That happens. End of story."

Chapter Forty-Five

De La Torre is in the hallway outside his office when his cell phone rings. It's eight-thirty and he's been at work for two hours. He tossed and turned on the living room couch before he gave up on the idea of sleep. That's two nights in a row with a total of three hours of sleep, and his nerves are humming and singing like a high power line on a hot summer's day. It's getting harder to hold it all together. But he has to stay strong.

It's Polaski again, the third call in the last twenty-four hours. De La Torre has ignored the others, but he figures he better take this one before things begin to look too suspicious. De La Torre doesn't want Polaski talking to anybody else at the Bureau, and he's liable to do that if he can't get ahold of De La Torre.

But he can't have anybody overhear him.

He takes the elevator back down, goes outside, and lights up a cigarette. If anybody wonders why he's outside, it'll just look as though he's taking a smoke break.

He takes out his cell, pulls up Polaski's number and hits the green button.

The phone rings a couple of times before Polaski answers.

"I've been trying to reach you," he says.

"I've been out of pocket," De La Torre says. "There's a lot going down. What do you have for me?"

"I've got some news. Bad news. Our witness is dead."

De La Torre stares at the passing pedestrians. He senses his heart beating, hears his respirations, and feels his knees grow weak.

Polaski says, "She got hit by car doing sixty as she was crossing the street."

"When did this happen?"

"Yesterday. Late morning. It was hit-and-run."

"Probably just an accident, don't you think?"

Polaski snorts with derision.

"No, we're sure it was intentional. Witnesses say the car ran a red light, and swerved into the other lane to hit her. And the car was stolen. Looks like a hit job to me."

De La Torre drops his cigarette on the sidewalk, rubs it out.

"You think it was related to this guy?" he asks.

"You mean Charlie McCoy? Sure I do. Too much of a coincidence, otherwise. I mean, she was a waitress, for chrissake, who would want to kill a waitress? The question is, how did he find out about her?"

"Maybe she talked to the wrong person."

"I don't think so. She didn't seem like the type to shoot her mouth off. Lived alone except for her three-year-old daughter, didn't go out much. So, who is she going to tell?"

"Who knows? Maybe a customer. I don't know what happened."

Polaski's voice gets louder, harsher.

"Somebody must've leaked the information to McCoy," he says. "Nobody knew about this witness in this office except me. Who did you tell at your end?"

"Nobody. Wait. I take that back. I mentioned it briefly to an assistant US attorney named Prescott. He wanted to know what was going on, so I told him."

"What do you think? Could he be the leak?"

"Let's say he's under some suspicion at the moment. That's strictly between you and me, understand? I'll need to look into this further. I'll get back to you."

As he goes up in the elevator, De La Torre thinks that if they check with Prescott he would deny knowing anything about the witness and that could be trouble. But it'll just be his word against De La Torre's.

Still, one more thing to worry about. He wishes he could talk with Malcolm, but that's out of the question.

He steps into his office. Cathy Hunt is sitting behind his desk, in his chair, talking on his phone. She's wearing the same clothes as last night.

"He just came in," she says. "I'll call you back."

She hangs up the phone, checks her watch.

"Hope you don't mind me using your office," she says.

"What's going on?"

"It turns out we got a call yesterday afternoon. A guy saying that he has some information concerning the Adonis crime family. I found it when I was going through the call logs this morning."

"You think he's that guy?"

"The guy that broke into Phil Adonis's house and stole a bunch of stuff and then got involved in a shootout with members of the Adonis crime family? That guy? Yeah, I think he's that guy."

"There's no way to be sure."

"I don't know about that. He said some interesting stuff."

"Like what?"

"He says he has information linking Phil Adonis directly to money laundering."

"Great. That's what we've been looking for all these years. If we can believe this guy, that is. You hear stuff like that all the time out on the street. Always turns out to be garbage."

She leans over the desk and looks him in the eye.

"But that's not all. This is the best part. He says he's got info regarding bribes paid to public officials. Some high ranking people, according to him. This could be something really big."

"That sounds a little farfetched, doesn't it?"

She stands, walks to the door, and pushes it shut. The office suddenly seems smaller.

She says, "I'm sure Phil Adonis has greased a few palms in his time. Lisk said he'd seen some records of bribe payments, right?"

"We assumed they were small time. Cops walking a beat or municipal judges or--"

"This guy who called wasn't talking small time. Do you know what this means? And why should this guy lie?"

"Maybe he's looking to make a deal and he's--"

"We can take down the Adonis crime family and a bunch of crooked politicians at the same time. It'll be the biggest prosecution since The Commission Trial."

The Commission Trial, the case that sent the leaders of New York's Five Families to prison. It was the case that made Rudy Giuliani's political career. She is practically drooling. This is her shot at the big time.

He says, "Why is this guy looking to deal? At this time?"

She leans back against in the chair and folds her arms across her chest.

"Beats me," she says. "I thought this whole robbery was a scam, something put together by Phil Adonis as an explanation as to why he didn't have any of the stuff we subpoenaed. But now I don't know. Maybe it was a real robbery, otherwise the thief wouldn't be calling us trying to make a deal, right? That doesn't make sense."

"Do we have a lead on this guy's location?" De La Torre asks.

"Nope. He called from a pay phone. Long gone now. We're checking closed circuit cameras in the area, see if they caught anything, but no luck so far."

"I didn't think there were any pay phones left."

"Evidently there is at least one. It's somewhere in the Poconos. Assuming he's the guy who shot Marco Delassandro, he's headed north and west. At least for the moment."

"What do we do now? This seems like a dead end."

"Dead end? No way, no sir. The Justice Department is going to use all its resources to find this guy. We're not giving up on this. There's too much at stake. Section Chief Winston's going to get the okay from upstairs. I'm proposing we offer a fifty thousand dollar reward for McCoy's whereabouts. We need information--"

"Wait a minute, you said McCoy."

"Did I?"

"Yes. Who's that?"

She gives him a sly grin. She's enjoying this entirely too much, he thinks.

"Hey, you caught me. That's what I figure the guy's name is. The one we're looking for. After reviewing the call logs, I searched for anything out of the ordinary in the police reports for that area. A gray Ford 150 pickup was found abandoned outside a diner in Coal City last night. So that got my attention."

"Where the hell is Coal City?"

"Northeastern Pennsylvania. Near Scranton. About seventy-five miles north of where the phone call was made."

"It's a gray Ford pick-up, but other than that, so what?"

"It has Jersey plates that belong to a Nissan. Turns out the address for the Nissan was near where that shoot-out occurred yesterday. One and one always equals two in my book."

"You did all this last night?"

She shrugs.

"I never get more than a two or three hours sleep," she says.

"You got insomnia or something?"

"No, it's some sort of genetic thing. Apparently my mother had it, too. Any more than three hours sleep and I feel sluggish. And I took a nap on the couch in the reception area, so I'm good. Thanks for asking. But wait, it gets better. We ran the VIN and the pickup is registered to a Charles L. McCoy, age fifty-three. And guess what? He's got a record and he's wanted for the murder of his ex-wife and her boyfriend. According to relatives, he's got his daughter with him, so he's guilty of transporting a kidnapping victim across state lines. That gives us federal jurisdiction right there."

De La Torre clears his throat.

"That statute doesn't apply if the kidnapper is a parent," he says.

"He had his parental rights terminated when he was in the slammer a few years back," she says with glee. "Legally speaking, he's not even her father, so there's nothing to stop us from taking over this investigation."

"That's great work. You told Winston all this?"

"Sure did," she says. "I was getting off the phone when you walked in. Section Chief Winston's approved all hands on deck. Interviews with all McCoy's relatives, his known associates, anyone who may know where anywhere he may run to. We're getting local law enforcement all up and down the East Coast to issue APBs on the double murder. Now we know who he is, we can get his photo out there. We're going all in on the media. We should have this guy in less than twenty-four hours. There's nowhere you can hide in this day and age."

"Unfortunately, we don't have a solid lead on where's he going or what he's driving."

"But we do. Turns out that a Seventy-Two Olds Cutlass was stolen two blocks from where the pickup was found. I'm figuring he switched vehicles and it's the Cutlass we should be looking for."

De La Torre thinks, none of this is good news.

"I am definitely impressed," he says. "I just want to reiterate that I need be included in this thing. I've been after Phil Adonis for sixteen years. To you it's a job, but I've been living it. If this guy's going to bring Adonis down, I definitely want to be in on it."

"Don't worry," she says with a smile. "We won't forget about you. One other thing. The name Moe Baker mean anything to you?"

Chapter Forty-Six

They're sitting in a donut shop. Phil, Dutch, Taco, Niko, and Ralph Tocco.

"You mind telling us what we're doing cooling our heels in this joint?" Niko asks, chewing on a jelly-filled.

Phil says nothing. He received a call from O'Brien an hour ago telling him that Niko may be the rat. Now he doesn't know what to say or do. Anything Niko suggests may be trap. He wants to talk to his father, but Dad is at the hospital for some tests.

"And why we aren't out looking for this guy McCoy?" Niko continues.

"I'm waiting on a phone call," Phil says, pointing at his cell phone.

"And that means we all got to be here for that?" Ralph says.

Phil gives him the side-eye. Niko telling him what to do is bad enough. Now he's getting shit from the likes of Ralph Tocco. There's definitely going to be a house cleaning when this is all over.

The phone rings and Phil picks it up.

"Phil here."

"We got a fix on that phone," a voice says at the other end.

"Took long enough."

"I've got to be careful. I'm not supposed to be doing this stuff. I'm probably breaking eleven different laws."

"I'll remember you at Christmas."

"Hope it's long before then."

"Whattya got? Time's wasting."

"He's in upstate New York. Near Lake Placid. That's the best I can tell you. The phone's not GPS enabled, so I gotta do this the old fashioned way by triangulating towers."

"That's enough. I'll call back in a few hours for an update."

Phil hits END.

Niko says, "Mind telling me what that was about?"

"I got some information on the whereabouts of our friend."

"How did you get that?"

"Don't ask so many questions. Isn't it enough that I know?"

"So where is he?"

"Upstate New York, headed north."

"That's not very helpful. Upstate New York's a pretty big place. We need to know where he's going."

Phil stands, tosses a fifty on the table to pay for the coffee and doughnuts.

"Don't worry," he says. "I know where he is and where he's going. And he has an eight hour head start on us. So we need to get moving."

They're walking toward the door when Taco stops and gawks at a TV set nestled in a corner near the ceiling.

"Look at that," he says, pointing. "It's that son of a bitch McCoy."

Chapter Forty-Seven

The car is a beater, a fifteen-year-old Honda Civic with bald tires, 200,000 miles on the clock, and serious rust issues. Fifteen winters of road salt have taken their toll. But it's transportation and that's what they need since Charlie dropped off the Olds Cutlass in the Lake Placid Police Department's parking lot. He left two grand under the driver's side floor mat to pay for repairs.

"I'll give you twelve hundred for it," Charlie says. They're standing outside a cottage that looks like something out of The Lord of The Rings.

"You ain't giving me anything, man. This is what's called an arms-length transaction."

The owner of the piece of crap is an obese white guy with a long gray pony tail and Nicotine-stained teeth.

"Twenty-two hundred and not a penny less," he says, nodding his head twice.

"I don't know. It doesn't look too great with that rust and all. I'm not sure it'll make it out of your driveway. Fifteen hundred is the best I can do."

"Twenty-three hundred."

Charlie shakes his head. "That's not how you do negotiations. I go up. You go down. We meet somewhere in the middle. That's how it works. It doesn't work if we go in the same direction."

"I saw you and the little lady getting off the bus, down at the bottom of the hill. You don't have a car, you don't have nothing. I'm betting everything you own is in those bags of yours."

He points at the two duffel bags and Amy's backpack and suitcase that are next to the door.

"And the next bus ain't for two hours."

He looks at the sky.

"There's rain coming. You'd best stop your bullshit negotiating and pay my asking price before I decide my car's not for sale no longer. And I'll need payment in cash."

Charlie turns his back and takes the wad of bills from his pocket and counts out twenty-three hundred-dollar bills.

"The pink slip's in the glove compartment," the guy says, counting the bills.

"That's a smart place to leave it."

The guy gives him a look as if he's not sure if Charlie is being sarcastic.

"You'll have to take care of transferring the title," he says.

"Not a problem," Charlie says.

***

The sky opened up ten minutes after they left. It's raining hard now, the wiper beating frantically in an unsuccessful effort to keep the windshield clear. They lost time dumping the Oldsmobile and buying the Honda, but

Charlie's feeling pretty good. There's not much chance of them being tracked to the Honda. They're practically invisible.

"About four hours and we'll be there," he says.

Amy doesn't say anything.

"What's the problem?" he asks.

"I don't like this car. It stinks."

It did reek of cigarette smoke.

"I'm getting a headache just sitting here," she says.

"It was your idea we ditch the Oldsmobile."

"It was stolen," she says. "And you promised you'd give yourself up to the police. I haven't forgotten about that."

"I said I'd think about it. And don't do that."

"What?"

"Roll your eyes like that."

"You promised you'd give yourself up. Don't lie."

He feels the bald tires hydroplane and for a moment he's not in control. He slows to forty-five and the tires regain their marginal grip on the roadway.

"Going to the police is a big deal," he says. "It's a one directional thing. You can't go back again. And there are some consequences to think of. Like prison, for example. Personally, I don't want to be forced into making an important decision by a thirteen-year-old girl with no real life experience."

She narrows her eyes.

"I don't know why it's so hard for you to do the right thing. Just for once."

"Because it means I'll go back to prison. I have a previous felony conviction. If I'm not careful I could end up with a twenty-year sentence."

That's not counting murder convictions for Moe and that guy at the Shore. Hell, they'll just throw the keys away and be done with him.

He doesn't know where she gets off telling him what he should do. When he was a kid, he never would've thought of telling an adult what to do.

And she's not getting the message that I don't really care what she thinks.

"I'll do anything to avoid going back to prison," he says. "I'd go crazy if I have to go back there. And I don't think I'd survive very long seeing as how I've gotten crosswise with the mob. Sometimes I think you just want me to be punished."

"Sometimes I think there are things you're not telling me. Maybe you won't have to go to prison. You don't know. We were at the police station. You could have done it then. Just walked in. Explained everything to them. Like you said you would."

"You should stop giving advice about stuff you don't understand. And there's something else bugging you, what is it?"

"Isn't it enough that I feel like I can't trust you?"

A sign says SLOW. He touches the brakes and the whole car shimmies.

"No," he says, "there's something else bugging you."

"That thing about you paying my school tuition. If you really did, that is. That doesn't make you special or anything. Hope you know that."

"I didn't think it did."

"And it doesn't make all of what happened my fault, either."

"Of course not. It was my decision to borrow the money."

They're driving slowly through a small town. He stops at a crossroads, the brakes squealing in protest as they come to a stop. He looks right and left. A police black-and-white cruises by without even slowing down. He spots a pay phone on the side of a Stop-and-Shop convenience store. He sits, thinking.

"There's a pay phone," Amy says, pointing. "Isn't that what you were looking for?"

He nods.

"What are you waiting for?" Amy asks.

"Just thinking."

He eases through the intersection and pulls into the Stop-and-Shop parking lot.

"I'll call the FBI again," he says. "Right here and now."

It's gotten colder and it's still raining, although not as hard. Standing next to the phone, he fumbles around for change to make the call. He calls the operator and asks to be put through to the FBI office he'd called the day before.

"Is this an emergency?" the operator asks.

He glances back at Amy.

"You could say that."

She asks for an additional three dollars for five minutes and he keeps feeding change until he hears the ring. Somebody answers and he asks for James. He explains that he called and spoke to James yesterday about the Adonis family. After a couple of minutes a man who is not James comes on.

"Where's James?" Charlie asks. "I asked for him."

"You've got me instead, partner. Think of me as his boss. You've got the big man now, and I've been meaning to talk to you. You need to come in, Mister McCoy."

Charlie gets a sinking feeling in his gut. This guy knows my name.

"Who are you?" Charlie asks.

"I'm not important. You're important. Tell me when we can get together and where."

The rain is soaking through Charlie's shirt and pants and he suddenly feels very cold.

"I'm not ready to meet," he says. "We've got to set some ground rules first."

"You're in no position to go setting any rules, Charlie. You have no power here."

"That's not how I look at it. From where I'm standing I'm looking at a lot of power."

"No, you're looking at a lot of trouble. You know your ex-wife is dead. Murdered. You're the number one suspect."

"Can't help you there. I know nothing about that. I wasn't involved."

"People here are thinking you did it. Tell me exactly what it is you have that makes you so powerful."

Charlie wipes the rain from his face with the back of his hand. He tastes salt and dirt. The call's about to end and he doesn't have any more change.

"I'd really like to know your name," Charlie says.

"The Adonis family is looking for you, but I expect you know that, given what happened at the Shore. You need to come in before they catch up with you."

"You're not listening. I need--"

"You need to make a deal, Charlie, that's what you need. Work with me here. Meet me somewhere. Neutral ground. A parking lot. An empty field. In the woods. A motel room. Somewhere private. Wherever you want. Bring the stuff with you. Just you and me. I'll take care of you."

"I don't like the sound of that."

"Let me ask you, have you looked at what's on those discs? Can you tell me something? What sort of information do you have about bribes? You know, what names can you tell me?"

Charlie stares at the phone as if it were a snake and it had just bitten him.

"If you wait until we have you in custody," the man continues, "you won't have any leverage. Best to come--"

Charlie hangs up and trots to his car.

Chapter Forty-Eight

"Did you ever wonder how they found out about Lisk?" she asks.

"How do you mean?"

They're in the cafeteria. He's eating a Cobb salad. She ordered a burger and fries. When she asked about Moe Baker, he denied knowing anything and asked who he was. She nodded her head in response but didn't say anything. As long as they don't speak to Polaski, he doesn't have a big problem.

But how did they find out about Baker?

Half an hour ago she asked him if he wanted to grab a bite to eat before the cafeteria closed. De La Torre was wary. She always seemed to have an ulterior motive for everything.

"There must be a leak somewhere, right?" she says. "Is there any other explanation?"

He knew this was coming and he was prepared.

"Lisk wasn't the sharpest knife in the drawer," he says. "He was book smart, had to be since he was a CPA. But he wasn't street smart, if you know what I mean."

"So, you figure he did something to give himself away."

"That's what I'm thinking, yes."

"I wonder what he did. I mean to be so stupid. You'd think he'd be extra careful."

"One thing is for certain," he says, probing for information. "Lisk didn't know the identity of the other asset."

"Why do you say that?"

"They worked Lisk over pretty bad. And I haven't seen any corpses of Adonis family personnel show up. And nobody's gone missing. I can only figure Lisk didn't know who the other guy was."

"Because, given the way he was tortured, he'd have given him up?"

De La Torre nods. She's buying it. They doesn't suspect him of anything. And they won't. Why? Because he's right in front of them, and you can never see what is right in front of you. And he's one of them. How many crooked FBI agents have there been over the years? A dozen or so who got caught--and that the Bureau admitted to. And then there's the monster-under-the-bed syndrome. There's no telling what the Bureau might find if it looked too closely.

No, he's safe. It's Prescott who has something to worry about.

"You got anything new on McCoy on your end?" she asks.

"Nothing."

He took McCoy's call on an unrecorded line, so he doesn't have to worry if she reviews the logs. In fact, no worries all around.

"Let me ask you a question," she says, squirting a bright red glob of ketchup on her burger. "What can you tell me about this guy Polaski?"

Chapter Forty-Nine

Charlie and Amy are in the deep woods now. Nothing but tall trees lining both sides of the road. They drive across a covered wooden bridge, the planks rattling under the car's tires.

"We should call ahead," Charlie says. "Let your aunt know we're coming. But I don't know her number."

A pause.

"You're not going to give yourself up, are you? Ever?"

"I made the call," he says. "I ran out of change."

"Seriously? What really happened?"

"It didn't go the way I expected. The guy made me suspicious. He asked the wrong kind of questions."

"You should--"

"Give it a rest. I've got bigger problems. It's been a while since I've been to your aunt's place. I don't know how I'm going to find it in the dark. If we hadn't wasted so much time changing cars, we'd be there already."

Silence.

"I have Aunt Louise's number."

"Really? How's that?"

"It's on my cell phone."

He jerks his head around.

"Your cell phone? We left that in the trash back at that diner."

"I took it out of the trash while you were stealing that car."

He slams on the brakes. The rear of the car slews right and left before the car slides to a stop.

"You've had it this whole time?"

Her upper lip quivers.

"So, where is it now?"

She points at her backpack that's lying on the floor next to the back seat.

"It's in my backpack."

"I told you. We had to get rid of it. You disobeyed me. You snuck around behind my back. You didn't even tell me what you were doing."

He steps out of the car, rips open the rear door, and drags out the backpack. He trots down the road toward the bridge, the backpack in hand. It's still raining. The cold drops sting his face, the rain runs into his eyes, blinding him. Amy's ten yards behind him, shouting. His brain is a jumble of thoughts. Moe Baker and the bullet hole in his forehead. Carol with half her head missing. The dead guy on the kitchen floor.

Charlie strides over to the edge of the bridge.

"What are you doing?" Amy cries.

"Getting rid of this damned cell phone. Once and for all."

He whirls the backpack above his head and then hurls it into the river below and watches it float away.

"I can't believe you did that," she screams, the rain running down her face.

"Believe it."

Chapter Fifty

De La Torre is sitting in his office, thinking he was stupid. He became impatient. He pushed McCoy too hard, and McCoy became suspicious.

He can't afford any more mistakes like that.

He has to keep his emotions in check. De La Torre had seen it a million times. A criminal can't control himself and he ends up doing or saying something stupid and then it's all over. If he'd just kept his mouth shut, everything would've been all right.

There are no do-overs in this game.

The conversation with Hunt concerning Polaski was awkward. She asked how many times he spoke with Polaski. He said he couldn't recall exactly, maybe a couple. She asked him when Polaski told him it was McCoy. He said he first knew about McCoy when she told him. She asked if he knew anything about how the witness died. He said of course not. She asked all the questions with that little smile on her face.

Was that call from Polaski about the dead witness some sort of set-up? Was the call recorded? He's going to have to watch his step. The walls were definitely closing in.

"So this coffee shop has a big picture window," she said. "It looks out on the street. Being late in the afternoon, business is slow and the witness is standing behind the counter, looking out the window when she sees this Toyota pull up in a no parking zone. A guy gets out carrying a big duffel bag. He walks real fast right past her and around the corner."

"That's my understanding."

"You betchya. The witness even noticed the guy had a cast on his right hand. A squad car had already found the van with Moe Baker's body. They checked the security tapes and saw the license number of the Toyota. It was easy to locate the Toyota because it had already been towed and so the plate was in the system. The local PD canvassed the neighborhood to see if anybody had seen the driver and they found the waitress. All within four hours."

"Yeah, it was good work."

"And that was a couple of days ago."

What was she implying? That they suspected him of slow playing the investigation? Or, worse yet, being complicit in the death of the witness. No, that's impossible. They would've suspended him pending review if they thought he was the leak. That's what the book calls for. And the Bureau always goes by the book.

He leans back in his chair. Things are still good.

He's closing his eyes when Cathy Hunt pushes open his door without knocking and steps into his office. She's beaming.

She says, "I've got some interesting news for you."

Chapter Fifty-One

Not a single sound out of Amy since he tossed her backpack in the river. Not even a grunt. Total silence. He preferred her when she was whining.

It's evening and they're on a county two-lane, somewhere in far Northern Maine. On the left is a small airstrip. A single-engine plane is taking off. It rolls down the runway, leaves the ground, and slowly disappears into the purple sunset. He wishes he were on that plane, just taking off into the wild blue yonder, wherever the hell that is. Hit the road and make a new life for yourself because the one you got is all screwed up.

The American dream.

He imagined flying to the wilds of Canada, touching down in a field somewhere, and hiding out. He had money and it wouldn't cost much to live in a cabin in the woods, all by himself. He could make it a couple of years. He'd change his appearance--shave his head or grow a beard or maybe both. He'd still have to go into town to get groceries and maybe pay some utility bills and people would wonder who he was and where that airplane came from. And he'd have to rent the cabin. And the cops would sooner or later wonder about the guy living in the woods all by himself, and they would pay a visit and ask questions and that would be the end.

Or maybe he could stage a plane crash and everyone will think he burned up in the fire. Or he might fly the plane toward the ocean, parachute out, and let the plane fly on auto pilot until it ran out of fuel and crashed into the water. He read about a guy who did that.

It's too bad he doesn't know how to fly a plane.

Sneaking across the border late at night might be another option, but the border is monitored by sensors in the roads, cameras in the trees, satellites in outer space, that sort of thing. On the other hand, it's the longest undefended fricking border in the world. Somewhere, there must be a place to sneak across.

If it were winter, the lakes would be frozen and he might be able to just walk across. Bootleggers did that during Prohibition. Unfortunately, it's not winter.

Idaho is another option. The federal government has a pretty weak hold on power out there. Of course, he'd have to travel 2,500 miles to get there while every cop in creation is looking for him. But they won't be looking for him in Canada, will they?

What about the mob? When would they stop looking for him? Approximately never. No matter where he went, his past would be nipping at his heels. How long could he go on like that before he got tired of running and simply gave up?

He realizes his mind is just going in circles again.

He'll think about what to do after he drops off Amy. He'll tell Louise and Richard to leave the house and go to a motel with Amy for a few days, just in case the mobsters show up looking for him. Then he'll make a dash for the border and figure out a way across.

"What are you thinking about?" she asks.

These are the first words she's said in a couple of hours. Since he slung her backpack into the river. He took it as a good sign.

"Nothing," he says. "I'm thinking about nothing."

"You can't be thinking about nothing. Nobody can."

"Sure I can. I do it all the time."

"So, you're saying that your mind is like a blank canvas."

"Yep. You got it. Absolutely empty. Its usual state."

"You just don't want to tell me about what you were thinking."

"That's not it," he lies.

"You were probably planning a heist."

"No, I'm not thinking about committing any crimes."

"Then why don't you tell me?"

"Jesus, you're a pest."

They roll into Cape Summit a little before nine. It's Maine in the middle of the summer, so it's still twilight. He stops at Louise's flower shop, The Blooming Lily. The lights are out. He bangs on the door, but nobody answers, which isn't surprising given the CLOSED sign in the window.

A restaurant is across the street with a sign that reads, YE OLDE LOBSTER HOUSE. Charlie tells Amy to stay in the car while he goes inside.

Business is booming in Ye Olde Lobster House. The ambiance is somewhere between tourist casual and vacation slob and every table is taken by customers with white and red plastic bibs tied around their necks. The wait staff is shuttling from kitchen to table, their trays loaded with steaming lobsters. After several minutes a waitress dressed in a medieval costume and with a face as red as one of the lobsters approaches

"There's at least a forty-five minute wait, sir," she says, wiping sweat from her brow.

"I wasn't looking for dinner," Charlie says. "I was hoping you'd be able to tell me how to find Louise Crowder. I went to her shop, the Blooming Lily, but she wasn't there."

"I haven't seen Louise for the last couple of days."

"Maybe you could give me directions to her house."

The waitress's expression changes, a sudden wariness.

"I know she lives somewhere near here in an old farmhouse," he says quickly. "But I'm not from around here and it's been a long time."

"Tell me again, why are you looking for her?"

"I'm her brother-in-law. Well, ex-brother-in-law."

Her eyes take on a suspicious look. Had Louise told her about her jailbird brother-in-law? He looks up at a TV that's over the bar. Jesus, it's showing his photo, a mug shot from his last bust, three years ago. He hasn't changed much. It's a damned good likeness. Now there's a photo of Amy, with the words KIDNAPPED CHILD in block capitals underneath.

Crap! Where did that come from?

"I have her niece out in the car," he says hurriedly, looking toward the door and away from the TV. "I'm dropping her off so she can stay with her aunt for the rest of the summer. Take a look, see for yourself. She's in the car."

"Why don't you call Louise? Get the directions from her?"

"I don't have her number. I figured I'd get here in full daylight. Now I'm bound to get lost looking for her place in the dark."

She glances at the restaurant that's full with customers waiting for their meals.

"Okay, listen. I only have time to say this once. You go down Main to the second light." She points to her right. "Take a left. That's County Road 516. Go about three miles. Take a right. That's Hapworth Lane. Louise's house is about a mile down on the right. You can't miss it. It sits on top of a hill and there're no other houses nearby."

He looks up at the TV. A pretty blond anchorwoman is talking about a train derailment near Chicago.

"Thanks for the directions," he says.

Chapter Fifty-Two

O'Brien's been wandering all day. He had breakfast and then he drove to the City. He stopped in at his favorite bar at the Four Seasons and knocked down a half-dozen Martinis in a couple of hours together with two orders of oysters on the half shell. He was ready to order another martini when the barman gave him a subtle shake of the head.

He didn't feel like being alone. So, looking for a little company, he called a hooker he knew named Janelle, but the call went straight to voice mail, and she hasn't called back.

His cell phone kept vibrating, and it was driving him nuts. It was the office, mostly. And some clients. And a number he didn't recognize kept showing up.

He ate an early dinner at one of his favorite steakhouses. A porterhouse, baked potato all the way, steamed broccoli because he was starting to feel bloated, and a bottle of pinot noir from the Russian River, wherever the hell that was.

He's had time to think about his discussion with Bernays. Bernays has his own cause for concern. The two of them had done some things the bar association would definitely disapprove of--bribery, witness intimidation, evidence destruction, jury tampering, that sort of thing. Fringe offenses, true, but the sort of thing that's frowned on by the authorities--but then what isn't these days? And who would he implicate in these shenanigans if he were to make a deal? Bernays wants O'Brien to disappear in order to save his own ass, that's obvious.

Going into witness protection won't be easy. Wherever he ends up, he won't be able to practice law. He'll be a nothing. Big Jerry O'Brien the man who can get congressmen--even governors and senators--on the phone will become a sixty-three-year-old nobody.

What will he do? How will he make a living? He's kidding himself. Steakhouses! He might have one good steak dinner a year if he's lucky. He scrapes up the last of his bread pudding, slaps down two hundred-dollar bills on the table, and wobbles off in the direction of the front door.

He drives slowly toward the office. He has forty grand in the office safe. Tomorrow, he'll get the fifty large out of his safety deposit box and then make a decision on his future.

He feels nauseated from all the food and drink. He's always overeaten when he's under stress, a form of self-medication, the doctors say. O'Brien knows differently. He overeats because he likes food.

He pulls in front of his office building, gets out, checks his watch. It's after nine PM, so he won't have to feed the meter. It's his lucky day.

He swipes his key card and the green light flashes. He punches the security code into the little keypad, but the door doesn't open. Damn his thick, sausage-like fingers. He hits the six digits again, but, still the door doesn't open. The numbers are swimming before his eyes--he tries to focus. He did have too much to drink. Maybe he should go sleep it off and get the money in the morning. He tries one last time. This time the door opens with a click.

He goes up the stairs, leaving the door open. He doesn't want to go through that business with the damned keypad on his way out.

The office is darkened and empty at this hour. He's walked this hallway so many times that he doesn't need to switch the lights on. Will he ever come back here? What will become of O'Brien & Associates, the firm he founded thirty-two years ago, and the employer of three associate lawyers, three secretaries, two paralegals, two law clerks, a receptionist, a file clerk, and an office manager?

It's his only lasting accomplishment in life and soon it will be gone.

He walks to his corner office, weaving slightly. The small iron safe is built into the bottom right cabinet of the credenza that's behind his desk. The safe also has a keypad. But he manages to open it on the first try, pushes aside a box of micro-cassettes, and takes out two brick-sized bundles of hundreds. He turns the banknotes over in his hands. It's damned little money when you get right down to it.

There's a shuffling noise. He looks up. A light is on in the hallway. Did he switch that light on? He's so befuddled he can't remember.

"Who's there?" he cries.

No answer. O'Brien opens the top desk drawer and fumbles around for his revolver. Looking up, he sees two man standing in the doorway to his office, pointing guns with silencers at his chest.

Chapter Fifty-Three

Charlie thinks, what an idiot I am. If the waitress in the lobster house sees his photo on TV, she's going to know exactly where to direct the cops. He's praying she's too busy serving lobsters to notice what's on CNN.

Louise and Richard's house is a rambling white clapboard structure on top of a hill. It's set back three hundred yards from the road. Charlie stops fifty yards from the house. The last glimmer of light is disappearing on the horizon.

Strangely, no lights are on in the house, only a porchlight outside.

"Stay here," he says to Amy.

He walks around the side of the house, the Beretta in his left hand. Is the Adonis family already here, waiting for him? Do they have Richard and Louise tied up--or worse, dead? Is this a trap?

There are no cars parked on the side of the house. He lifts the garage door and switches on the overhead light. Louise's ancient Volvo station wagon is parked inside. The space next to it is empty. He bends down. There's a small, damp oil patch on the concrete. A car was here recently, at least within a couple of days.

He walks around to the front of the house, thinking if the mob was here he'd know it by now. He knocks on the front door, waits. He's hoping Richard answers. He doesn't want a knockdown, drag out confrontation with Louise right here on the front porch--he just wants to drop off Amy and leave.

He knocks again. No answer. He checks his watch. It's nine-thirty. Where can they be at this hour? He tries the knob, but the door is locked. Then it hits him. He's been an idiot again.

They've gone to Carol's funeral. They're 700 miles away.

He stands in the doorway, thinking, and now what?

He doesn't want to go back on the road--he has nowhere to go. The police are looking for him and his picture is on TV. If he tries to check into a motel with Amy, he's sure to get a visit from the police before morning. They know she's with him, so they'll be looking for a middle-aged guy with a kid. Word will have gone out to all the motels.

And this is as good a place to make a stand as any.

No, best to stay here. At least for the night. He can think about what to do with Amy in the morning.

He waves to Amy, tells her to come on. Out of the darkness, she approaches tentatively, carrying the little plaid suitcase.

"Where's Aunt Louise and Uncle Richard?" she asks.

"They're not here. We'll just have to let ourselves in."

"Isn't the door locked?"

He pulls a key ring from his pocket and then examines the lock. It's an old Kwikset deadbolt, a nearly worthless lock with a shallow keyset that's easily opened by a gentle bump. He selects a key from the ring.

"You've got Aunt Louise's house key?" she asks.

"Sort of."

"What are you going to do?"

"Watch. This is like a magic trick."

He inserts the key and then pulls it out slightly. He takes a leather tool kit from his jacket pocket. Inside are a variety of small screwdrivers and a small hard rubber hammer. He removes the hammer and taps it on the end of the key. He tries to turn the key, but no luck.

"This doesn't always work the first time," he says.

He pulls the key out again and gives it another tap. Still, the key doesn't turn.

"Maybe we should stay at a motel tonight," she says.

"I'm good. Just give me a second."

The third time the key turns and the door opens.

"You should have a little confidence in your old man," he says.

"Yeah," she says. "Sure. Confidence. That's the ticket."

He steps inside. To the right is a living room and to the left is a dining room. Straight ahead are stairs. The ceilings are low and the walls are paneled in a dark-stained pine. Jesus, it's like a cave in here. He half expects to see a guy in an animal skin wandering around.

He walks through the living room to the family room. The creepy black-and-white photographs of trees cover the walls.

To his right is a large stone fireplace. A rifle hangs over the fireplace, exactly where he remembered. He takes it down, examines it, and works the bolt. The rifle is a Remington 700 model with a black fiberglass stock and stainless steel barrel. The Remington 700 similar to the M40 sniper rifle he trained on when he was in the Marines many years ago. The gun is clean and well oiled. The bolt action is tight and the gun is free of wear except for a few superficial scratches. He hefts the rifle a couple of times, trying to re-familiarize himself with the feel of the weapon. He turns his head and sees that Amy is watching him. She has an inquiring look on her face.

He hangs the rifle back on the wall.

Between the kitchen and the family room is a door that opens to stairs that go to the basement. He opens the door, switches on the light, and goes half-way down the stairs. A single sixty-watt bulb hanging from the ceiling illuminates a small room of old junk, cobwebs, and cardboard boxes that probably contain more old junk. Not a mobster in sight.

Upstairs, Amy gives him a puzzled look.

"Where are Aunt Louise and Uncle Richard?" she asks.

"I don't know. I'm sure they'll be along in a little while."

She is chewing on her lower lip. When did she start that?

"There's something I want you to do," he says. "It's important. Can you do this for me?"

"What is it?"

"I want you to go down in the basement and stay down there until I say it's safe to come up. Understand?"

"Why should--"

"And hide. Get behind something where nobody can see you. And be real quiet. And don't come out, no matter what. Understand?"

"I don't want to go down there. It's dirty and--"

"Are you listening?"

"Why were you looking at that gun? Are those men coming here?"

"Just do what I say."

She steps away from him, fear in her eyes.

"I don't want to go in the basement," she says. "And what about mom? We need to talk to her. Tell her what's going on. She'll be worried."

"I don't have time to talk about that right now."

"I should call her. She may have--"

"Don't worry about it," he says, raising his voice.

"Why? What else do you have to do? Do you have somewhere to go? I don't think so. I want to know why Mom doesn't answer when I called. Or why she didn't return my messages."

"I can't help you there," he says. "Maybe her phone isn't working. You know, the batteries are dead or something. Or she's just not answering."

"That's not it. She would never ignore my calls. There's something you're not telling me."

He rubs his jaw.

"It's late. I'm tired. I've been driving all day. We'll talk about it in the morning."

"I want to know right now. Did something happen to her? Did you do something to her? Has she been hurt?"

"You just don't know when to stop asking questions, do you? And I haven't done anything to her."

She grabs his sleeve.

"What's happened to her?" she says, her body shaking. "Why didn't she call me? Where is she?"

"Stop it. Sometimes it's better not to know things. Especially when you can't do anything about it. You should know that by now."

She looks him straight in the eye and flinches as if she had been slapped.

"Oh my God, she's dead. You knew and you didn't tell me."

He pulls away, trying to think of the best thing to say, coming up blank. Everything is happening too fast.

"She's dead," he says. "Some men killed her. And they're going to kill us, too, if they have the chance."

She's suddenly weeping, tears flowing down her cheeks.

"How long have you known?" she says between sobs. "My mother's gone. When were you going to tell me?"

"We're not going to give them the chance to kill us, that's what's important. Now just do what I say and go down in the fricking basement and stay there until I tell you to come out. Stay there for as long as it takes and don't come up."

"Is that it? Is that all you can say?"

"What more do you want me to say?"

She glares at him.

"Say that you're sorry. Show some emotion. At least act like her death means something to you."

"I still don't know what you want me to do. Yeah, I'm sorry she's dead, of course. But we can't do anything about it now. Dead is dead."

"Her death doesn't isn't important to you, is it? Nothing's important to you."

"Staying alive is important to me. We're not talking about this anymore. Get in the basement or I'll drag you down there myself."

She backs down the stairs, her eyes awash with emotion. Fear, disgust, horror. Contempt. All those things. He'll try to make this up to her at some point in the future. When this is all behind them.

"I'll never forgive you," she screams. "I hate you."

He says, "I hate me, too. Now you have something in common with your old man."

He slams the door shut.

What to do? The original plan--drop off Amy and make a dash for it--is no longer operative. What are the choices? Get back on the road. Problem? There's nowhere to go. And the Adonis family may be out there, waiting. Alternative? Wait until first light and then make a break for it. Problem? If the Adonis family isn't here already, that gives them another six hours.

Then again, maybe they haven't been tracking him. Maybe they didn't know about Amy's cell phone. Maybe there's nothing to worry about. Call that the logic of wishful thinking.

The final alternative? Wait until morning and then call the police, tell them to come over and take him into custody, and take his chances with the law. He could give himself up, and maybe Amy will be safe with the police.

Why not call the cops right now?

Because he needs time to cogitate on the best solution, that's why. He can't think straight right now--the argument with Amy has him too upset. And he's not going to make a life defining decision while he's upset.

That's what he'll do. Think about it. The trick is to just last until morning.

He takes a pair of white latex FoodHandler gloves from his pocket and puts one on his left hand. He spends ten minutes searching drawers and cabinets and comes up with a half-full cardboard box of shiny brass Remington .30-06 150 grain cartridges, ten in all. The box indicates they're suitable for killing deer and elk. It doesn't say anything about mobsters, but Charlie is sure they'll do the job. He hopes ten cartridges will be enough. What did they say in the Marines? One shot, one kill. But that was a long time ago. And he wasn't comfortable with the idea of killing back then. What would happen when the time comes? Would he freeze up? He shot Moe and that guy at the Shore, but that was self-defense, which made it easy.

He trots up the stairs, carrying the rifle in his left hand. The cartridges are in his pocket and the duffel bag is slung over his shoulder. The bag contains the shotgun and the shotgun shells as well as the CDs, and the strap digs hard into his shoulder.

As he mounts the stairs, he thinks about what Amy said. I'll never forgive you.

He's not surprised. Any closeness he felt was a figment of his imagination brought on by being in proximity to her for two days. They were strangers. Any shot he had for a relationship with Amy disappeared when he was sent to the joint all those years ago. You don't get any second chances in life. Hell, you get damned few first chances.

He gazes out one of the upstairs windows, trying to remember what he was taught in the Marines. He has the high ground, which is good. And a clear line of sight, which is also good. But he has a large perimeter to defend, which is bad. And there will be more of them than there is of him, which is very bad.

When they come, they'll have to come from the road. If they try to approach from the back of the house or from the south, they'll have to make their way through a thicket of pine trees and brush, and he's betting those city boys aren't dressed for a cross-country hike in the woods. And they can't come from the north. They would have to ford a river if they came that way. He's betting they drive straight up the driveway, which would be the stupidest thing to do. Their vehicle will be a death trap.

When will they make their move? First light or soon after. They wouldn't want to take a chance that he'll escape in the darkness. They'll have the sun at their backs when they come, another tactical advantage for them, although Charlie doubts that they will be aware of it.

He opens the windows in all the upstairs rooms, so they won't know where the shots are coming from. He grabs a straight-backed chair and drags it next to the window in a small bedroom overlooking the drive.

Nothing to do but wait. He might go down to the basement and try to talk with Amy. But that will only make things worse because he would say the wrong things. He has never been good at discussing matters of the heart.

So he sits, looking out the window, the rifle on his lap and the shotgun by his feet. Off in the far distance, there are fireworks. Happy Independence Day.

Chapter Fifty-Four

Phil opens the plastic box and removes the twelve-volt cordless drill. He examines it closely and then squeezes the trigger. The drill emits a high-pitched whine. He imagines it chewing into McCoy's flesh and grinding into bone. Maybe a 3/8 inch drill bit to the eye will get McCoy's attention. Satisfied, he puts the drill back in the box. He feels better than he has in days.

"Taco," he says. "Did you bring the propane torch?"

Taco holds up a plastic Lowe's bag.

"Got it right here, boss."

Niko says, "I don't know why you're keeping me in the dark here."

Phil thinks this is funny, since he knows that Niko is a goddamned rat who's been keeping everybody in the dark, probably for years.

Phil says, "Keeping you in the dark? How's that?"

"Like, how are we going to find McCoy?"

Phil pulls a cell phone from his pocket, holds it up.

"You're tracking the guy's cell phone?" Niko says. "I thought he didn't have one."

"Not his. He doesn't have one. It's his daughter's we're tracking."

"How do you know her number?"

"This cell phone in my hand is her mother's. It's got the girl's number on it. In fact, she's called it several times in the last twenty-four hours, no doubt looking for mommy. I have a source at the cell phone company. He's been tracking the girl's phone, keeping me informed of their whereabouts."

A ringing erupts. Phil takes another cell phone from his jacket pocket.

"Speak of the devil," he says. "There's my source now with an update."

Phil listens as the guy explains that he lost the signal to the phone.

"They must've ditched it," the guy says.

"Okay, I understand," Phil says, hanging up, disappointed.

Have they lost McCoy again? At this point they have no choice but to keep going. There is nothing else he can do.

Niko says, "There a problem?"

"No problem. Why do you ask?"

"The expression on your face. You don't look happy."

"No everything's fine. I know exactly where they are. Or at least where they're going."

"You got a plan to handle McCoy?"

"Don't worry about McCoy," Phil says. "He won't be a problem. He's soft. He could've taken us all out with that shotgun of his when he had us trapped. Just stick it in a window and start firing. But he didn't take advantage of the situation. Like I said. Soft."

He snaps shut the plastic box containing the drill.

"You gonna get involved this time, Niko?" he asks.

"Involved? What do you mean?"

"You didn't seem interested when we had our conversation with Mister Lisk. I kind of wondered about that. You know what I'm saying?"

"What're you saying, Phil?"

"I'm saying buck up or stay in the truck, Niko. That's what I'm saying."

Niko gazes out the window at the darkness.

"I didn't want to interrupt your quality time with Lisk," he says. "You were having so much fun."

Chapter Fifty-Five

Dawn is a tiny sliver of light on the horizon. The white four-seat Cessna 182 Skylane makes a hard turn around the runway below and then drops a hundred feet. De La Torre knows the model of the plane because he's read and reread the brochure in the seat pocket a dozen times.

De La Torre's thinking about what Cynthia said. *Sometimes I wonder what really pays for all this.*

What did she mean by that? Did she want to take a peek at the monster under the bed? Was that what she was saying? Or was she just screwing with him? He figures it's the latter. He has nothing to worry about. The family situation is still firmly under control.

The Cessna makes another abrupt turn. It's been a bumpy ride. During the four hours they've been airborne, he's been able to avoid vomiting, but this latest turn is too much. He grabs the brown paper bag and hurls the undigested potion of last night's Cobb salad.

"Sorry about that," the pilot says. "Unexpected turbulence. A weather front just went through. You doing okay back there?"

"Fine," De La Torre grunts, feeling the stomach acid burning the inside of his throat and the smell of vomit permeating his nostrils.

"What about you, ma'am?" he says to Cathy Hunt.

"I'm fine, too," she says. "Thanks for asking."

She finishes applying a fresh coat of lip gloss, purses her lips, and makes one last inspection in her compact's mirror.

Six hours earlier, she told De La Torre that a guy near Lake Placid had called the Bureau, saying he'd sold a Honda Civic to a man matching McCoy's description. The man had a girl with him. The guy also wanted to know how big the reward was.

"Sounds like our fella," she said. "And I know where he's headed. Cape Summit, Maine."

"How do you know that?"

"Female intuition. Plus that's where his ex-sister-in-law lives. Plus his last known location and his general direction of travel--basically north. Plus a tracking device on Ralph Tocco's Suburban tells us that's where the Adonis family is going, and I'm guessing they know something."

"All you really have," De La Torre said, "is the word of this guy who sold the Honda Civic. We don't even know it was McCoy."

"And don't forget that Olds Cutlass, too. The one that was stolen. We found it. In Lake Placid. A couple of miles from where McCoy bought the Civic. And you know what's really strange?"

De La Torre says he doesn't.

"He left the Olds in a police station parking lot."

"That is weird. Like he's asking for trouble."

"And something else. He left a couple of grand under the floor mat along with an apology for taking the car."

Two hours later they were boarding the plane.

She runs her fingers through her hair and, apparently satisfied, puts her compact away.

They land and De La Torre climbs out and then Hunt. De La Torre bends his knees a few times, happy to be on firm ground again.

A government-issue black Crown Vic with federal plates is at the edge of the runway, together with three police cruisers, and a hulking SWAT truck. He's not happy with the excessive law enforcement presence. The more cops involved, the more people who stand between him and McCoy and the information he needs.

A young guy in a three-piece suit approaches--must be the agent from the Boston Field Office. He has a ballistic vest and a navy-blue FBI windbreaker in each hand. De La Torre slips off his suit jacket and dons the vest and windbreaker. The three-piece suit says his name is Reynolds and that it's about forty miles to the suspect's location.

"It's a fifty minute ride," he says. "At legal speeds."

"Where're the mobsters?" she asks.

"Tocco's Suburban is about twenty minutes away from the location. That's as of five minutes ago."

"Then we need to step on it." Hunt says. "Make sure everybody knows that McCoy's armed and dangerous. So are these other jokers. McCoy's suspected of killing

322   THE REDEMPTION OF CHARLIE MCCOY

three people and seriously injuring another. The others are known hoodlums. Don't take any chances. Rules of engagement are one verbal warning, then shoot." She points at the other vehicles. "Make sure they all understand. And tell them that we will definitely be exceeding legal speeds."

A cell phone rings and Hunt extracts it from a little holster on her belt. She listens intently for a few moments, nodding her head.

Then she says, "No kidding."

Chapter Fifty-Six

Charlie awakens to the sound of a phone ringing. Without thinking, he picks up.

"Who is this?" he says.

"Is this Charlie McCoy?"

"What? Who is this?"

"Good morning, Charlie. We're just giving you a wakeup call. Kind of a courtesy. Let you know we're coming."

"I don't know who this is."

"Yes you do. We're coming for you, Charlie. And for your darling little girl."

There's laughter at the other end of the line.

He jumps to his feet, looks down the drive.

A thick fog formed overnight and with that and the weak morning light he can barely see the road.

He picks up the rifle and looks through the scope. It's a three-power scope and he can make out the end of the drive. There's some movement. Or maybe not. Maybe it's his imagination. He takes a look through his binoculars.

The trees with their full summer foliage obscure his view. Then something. Definitely some movement this time. A man. No, several men, like ghosts in the mist.

He drags the bedside table in front of the window. The table is six inches higher than the window ledge, which makes it the perfect height. He removes some books from a bookcase and makes two piles on the bedside table, each pile three inches high. He loops the cord from blinds around the end of the barrel three times to provide some stability. Resting the rifle on the bedside table, he pushes both piles of books in against the forestock of the rifle. Together with the table, the books act as a makeshift rifle rest.

Getting on his knees, he rests his arm with the splint just in front of the trigger guard. Not an ideal arrangement, but it'll do.

He looks through the scope again.

Chapter Fifty-Seven

They've been joined by two black SUVs with K-9 placards on the side, making their little convoy seven vehicles.

"In case McCoy tries to get away on foot," Hunt says.

De La Torre nods. He's impressed that she's been able to get this organized in just a few hours, although the more cops that appear, the more uncomfortable he gets.

"Guess what?" she says. "Jerry O'Brien is dead. The Adonis's lawyer, right? Shot to death."

"What? When?"

"Last night. That's the call I got at the airport. His corpse was found a few hours ago by a late night cleaning crew. Four slugs to the chest."

De La Torre fights hard to stop from smiling. The only member of the Adonis family who could personally identify him as their mole is dead. That leaves Big Phil and Little Phil, but their testimony would be hearsay and inadmissible because he never actually spoke with them.

The only person I have to worry about is McCoy.

"What do you make of that?" he says. "Who would want to kill a lawyer?"

"Most of the population at one time or another."

"You think the shooting's related to McCoy?"

"Hard to tell. Maybe it's just part of a reorganization."

"Is that what our mole says?"

She flashes him a wide grin.

"What do you think of this guy McCoy?" she says.

"An average, run-of-the-mill thief. That's all."

"He's caused a lot of carnage in the last two days for an average run-of-the-mill thief. Why do you think he's doing it?"

He shrugs. "I guess he flipped. Maybe it had to do with his ex-wife and her boyfriend. Jealousy, that's all."

"He wasn't convicted of anything until he was in his forties, did you know that?"

"What's your point?"

"He went a long time before being sent to the joint. That's unusual for a career criminal."

"He's a more successful than average thief. So what? Sounds like you got the hots for him, if you don't mind my saying."

She smiles. "He is kind of attractive. Something to do with his eyes, I think. Do you know he was in the Marines?"

"No, I didn't. Doesn't mean anything, though. Plenty of ex-Marines become crooks."

"There's no such thing as an ex-Marine. Retired Marine, maybe. Not ex-Marine. My dad was one."

"Doesn't change what McCoy is," he says.

"I reviewed his DOD file last night. He was on embassy detail for several years. That's an important assignment. They don't just give it to anybody. He was one of the Marine guards at the American Embassy in Iran when it was taken over."

"No kidding."

"Apparently he was beaten and subject to severe psychological torture by the Iranians for months. He lost sixty pounds while he was in captivity. He was only nineteen at the time."

"Psychological torture. That could explain his behavior."

"He was awarded the Defense Meritorious Service Medal by Reagan himself."

De La Torre sneers and shakes his head.

"Doesn't change the fact that he's a crook," he says. "And a suspected murderer. Look what he did to his ex-wife. That was pretty sick."

She sits up straight, adjusts her holster.

"I don't think he killed his ex-wife," she says.

"How come?"

"I reviewed that information from the tracking device on Marco Delassandro's Mercedes. The Adonis family was at the wife's house at about the time of death. My thoughts, they were trying to find Charlie McCoy and they tortured his ex-wife to death to get information. That's my theory."

This bitch never quits, he thinks.

"I'm surprised you didn't notice that," she says. "Since you got a copy of the printout."

"When I got that printout, I wasn't looking for where they'd been, only where they were. And we've got McCoy on plenty of other things we can charge him with. Even if he didn't kill his ex-wife."

"It does make me wonder," she says. "What makes a good guy go bad? Do you ever think about that? Is it just money? Or is it the excitement? And what's this whole thing about his kid? She's not even his kid, strictly speaking. Why not just dump her somewhere? She must be slowing him down."

"Maybe he intends to use her as a hostage if things go bad."

Hunt says that's possible, but in a way that suggests she doesn't really mean it.

"I got a question," he says. "You said you have that genetic mutation so you don't have to sleep much."

"What about it?"

"And you said apparently your mother had it. What did you mean by apparently?"

"I never knew my mother. She died in child birth."

"So, you were raised by your father. The Marine."

"Marine sergeant major, in fact. Yeah, that was me."

Chapter Fifty-Eight

"Damn, it's cold," Dutch says, stating the obvious. "I'm freezing my nuts off here."

"Why's it so cold in the middle of the summer?" Ralph Tocco whines.

"In case you didn't notice," Niko says, "we're way north. You can cross into Canada by going southwest from here. Take a trip to Montreal, if you want."

Phil takes another look through the binoculars. There's no sign of life, but all the windows in the house are open. That's strange, given as cold as it is. A beat-up Honda is parked in front of the house.

"What's with the POS in the driveway?" Niko asks. "If that's McCoy in there, where's the pickup?"

"Probably dumped it," Phil says. "That would've been the smart thing to do."

"How do we know he's actually here? That could be somebody else's."

"He answered the phone."

"How do you know it was him? Did he say it was him?"

"It was him."

"You don't know. It might've been the guy who lives there."

"It's not. That guy was at the funeral home yesterday. Tino checked it out, saw him there. His sister-in-law's cremation's today. He wouldn't have come all the way back here for one day." Phil pauses. "You ain't getting cold feet are you, Niko?"

He laughs at his little joke, but nobody else seems to get it.

"We still don't know whose car that is," Niko says. "And maybe that guy you talked to was just watching the house."

"It's his ex-sister-in-law's house," Phil says, annoyance creeping into his voice. "And he was heading straight here when the cell phone signals stopped. And that was seventy miles away. Some coincidence. And I know I talked to him. I'd bet my life he's in there with his daughter."

Niko gives him a funny look.

"How are we going to do this?" Niko says. "So that we don't lose any more men in the process. That is if he's even in there."

"No worries," Taco says. "This guy's a shlub."

Niko says, "Don't be too cocky. He put a bullet in Moe Baker."

Taco says, "Moe Baker was a mook. A shlub shoots a mook, no big deal."

"And don't forget he took out Marco," Niko says.

They all fall silent at the thought of Marco.

"All he's got is that shotgun," Phil says. "And maybe the handgun he used to shoot Moe."

"That's what we know about," Niko says. "Maybe he's got more guns. Maybe he's got a whole fucking arsenal up there."

Phil says, "The guy's got a felony record. I doubt he's been stocking up on firearms while he's on the run with us and the cops looking for him. We just have to make sure we stay out of range of that shotgun."

Phil reaches into the back seat of Ralph Tocco's Chevrolet Suburban and holds up a Colt AR-15 assault rifle.

"That's why we have these," he continues. "Highly accurate at two hundred yards. McCoy's shotgun is pretty useless beyond a couple of hundred feet, so we have the advantage. We drive up to about a hundred yards, get out and scatter. We'll be safe."

"How do we get him out of the house?" Taco says. "He could stay holed up in there forever."

"That's why I told you to save these," Phil says, holding up a beer bottle. "I'm going to fill them with gasoline. Put a lighted rag in the top. Run up to about forty feet from the house and throw a couple through a window."

Niko says, "You'll be in range of that scatter gun of his."

"The rest of you will have to create a diversion. Start shooting at the house. Shoot out all the windows. That'll make him take cover. Suppressing fire is what that's called. I figure a couple of bottles should be enough to smoke them out."

Dutch comes trotting toward them, a foot-long pair of wire clippers in his right hand.

"All taken care of boss," he says, holding up the clippers.

Chapter Fifty-Nine

We're going to die, Charlie thinks. He picks up the phone. Time to call 911, assuming the cops can get out here in time. He listens. No dial tone. He punches the little button a couple of more times. Still nothing.

The phone line's been cut.

This would be a good time to have a cell phone.

He looks up. A slate-gray late-model Chevrolet Suburban turns into the drive. It's over three tons of steel, glass, plastic, and rubber. A huge target. The windshield is heavily tinted and he can't see any of the occupants. But the vehicle definitely isn't Louise's or her husband's, ardent environmentalists that they are.

He looks through the scope.

New Jersey plates.

That's all the confirmation he needs.

The Suburban is now two hundred and fifty yards away, rumbling along at about twenty miles per hour, twenty-two feet per second.

They've done just as he expected.

Charlie's betting the rifle is sighted in for two hundred yards, but there's only way to be sure. He looks through the scope with his right eye, his dominant eye, but he wraps his left index finger around the trigger. This isn't quite as awkward as he thought it would be.

He counts to seven and aims at a spot twenty-four inches below the roof line and twelve inches from the A-pillar on the driver's side. There was a time when he could've made this shot in his sleep. Of course there was a time that he could hit a six-inch bull's eye at 500 yards three times out of four.

He breathes in. He breathes out. He squeezes the trigger. The rifle kicks.

A bullet hole appears in the windshield, an inch higher and two inches to the right from where he aimed. The Suburban keeps moving. He thinks he's missed the driver. The bullet probably went over the guy's left shoulder. Then the Suburban veers to its left and travels twenty feet before it collides hard with a tree, crumpling the front bumper. It's now stationary--it'll be as if he's shooting fish in a barrel.

Hurriedly, he works the bolt, chambering another round. With two good hands he can do this do this in less than two seconds, but with one hand it takes twice as long. He aims at the left side of the windshield, where a passenger would be sitting, and fires. Another bullet hole appears.

Chapter Sixty

Phil throws open the car door. A stand of trees is fifteen feet away. He jumps from the Suburban and races to the trees. A bullet hits a tree trunk off to his right and splinters of wood fly in the air. It's not until he gets safely behind a tree that he realizes he left his rifle behind and the beer bottles and the gasoline.

Time to rethink the plan.

What just happened?

Ralph Tocco turned into the drive and the Suburban bumped along the rutted gravel drive. Dutch was in the front passenger seat and Niko and Phil were in the back seat. Taco was by himself in the third row. Dutch was idly releasing the magazine from his Colt AR-15 and then sliding it back into place.

Phil was thinking about Marco, who was going to go through the rest of his life with one arm. All thanks to this guy McCoy. Phil couldn't wait to set fire to that house up there. It looked like it was mostly wood. And old. Dried out. It would burn to the ground in minutes.

Maybe McCoy would burn to death in the house. But Phil hoped not. He wanted a little one-on-one personal time with Charlie McCoy and his daughter. And he'd need to find those discs before he let McCoy die.

"This shouldn't take too long," Ralph said. "McCoy will be dead before breakfast. He's probably hiding in a closet with his daughter right now. He'll never know what hit--"

Ralph's head snapped back and then with a groan he slumped forward on the steering wheel. The Suburban veered to the left. There was a hole in the windshield, big enough to push a pencil through. Fractured glass surrounded around the hole.

"He's been shot!" Dutch yelled. "He's shot in the eye. In the goddamn eye."

The Suburban slammed hard into a large tree, and Phil was thrown forward. His face hit the head restraint in front. He felt pain and blood trickled from his nose.

Another hole appeared in the windshield, on the passenger's side this time. Dutch grabbed his throat, blood seeping through his fingers. He dropped the AR-15, then emitted a deep gurgling noise.

"We gotta get the hell outta here!" Niko yelled. "He'll kill us all. We're sitting ducks."

Everything changed in less than ten seconds. Now, Ralph and Dutch are dead and Niko and Taco are trapped in the Suburban.

Niko is looking out the open door, trying to decide whether he should make a run for it.

Another shot hits the windshield, and Niko jumps from the Suburban. A bullet kicks up dirt at Niko's feet, but he makes it behind a tree trunk to Phil's right with his rifle still in hand. Taco struggles to get out of the third row seats, unable to get the seat in front of him to slide forward. He's screaming and cursing at the seat back.

Another shot in the windshield and then another and then another.

Phil retreats further into the trees.

He shouts, "Taco, get the hell out of there."

Silence, except for the cawing of blackbirds overhead.

"Taco, get out of there before he kills you."

There's no response.

Niko says, "He must be dead."

Phil crouches down and heads deeper into the trees. Niko follows close behind.

Chapter Sixty-One

The magazine's empty. Charlie loads the magazine with the three remaining shells from the box, jams the magazine into the rifle, and works the bolt so he has one in the chamber.

Charlie looks through the scope at the ruined Suburban. He heard the shouting. One of them is still inside the SUV. The guy's either dead or doing a good job of playing possum.

Looks as though there are only two left to worry about. But that's two too many. They will go through the woods and try to come around to the back door or a side door.

Amy must have heard the shots. Should he go down and try to reassure her? No time. And he has to face facts. She isn't going to listen to him, anyway. And this isn't the time to get distracted.

And he has other things to worry about.

He races into the hallway, looks both ways. To his left, a window overlooking the woods. He sidles up next to the window, the rifle in his good hand and the shotgun under his right arm.

There's nothing. He waits and then he sees movement fifty yards out. They're headed toward the back of the house. One of the men emerges from behind a tree. Charlie drops the shotgun, aims the rifle, and shoots, but his aim is unsteady and he hits a tree trunk six inches to the man's right. He curses himself for missing an opportunity. Two cartridges left.

He moves again, this time into a tiny bathroom in the rear of the house. The single window is a small casement. He cranks the winch as far as it will go, which opens the window only a foot, but it's enough to shoot anything approaching from the rear.

A large open area is behind the house. If they try to cross that, they'll be sitting ducks for his shotgun.

There's some movement a hundred yards out. He shoulders the rifle, but then he loses track of the target in the dense woods. Or perhaps there had been nothing. It could be his nerves getting the better of him.

He checks his watch. It's been five minutes since the first shots. Maybe somebody heard the shots and called the police. Maybe it's just a matter of a few minutes before a couple of cruisers come rolling up the front drive. Or maybe nobody heard the shots. Or perhaps they heard and decided it was somebody enjoying some out-of-season deer hunting.

Then the sound of breaking glass.

Chapter Sixty-Two

Phil ran through the woods on the side of the house. A bullet had taken a chunk out of a tree trunk just inches from his head. Too close. He was lucky. He went further into the woods and toward the back of the house. A small window was open on the second floor and a rifle barrel poked out. Where did McCoy get that from? Ducking behind a tree, he took his cell phone and called Niko's number.

"Do it now," Phil said.

He trotted through mud that was up past his ankles. Freezing water seeped through the tops of his shoes. He's ruined his $600 Bruno Magli slip-ons and probably his slacks as well. All because of McCoy, a man who should be dead twice-over by now. Overhead, the blackbirds cawed, a mean and nasty sound. He imagined they were mocking him for his ineptitude. Taco's dead. Dutch's dead. Ralph's dead. You'll be dead soon.

He waited behind a tree, two hundred feet from the back of the house. After a few seconds, the sound of breaking glass, meaning Niko's going in the front door as planned. He looks at the window. The rifle is no longer there. It's now or never.

He counts to five, hesitates for a moment, and then runs toward the back door, hoping McCoy has taken the bait. He emerges from the woods, now an easy target for McCoy's shotgun. He runs past a wood chipper and a large stack of branches. Only twenty feet now. He feels slow, clumsy. He trips, falls in the mud, drops his pistol, picks it up, crawls, and scrambles to his feet. He's going to make it. He takes a quick glance at the window. Nothing.

He's under the eaves now, too close to the house to be a target from the upstairs window. Staying close to the wall, he edges toward the back door. He tries the knob. Locked. Ten feet away a pair of metal doors set into concrete-- storm cellar doors. He tries one of the doors. Unlocked. He pulls it open and descends into the cellar.

Chapter Sixty-Three

Charlie descends the narrow, steep stairs, the floorboards creaking under his weight, the shotgun extended before him, sweeping right and left. The glass in the front door is broken and the door is open. Where did he go? Left to the living room or right to the dining room? Charlie goes right. Nobody. He crouches and then uses the shotgun to push open the swinging door that leads into the kitchen.

He steps into the kitchen, staying close to the wall. He's thinking maybe the guy isn't even in the house. Maybe he got scared and took off. Then he silently curses himself. That kind of thinking will get you killed.

Charlie drops to the floor and crawls on his belly toward the back of the house. He peeks around the edge of a cabinet.

There he is, ten feet away, a skinny guy, crouching behind the sofa, with an AR-15 rifle. Charlie recognizes him as Niko Falcone.

"Don't move, asshole," Charlie whispers. "Or I'll kill you right where you are."

The guy's head turns.

"Drop the gun," Charlie says. "Now."

The gun clatters on the floor. Falcone raises his hands.

"Don't shoot," he whispers. "I'm an informant for the FBI. I want to help. We can work together."

Charlie stands and walks toward the man.

"Where's your little friend?" he says, thinking this is almost over.

There's a scream, and then a triumphant shout. "McCoy, I've got your daughter. We're in the basement. Come on down. Join the party, why don't you?"

Chapter Sixty-Four

Falcone walks down the basement steps, two steps in front of Charlie, who is pointing the shotgun at the middle of Falcone's back.

Another guy, whom Charlie recognizes as Little Phil Adonis, sits crouched in an old wooden chair in the back of the basement, in the darkness. Amy is in front of him, acting as a shield. His left arm is around her neck and he's pointing a large caliber automatic pistol at her right ear.

Charlie stops at the bottom of the steps. He jabs the shotgun into the back of Falcone's head.

"Stop right there," he says to Falcone.

"Drop the shotgun, McCoy," Adonis screams.

"And then what happens?" Charlie's voice is hoarse. He doesn't recognize it.

"You don't drop it, I'll shoot your daughter. I swear."

"You'll shoot her anyway. Then you'll shoot me and I won't be able to defend myself because my gun will be on the floor."

"Doesn't matter. I will shoot her. And it'll be your fault. Just like it was your fault her mother's dead."

"I didn't kill her mother. You did."

"I only pulled the trigger. You killed her when you took our stuff, you thief. It's all your fault. Everything. And I will shoot your daughter, most certainly. It'll be my great pleasure."

Amy whimpers. Charlie jams the shotgun into Falcone's back, pushing him forward.

"You shoot her, then I'll shoot you and your friend," Charlie says. "Then I'll be the only one alive. I win."

Adonis cackles. "I don't believe you. You won't allow your daughter to die, you're too soft. I'm counting to three. Then I pull the trigger."

"Let her go first. I'll drop my gun. Then I'll give you what you want."

"One."

Amy cries, "Daddy, help me, please."

Charlie says, "Stop right now or I'll shoot your buddy. I'll--"

Adonis's eyes glitter. They're hard, black, and predatory.

"I don't care," he says. "Go ahead. Do it. Save me the job. Two."

"Daddy, please . . ."

"Listen, don't kill her. Kill me. I'm the one you want."

"Drop the gun. Now."

Charlie takes a deep breath, bends his knees, lays the shotgun on the ground, and then stands.

Adonis laughs in triumph.

"I knew you'd chicken out. You got no guts. Now kick the shotgun over to me."

Charlie does as he's told.

Adonis says, "Now you've decided to cooperate, I'm telling you what we're all going to do. We're going outside and I'm going to take this darling daughter of yours and feed her into the wood chipper. Very slowly. Feet first. Think of the noise it'll make. Grinding and cracking. Make a little hamburger out there."

Amy screams in terror, tears streaming down her face.

"Tell you what," Adonis says. "I'll stop just above the ankles. Show you what a great guy I am. They can do amazing things with prosthetics nowadays, you know, those metal flippers."

"You don't need to do that," Charlie says. "I'll give you the discs."

"Yes, you will. But I want to see you beg for your daughter first. Go on, get on your knees and beg that I don't feed her into the wood chipper. You caused me a lot of trouble. I deserve to see you beg. I deserve some satisfaction. It's the least you can do for me. Go on. Beg."

Charlie takes a step forward.

"Let her go. You can have me. I'm the one you want."

"Get down on the floor and beg."

Charlie takes another step.

"Stop or I'll shoot her."

"I'll give you the discs and then you can kill me. Just let her go."

Charlie takes another step.

"You don't believe me," Adonis screams. "Watch this."

He swings the pistol around and squeezes the trigger. Falcone's head explodes in a spray of blood and his body crumples to the floor. Charlie raises his right arm and there's another explosion. A red crease appears above Adonis's right eye and extends over his right ear. He stands, staggers backward, clutching at his head.

Amy screams, terror etched into her face.

Chapter Sixty-Five

Charlie grabs Amy and pushes her toward the stairs and away from Adonis. He gives Adonis a shove and he falls to the floor.

"Get out of here," he says. "Go upstairs and hide somewhere. Stay there until I get you."

"Are there more of them?"

"I don't think so. I think they're all dead now. But don't come out until I tell you to. Now go."

She stumbles up the stairs as Charlie strips off the ace bandage and removes the Beretta from his now throbbing hand. Those bones are never going to heal right.

How does he feel? Not great – his hands are shaking. But not as bad as he thought he'd feel after killing or seriously injuring four men. Is he getting accustomed to violence? He puts the thought out of his head. It's not the right time to grow a conscience.

Adonis is lying on his back, a low moan emanating from his throat. His gun is still in his right hand. Charlie leaves it there.

Blood streams down the side of Adonis's head. He examines Adonis's wound. The bullet grazed the side of his head, just above the ear, leaving a wound a half-inch wide and three inches long. Charlie aimed as far left as he could to avoid hitting Amy and he almost missed Adonis entirely.

Adonis has stopped moaning, but he's still breathing. Charlie thinks about putting another bullet in his head to finish the job--something for Carol. But he has another idea. He walks over to Falcone--still keeping an eye on Adonis--and places his gun in Falcone's right hand. He points it toward the wall behind where Adonis stood and fires it once. Any police test for gunshot residue on Falcone's hand will now be positive and it will look as if he fired at Adonis and missed.

He rummages through Adonis's pockets and finds a thick roll of hundred dollar bills. He goes through Falcone's pockets and finds another, smaller, roll. Together, there must be ten grand. He stuffs a few hundred dollars back in each man's pocket so it doesn't look too much like a robbery. He looks at Adonis's watch. It's a solid-gold Patek Philippe, probably worth forty grand. He takes it off Adonis's left wrist and sticks it in his pocket. He figures this won't look too suspicious. In this day and age, some men don't wear watches.

When he gets upstairs, he calls out to Amy.

"Come on, we're leaving."

She peeks from around a wing chair. Her face is still pale, her lower lip quivering.

"What about those men?"

"Don't worry about them."

"You shot that man."

"Yes. I had to. But it's better that you forget about that. In fact, it's better you forget about this whole thing. Everything. If anybody asks you what happened, tell them you don't know."

"But I saw you drop the gun."

"I had another gun hidden inside my splint. A small gun."

"So, you had a backup plan."

"If you want to call it that."

She starts crying and he grabs her and pulls her close. Her body is quaking. He feels the dampness of her tears soak through his shirt. The scent of her shampoo fills his nostrils. They stand like this for several minutes.

"I'm sorry," he says. "This never should've happened. Never." He waits for a minute, not knowing what else to say. Then he says, "Now, wait here while I clean up."

Charlie finds a towel in the downstairs powder room and rubs every surface he thinks he touched. Even with a glove on, you can't be too careful. He unloads the rifle and puts the remaining two cartridges back in the box and wipes down the cartridges, the box, and the rifle. He takes a skewer from the kitchen and uses it to scour out the inside of the rifle barrel, altering the rifling. Now the ballistics of any bullets fired from the rifle won't match the bullets in the mobsters. He puts the rifle back over the fireplace.

He spots Falcone's rifle, on the floor, behind the sofa. He puts that in the Honda.

He goes upstairs and collects the spent cartridges.

None of this is going to confuse the FBI. They'll quickly figure out the deer rifle was used. But there's no reason to make it easy for them to prove it. His efforts might be enough to create reasonable doubt if he were hauled in front of a jury.

They get in the Honda, Charlie in the front seat and Amy in the back seat. On the way out, Charlie stops next to the Suburban with the blown-out windshield. He ejects the remaining shells from the shotgun. They could have his fingerprints on them. He puts the shells in his pocket and he wipes down the shotgun and throws it and Falcone's rifle in the Suburban.

For the first time in four days, he's not carrying a firearm.

They pull out into the street and head toward town. Amy's curled up in a blanket she took from the house. He's not sure, but he thinks she might still be trembling.

He ought to say something. Something that will make her feel better. But he doesn't know what to say. He can't think of anything he can say that won't make things worse, so he doesn't try. Is there something he should say? Something that another person, a better person, would know to say. Is there something so fundamentally wrong with him such that he can't even communicate with his daughter when she needs him?

Even if there is, how would he fix it?

He needs to do something. He needs to change.

A mile outside of town, Charlie passes two black Cadillac Escalades with blacked out windows and New York plates that're traveling twenty miles per hour over the speed limit. He shakes his head. That's probably not a sight you see often in these parts. They got out just in time.

Chapter Sixty-Six

All he knows is pain. A sharp, throbbing pain, as if a metal stake is being pounded into his head by a giant's sledgehammer. Is he dead? Has he been consigned to some sort of Hell, where all he will know for eternity is this intolerable pain?

He climbs to his knees. Through the haze, he sees the body of Niko lying in the corner and this reassures him. He must be alive, after all. What would a dead Niko be doing in Hell? A live Niko, maybe, probably. Not a dead one. He staggers to his feet, falls, and then stands again. The pain is blinding. He can't see more than a few feet. There's something in his hand--his gun.

He teeters backward and forward and then falls backward, the back of his head hitting the concrete floor. The pain in his head surges like liquid fire and his vision, what remains of it, goes blurry. Better to crawl up the stairs rather than to risk falling backward again.

The stairs are unfinished wood and splinters drive into his hands and face as he climbs. He pushes open the door at the top of the stairs, and the gray daylight sends another spike of pain through his right eye. He waits for a moment, gathers himself, and then struggles to his feet. Tears run down his face.

The front door is twenty feet to his right, but it seems like twenty miles. He leans against the wall for support and slowly drags his feet toward the door. He's not sure he wants to go out that door. The light's going to be even worse, blinding. And then what? Is there a car? He can't even remember where the hell he is.

His cell phone. He checks his jacket pocket. It's still there. But who does he call? The police? There's a dead body in the basement and . . . others, too, he remembers. He'll have to answer for those.

His father. He'll call Big Phil. Big Phil will know what to do. He's always known what to do. Like that time with that sorority girl who got drunk and passed out and didn't wake up again.

He pushes open the door, steps outside, and takes a moment to get used to the light.

A group of men stand outside. Thank God. They'll be able to help him get to a hospital. One of them steps forward, looking at Phil in a strange way. He's a big man with a rough face. He looks familiar. He's staring at Phil's right hand. Phil glances down. He's still holding his gun. He looks back and the man is pointing a pistol at Phil's head. Then he remembers where he's seen the man before. He's a hitter for the New York family. His name's Donald. Or O'Donald. Or something like that.

Chapter Sixty-Seven

They've just turned into the drive when De La Torre hears the gunshots.

The cruiser in front of them lights up, which might not be the smartest idea since it lets everybody know they're coming. They drive past a Suburban with a blown out front window that's lying on the side of the dirt drive like a beached whale. Inside the Suburban are bodies.

De La Torre unholsters his Glock and racks the slide. Up ahead, on the top of the hill are two black SUVs and a group of a dozen armed men.

What the hell is this?

The cruiser pulls to the left and stops. De La Torre's Crown Vic pulls fifty feet to the right. He tumbles out the passenger door before the car even comes to a stop. Hunt crawls up next to him. She hands him a small pair of binoculars.

"Do you know who those men are?" she asks.

He peeks his head above the car's trunk and aims his binoculars at the men on the hill. None of them are McCoy. They're all too young, in their twenties and thirties. So, where is McCoy? Maybe he's inside the house. Maybe he's dead.

"No, I don't recognize them," he says.

"What about McCoy?"

"I don't see him."

"What do you think happened back there?" She jerks a thumb at the Suburban. "Looks like World War Three broke out."

The SWAT van has filled the gap in the middle of the drive and out swarm guys in black body armor and carrying fully automatic assault rifles. They take positions in the woods, in a flanking maneuver.

"Give me the microphone," Hunt says to Reynolds.

He does as he's told.

"Switch the loud hailer on," she says.

She fumbles with the microphone for a moment until she finds the on-off button.

"You men up there," she says. "This is the FBI. Drop your weapons, right now."

The men look at each other, shrug. One points at the police cars, but they don't drop their guns. A couple back up toward the house, pointing their guns at the police. From what de La Torre can see, they appear to be carrying submachine guns and pistols, horribly inaccurate beyond a hundred feet. Strictly spray and pray at this range. But the SWAT guys get the message. The sounds of safeties being released and bolts being unlocked fills the air.

Their assault rifles will be deadly accurate at this distance. De La Torre wants the men on the hill alive. He needs McCoy's whereabouts and they may know.

"Don't fire," he shouts. "Let them surrender."

The men continue to back up. De La Torre doesn't like the way this is going. At best it's going to be a siege. Four or five more SWAT teams called in. A perimeter established. Armored vehicles. A couple of communications vans with satellite uplinks. A helicopter or two prowling overhead. Reporters. TV trucks. The director of the closest Bureau office will show up and take charge. A big mess. And everything will be out of his control.

At worse it'll be a massacre.

Meanwhile, McCoy could be anywhere.

The men continue to back up, talking to each other. They're a few feet from the front door of the house.

Then one of the men steps forward with his hands in the air. He has a gun in his right hand. He drops it. He says something over his shoulder to the others, who drop their guns and follow him down the hill.

When they get to fifty yards away, Hunt tells them to stop and get on their knees with their hands behind their heads. They do as they're told, and the SWAT guys emerge from the tree line, moving as fast as they can in their bulky gear and making sure not to get in the line of their own fire. In five minutes, all the men are cuffed and in the back of the police cruisers.

De La Torre walks from cruiser to cruiser, checking. They didn't get McCoy, but he's guessing that there are a few warrants out on this bunch. These arrests will look good to the folks in DC.

Still, not what he needed.

Hunt is on her cell, nodding and looking pensive. She glances at de La Torre, folds up her phone and, puts it away. She motions to the agent from Boston and whispers in his ear. The two of them walk over.

"We're finished here," she says.

Chapter Sixty-Eight

De Le Torre and Prescott are sitting in a conference room at Bureau headquarters.

A search of the Crowder's house revealed two more dead bodies. Neither was McCoy, but they were Little Phil Adonis and Niko Falcone, which was interesting. On the flight back, Hunt was quiet the whole way. It was after five when they landed, and he went directly home.

The next day was Saturday and he slept until late morning, which felt good after getting a total of six hours sleep over the previous three days. That night, after dropping his daughter off at a friend's house, Cynthia and he went to the City to eat at a French-Japanese Restaurant that is all the rage. He felt rested and relaxed and Cynthia seemed to be in a much better mood. No more talk of secrets. The monster was back under the bed. It was amazing what a fine meal at an expensive restaurant could accomplish. After dinner they got a room at the Ritz-Carleton on Park Avenue.

In the middle of the night he awakened with a gasp. He'd had a lot on his mind when he went to sleep. Malcolm's monthly payment was due by the seventh -- Monday. He should've paid it when he saw Malcolm but he had no way to know things would get so crazy.

But there was something else. A feeling of dread crept over him like an ice water bath. He always trusted his feelings, but there was nothing to be concerned about now, was there? O'Brien was dead. Little Phil Adonis was dead. McCoy? Probably dead.

But maybe not. And what about McCoy's daughter? Probably in the same swamp as McCoy. But whatever happened to the discs?

He picked up his cell phone. There were a half-dozen calls from the office. They can go to hell. He was entitled to a day off.

He called the surveillance unit and told them he wanted tracking devices placed immediately on any vehicles owned by Louise and Richard Crowder. He said he already had the warrant and he'd drop it off on Monday. A lie, sure. But since the existence of the trackers would never be disclosed in a courtroom, it didn't matter.

Satisfied that everything was back under control, he went back to sleep.

When he returned home the next afternoon there were a number of calls on the house phone from the office. He spoke to Prescott and was told their presence was required in Washington first thing Monday morning.

The next day, he left the house at four a.m., went to the office, and printed out the latest on the Charlie McCoy case before driving to the airport. It was a little after eight when he arrived at FBI Headquarters in DC.

"They've been in there for an hour," the receptionist said. "They need to speak with you."

In the conference room, Winston, Prescott, and Hunt were sitting around the table. The presence of Winston was surprising. What's he doing here?

"Good of you to join us, Mike," Winston said. He turned to the others. "So, what do we have?"

De La Torre said, "A dead Niko Falcone. A dead Little Phil Adonis. Miscellaneous other dead mobsters, formerly of the Adonis crime family. A bunch of hoodlums from the New York mob in custody and facing weapons charges. A dead Jerry O'Brien. Big Phil is in hiding, nobody knows where, maybe out of the county."

"I asked, what do we have? What does this all mean?"

Prescott said, "It looks like Little Phil shot Niko. The ballistics of the gun that was found in his hand matches the bullet in Niko's head."

Winston asked, "Why would Little Phil shoot Niko?"

Hunt said, "Maybe Little Phil found out that Niko was our informant. That would do it."

Inwardly, De La Torre rejoiced. Niko was the informant. And he's dead. Things were getting better and better.

Winston said, "And they went all the way to Maine so Little Phil could shoot Niko in the head?"

"That's the way it looks," Prescott said. "Niko got off a shot that missed and another that grazed Little Phil's head. Little Phil then shot Niko squarely in the forehead."

Winston said, "Presumably in that order."

"Then Max Donnelly arrived and finished off Little Phil."

"What was Donnelly and those other apes even doing there?"

"Turns out," Hunt said, "we weren't the only ones with a tracking device on Ralph Tocco's Suburban. We found another. We're thinking the New York mob put it there. There must've been a falling out between the two families, and Donnelly and the others were there to take care of business."

"There are some problems with the scenario," Prescott said.

Winston said, "You mean, like how did Niko manage to basically miss twice from close range?"

"There's that. And some of the angles of the shots don't match up a hundred percent."

"That stuff never does," De La Torre said. "Everybody knows that. And we also found the shotgun that injured Marco Delassandro. It was in Ralph Tocco's Suburban. Ballistics matched the firing pin impression from the shotgun with the spent shells found at the scene where Delassandro was shot."

"So Ralph Tocco shot Marco Delassandro? One Adonis capo takes out another? In the middle of the street? In broad daylight? How does that make any sense?"

"Obviously there are problems inside the Adonis family," De La Torre said. "Or at least there were. Not much of it left now. That's good news, right?"

Winston shook his head.

"And it's all a big coincidence that all this happened at Charlie McCoy's sister-in-law's house that's way in the middle of nowhere? I don't believe that for a minute."

"Obviously, Little Phil went there looking for McCoy," De La Torre said. "And the New York mobsters followed him."

"But did he find McCoy, isn't that the question?"

De La Torre said, "I'm betting they found him and McCoy's dead and buried. In a landfill somewhere. Little Phil caught up with him, tortured him, and got what he wanted."

"That doesn't make any sense," Hunt says. "If they found McCoy somewhere else, why go to the house? And if they found him there, where's the body?"

"What about these rifle shots?" Winston asked. "Three dead. Who did that?"

De La Torre said, "That's a mystery right now."

"Where did the rifle come from?" Winston asked.

"We're thinking it belonged to Richard Crowder, but even that's not clear. The ballistics don't quite match."

"What do these people know, Louise and Richard Crowder? They were McCoy's in-laws, right?"

"Ex-in-laws. They know nothing. They were at her sister's funeral in New Jersey. A bunch of witnesses support their alibis, including two priests."

"Do you believe they know nothing?"

"I see no reason why they'd lie."

Winston sneered.

"To stay out of trouble with the mob," he said. "That's why they'd lie. So where are these discs with the information? They weren't in the Suburban. They weren't at that house."

De La Torre shrugged. "Little Phil destroyed them," he said.

"So, all this was a giant waste of time? We've been chasing our own tails for a week? I refuse to believe that."

"Why wouldn't Little Phil destroy that information?" De La Torre asked. "It probably incriminated him."

"That's assuming Little Phil found McCoy and found the discs. Maybe he didn't. Maybe McCoy's still floating around. There's a lot here that doesn't add up." Winston frowned. "More questions than answers."

De La Torre said, "It's been four days and nobody's seen hide nor hair of our friend McCoy, or his daughter, even with a nationwide search, so I'm betting landfill."

Winston turned to Hunt. "What do you think, Cathy?"

She shook her head. "I don't know. I'm sort of with Mike on this one. I think we've reached the end of the trail. At least for right now."

De La Torre breathed a sigh of relief. This is over.

A guy poked his head in the door, glanced at De La Torre and then motioned to Winston. Winston nodded and stepped out, followed by Cathy Hunt.

That was fifteen minutes ago.

"What do you think is going on?" Prescott asks, looking at his watch. "Why are they taking so long? Why are they making us wait?"

"Beats me," de La Torre says. "Obviously it's something above our pay grade."

They wait a few more minutes and then the door opens and Winston and Hunt come back in. Winston has a sheaf of papers in his hand and he's riffling through them.

Winston says, "Excuse us for a few minutes, Rusty. We need to speak with Agent De La Torre. Alone."

Prescott jumps to his feet and rushes out the door, obviously relieved to be excused from whatever was about to come down.

Even before Prescott closes the door behind him, De La Torre knows something is badly wrong. He can feel it.

Two agents step into the room. He doesn't recognize them--they must be from the DC Office.

Winston says, "These gentlemen are from the Internal Affairs Division, Agent De La Torre."

One says to De La Torre, "You need to come with us, sir."

The "sir" sounds like an afterthought.

The two agents accompany him to the interrogation room, where he sits for two hours, mentally preparing an account that explains the entries on his computer, his failure to inform his superiors that he had identified McCoy, and his failure to inform his superiors about Polaski.

He figures he's in a good position. There are all kinds of procedures he's entitled to before they can do anything to him. They can put him on leave, but he'll still get paid.

And the Bureau won't make a big deal out of this. It would be too embarrassing.

He can handle this.

On the other hand, the high paying job with a private security company is quickly receding the rear view mirror as those don't usually go to people drummed out of the FBI on suspicion of corruption.

The door opens and Winston and Hunt enter with the two guys from IA. Winston leans over the table, an expression of barely suppressed fury fixed on his face.

"Do you want to tell me the nature of your relationship with the Adonis family?"

"What relationship? What's this all about?""

Hunt says, "Come clean, Mike. We've got conclusive evidence you were working for them the whole time. It's best you be honest and not make things worse."

He starts to rise.

"That's insane. I don't know what you're talking about."

Hunt says, "Tell you the truth, I've wondered about you from the beginning. Some things just didn't add up. Like Polaski and that business with the witness who ended up dead. His version of events was different than yours. That had me real confused. But then we got the tapes and everything fell into place."

Tapes? He doesn't say anything.

"We found a box of microcassettes in Jerry O'Brien's office. O'Brien recorded your conversations. The one where you told him about Lisk. The one where you told him about the bugs in Big Phil's house. The time you told them about the upcoming raid on their heroin distribution center. Everything."

"I don't believe you. This is some sort of crazy bluff you're pulling. Somebody's trying to make me the fall guy here."

Hunt pulls out a chair and sits, a glint in her eye like a cat who's just caught a mouse and has decided to play with it for a while.

"Believe it," she says. "I have to say I was impressed with the job you did framing Prescott. That must've taken some effort. And the guy never knew what you were up to. Of course every time something suspicious was done on his computer, you were in the building. Quite a coincidence."

"Am I under arrest?"

"Not yet."

"You've got nothing. If you had something, you'd be arresting me."

"We're working on it."

"If I'm not under arrest, I'm leaving."

Winston holds up his hand and says, "Don't go too far. And we'll need your gun and your badge and your ID before you leave."

As he's walking out, Hunt says, "Hey, Mike, you remember how they found Lisk's body with his severed penis stuck in his mouth, right? That's all on you, buddy."

***

Meeting over, De La Torre walks down the hall, pulling his cell phone as he goes. He's figuring word hasn't gotten out yet.

"Need an update on that Subaru," he says.

"They're about two hundred miles north of town."

Chapter Sixty-Nine

Charlie climbs into the Honda, next to Amy. They've been on the move for three days. Right now, they're parked in a lot across from the bus station.

He figures it's time to facilitate another attempt at parent-child communication.

"I don't know what to say," Charlie says. "I didn't mean for any of this to happen, but it did. So maybe that makes it my fault."

"That's all you've got?" she says, not looking at him. "Maybe it's your fault? How about it is your fault, just admit it."

He shrugs. "You did have a July Fourth to remember."

"That's not funny."

She's gives him a look of scorn. Her face is pale and she has dark circles under her eyes.

"I shouldn't joke," he says.

"I swear you've got a heart of stone."

"I may not feel all the same things that most people do. I realize that."

She looks at the door.

"You don't have any feelings at all," she says. "You just aren't like a normal person."

"Don't be so melodramatic about everything. We're alive, aren't we?"

"You haven't even said you're sorry that mom's dead."

He studies the entrance to the bus station, watching the people go in and out.

"Of course I'm sorry your mother's dead," he says. "I'm sorry about everything. Most of all, I'm sorry you were involved. This has been a long time coming. I've been pretty lucky over the years. At least I've been pretty good at outrunning the bad luck or bad karma, if that's what you want to call it. But all that time it had been getting bigger and bigger, like a snowball rolling down a mountain and then it caught up with me. All at once. And you happened to be there when it did."

"Are you saying you're not responsible? It was just bad luck?"

"I'm saying I've done a lot of things I shouldn't have done, and for a long time I got away with it, and I'm responsible for that. But--"

"Will you just stop talking? Please. I don't want to hear it."

"--that's in the past and I don't have a time machine. If I did, I'd go back and fix everything. I'm not a very good person. I know that. Somewhere along the line I got off track."

Her expression softens.

"Maybe you can fix who you are?" she says. "You know, get back on track. It's never too late."

"Yeah I wish I could go three thousand miles away, where nobody knows me, and start everything all over again as a better person. But I can't do that."

"You can start over again right here."

"It's not that easy. You can't fix who you are, okay? As you get older, all that happens is you get older. You don't get better or smarter. You don't really learn anything you didn't already know. You just get more like who you are and so things get impossible to fix. I'll always be the way I am."

"What is that?" she says, her voice getting louder. "A thief and a liar. When are you going to realize you can be better?"

He looks away.

"I've often failed to live up to people's expectations. Including yours apparently. Maybe this is a good as I can be."

"You're just a bitter old man who refuses to change," she shouts. "That's all."

"Enough. Right now we have to make sure things don't get any worse than they are."

Her mouth turns down.

"You mean what I'm supposed to tell the police," she says.

"Right."

"I'm supposed to lie to them, right?"

"Thanks."

"You put yourself there. It's against the law to lie to the police."

"Not if they don't catch you," he says. "They're going to treat you with kid gloves, okay? You're a pretty little girl.

Just start crying and they'll back off. You stick with the story and you'll be fine. We'll all be fine. It'll be all over."

He hands her a brown paper bag with his right hand, which is now out of the splint.

"This is full of cash," he says. "It's a lot. About forty grand. I'd give you more, but it's all I've got. I--"

She starts to say something.

"Just take it," he says. "Don't argue for once. Now, go on. Your aunt and uncle are waiting for you."

There are tears in the corners of her eyes, and it's one of those times he's supposed to say something, but he's not sure exactly what. Perhaps he should say he loves her. But he doesn't even know what that means.

"Seems we're done here," she says, wiping away a tear. She turns back toward him.

"The only thing you ever paid for is my school tuition, right?"

"Basically. And part of your braces. And summer camp last year. And I gave your mother cash according to our agreement."

"Did you borrow money to pay for that stuff?"

"No," he says. "Jewelry stores, mostly. And a couple of mansions. And a drug store. And a currency exchange in Illinois."

Chapter Seventy

De La Torre watches the girl climb out of the beat up Honda with Rhode Island plates carrying a little suitcase and a brown paper bag. She dashes across the street to the Subaru Forester with Maine plates. She jumps in and the Subaru drives off.

He figures the paper bag must have her lunch in it.

He's going to have to keep a close eye on the rust-infested Civic because he didn't have a chance to put a tracking device on it, unlike the Subaru driven by Louise and Richard Crowder that the Bureau tracked all the way from Northern Maine.

This is going to be strictly old school.

His cell rings. It's his wife, the last person in the world he wants to talk to. He lets it go to voicemail.

What does the Bureau have on him? Probably not much. Maybe some half-garbled recordings, at most. He's betting they told him that stuff to mess with his head, make him lose his nerve, make him run. They'd have a better prosecution if they caught him at an airport trying to leave the country, so that'll be the last thing he'll do.

His best chance is to find McCoy and that disc before the authorities. The disc has information concerning bribes taken by powerful people. Those people would do anything to prevent the information from coming out-- even lean on the Bureau, if necessary. If he can get that information it will only take a couple of phone calls to get the investigation halted. But he has to act quickly. If the government finds his offshore account, then no amount of leverage will be enough.

The Civic pulls away from the curb and heads east. De La Torre saw McCoy come out of the bus station and he's thinking McCoy deposited the discs in one of the lockers. But there's no way to know which locker. He'll have to get that information out of McCoy. And the key to the locker.

McCoy drives a few blocks on Main Street. He stops at a light and then turns right onto Church Street. He goes down a block and makes another right. De La Torre hangs back because it looks as though McCoy is circling the block to see if he's being followed.

De La Torre slowly makes two more rights and comes back onto Main Street. McCoy's car is two blocks up. De La Torre's instincts were correct, as usual.

He stays back as far as he can while still keeping the Civic in sight. The Honda travels a couple of miles before pulling into a parking lot behind a burned out warehouse.

De La Torre drives past, parks a block down, and walks back. His cell rings and it's Cynthia again. He answers it this time.

"What the hell is going on?" she screams.

"What's the problem?"

"What have you been up to? There are FBI agents and federal marshals here at the house. They have a search warrant and they're turning the place upside down. Your daughter is scared out of her wits."

"I don't know what it's all about," he says. "I don't know what's going on. I'll talk to you later."

"Later will be too late. If you--"

He switches the phone off. You don't have family, you don't have nothing.

He laughs. Family.

With the FBI closing in, he's going to have to move fast. There's nothing incriminating in the house. All the bank statements for the Bahamas bank account are in a safe deposit box he took out in his aunt's name in a small community bank in a neighboring state. He always paid cash for that box, so it might take the Bureau a while to find it.

But they will eventually find it.

The Honda is parked next to some huge double doors, one of which is open. You don't see people leave doors open in this city. De La Torre unholsters a Ruger 22, which he removed from a police evidence room ten years ago. The gun is completely untraceable, a true throw down. It has a threaded barrel, and he takes a silencer from his jacket pocket, screws it onto the end, and then releases the safety. Loaded with subsonic rounds, a gunshot from the small-caliber weapon will sound like a baby's fart.

He steps through the open door, pointing his gun right and left, thinking this is a trap.

But it's empty inside. He waits as his eyes adjust to the darkness. The floor is covered with soot and there numerous footprints in the soot. Which are McCoy's?

A noise comes from above. Somebody's moving on one of the upper floors. De La Torre trots up some metal stairs, his gun hand extended in front of him, his eyes focused on the floor above, anticipating an ambush. Usually, he wouldn't be doing this without a half-dozen SWAT officers in ballistic vests in front of him, but this time he doesn't get the benefit of a tactical team.

He steps off the stairs. It's dark. Only a dim light filters through holes in the walls where windows had been. A red-and green plaid sheet is laid out on the floor with a pillow.

So this is where the guy was hiding out, a burned-out warehouse. That's just beyond sad.

Movement in the far corner. De La Torre raises his pistol.

"Hold it," he says. "FBI. Stop or I'll shoot."

A man steps out of the shadow. He's tall and lanky, with a three-day beard and matted hair.

"You're Charlie McCoy," De La Torre says. "Don't deny it."

"And you're Mike De La Torre."

The words surprise De La Torre.

"How do you know that?"

"I've seen the information on the disc. I know all about you. You're a crooked agent. And now you've found me. Where're all the others? You know, your team. Or is this a solo operation?"

He pauses.

"This is solo, isn't it?" McCoy says. "You're here for the stuff, not to arrest me."

"You did a pretty good job up there in Maine," De La Torre says, inching closer. "Got to hand it to you. Taking out all those racket boys by yourself."

"Haven't a clue what you're talking about."

"You're one cunning badass son of a bitch, aren't you? Speaking of the discs, where are they?"

"It's not going to do you any good even if you get them and destroy them. That information's been copied. It's been saved on three different emails. Anything happens to me, the information will be sent to the authorities."

"I don't believe you. The discs are formatted so they can't be copied. I know that for a fact. Now where are they? Did you leave them at the bus station?"

"If I tell you, then you'll kill me."

"I won't. Promise. My word. I just want the discs."

McCoy looks over at a duffel bag next to the wall on his right.

"You're right," McCoy says. "They're at the bus station."

De La Torre grins.

"They're in that bag, aren't they? You're easy to read, man. Just like a book. Now, throw that bag over to me, nice and easy."

McCoy picks up the bag and tosses it underhand. It lands a foot short of the sheet. De La Torre looks at the bag, momentarily taking his eyes off McCoy. As he does, McCoy steps quickly into the next room.

"Stop," De La Torre says.

He steps forward, onto the sheet, attempting to follow.

***

Charlie hears the cry and then a second later the thud. He steps over to the edge of the jagged hole in the floor. De La Torre's body lies on the concrete slab, a drop of forty feet, face down, with blood oozing from under his head. Charlie watches for movement. He sees none.

After several minutes he descends the stairs. Up close, he can see that De La Torre's head is turned at an unnatural angle, 130 degrees from the front of his body. He takes De La Torre's cell phone from his pocket--he'll toss it in the back of the first dump truck he sees. He doesn't want anybody finding De La Torre's body just yet.

He checks De La Torre's wallet. There's about three hundred in cash, some credit cards, and a driver's license. And a photo of De La Torre with a beautiful black woman and a young girl. His wife and child?

Charlie puts the wallet back without taking anything.

In another pocket he finds a sheet of paper. It's a computer readout. At the top it reads, MERCEDES BENZ G550. There's a VIN number. And a date--July 2nd.

Charlie's guessing it's the black Mercedes that was chasing him.

Below are two columns. One is a series of military times and the other is GPS coordinates.

The time of 10:15 to 10:34 is circled. He's betting the GPS coordinates are for his old house. Carol's murder. He folds the sheet of paper and places it in his shirt pocket.

He removes the sheet and pillow, being careful not to disturb the position of the body, and stuffs them in his duffel bag, which is empty because he left the Adonis discs back at the bus station.

On the way out, he walks backward, rubbing out the foot prints in the soot.

Chapter Seventy-One

Charlie sits in a plastic chair in a small room with a metal table in the middle. His hands are manacled and the manacles loop through a steel ring that is welded to the table.

Six hours earlier, he met with a lawyer. Charlie had called around and found that a guy named Melvin Hanks had a pretty good reputation, so he called and made an appointment.

Melvin Hanks--short, stubby, bug-eyed--sat in his office chair like a toad on a lily pad as he listened to a highly expurgated version of Charlie's story.

"So I want to give myself up," Charlie said.

Hanks said he saw some problems.

"Like what?" Charlie asked, hoping Hanks would give him a reason to back out of his decision.

"Biggest problem? How will my fee be paid? That's always my first concern. My usual retainer for a case this complicated is fifteen grand." He eyed Charlie. "You don't exactly look like you're rolling in the dough, if you don't mind me saying."

Charlie pulled Phil Adonis's watch from his pocket and held it up.

"Solid gold Patek Philippe Chronometer," he said. "Take it to a pawnshop. I'll split whatever you get fifty-fifty. It'll be enough to pay your retainer. Make sure you get a bill of sale."

Hanks had been around for a while, so he knew not to ask where Charlie where got the watch.

"You're doing the right thing turning yourself in," Hanks said as he shoved the watch in his jacket pocket.

"So I've been told," Charlie said.

***

The door to the interrogation room opens and Hanks shuffles in.

"I met with the prosecutors," he says, looking at his yellow pad. "So, let me tell you, we got some real problems here."

Charlie says, "We? Are they threatening to send you to prison, too?"

"I like to identify with my clients." He glances at his yellow pad. "They think they've got you over a barrel."

"Melvin, you only see the negative side of things."

"That's what makes me such a good lawyer."

"So what do they think they have on me?"

"First up, we got the killing of this guy Moe Baker. Did you know Moe Baker?"

"Sure, everybody knew Moe. But that's not important. The evidence will show that he was killed by Niko Falcone, the underboss of the Adonis family."

"Mind sharing with me the nature of this evidence?"

"Maybe the gun that killed Moe Baker was later found in Falcone's possession."

"And how do you know this?"

"Like I said, it's a well-informed guess. What else do they think they have?"

"The death of your ex-wife and her boyfriend."

"I've got an alibi for that."

"Who is your alibi?"

"My daughter."

"I'll need to talk with her."

"That's not happening. Leave her out of this."

"If she'll help--"

"No, that's not an option. Anyway, I'm guessing the gun that was used to kill my wife and her friend was found up in Maine in Little Phil Adonis's possession, so any charges on that are bogus."

"I'm not going to ask how you know that."

"Good idea."

Hanks shakes his head and his jowls waggle. "You're in a lot of trouble. I'm beginning to wonder why you gave yourself up."

"It was the right thing to do. What else is there?"

"There's a burglary of Big Phil Adonis's house."

Charlie laughs. "Next."

"I'm starting to get a feeling of what's going on here. What kind of beef did the Adonis family have with you, anyway?"

"That's a long, complicated story that we don't need to go into right now. Is that all the feds have?"

"There's also some guy named Marco who got blasted with a shotgun down at the Shore."

"I believe all the witnesses to that incident are dead. Including the guy who got shot. He had a misadventure in the hospital. Or so I hear."

Chapter Seventy-Two

It's twenty-two hours later. A different room. But the same story. Charlie's once again manacled to the table. The US Marshals seemed to take some pleasure in making the handcuffs extra tight today.

Charlie spent the night in a federal lock-up, which was a first for him. And just when he thought there wouldn't be any new experiences in his life. He slept poorly as he turned everything over in his mind. He made a mistake hiring Hanks. The guy's too nervous. And not terribly smart. He's the kind of lawyer who pleads all his clients out--after the retainer has been used up. Charlie can't imagine him in front of a judge and jury.

He doesn't know how long he'd survive in jail. There are remnants of the Adonis family that will be looking for him, not to mention the people implicated on that disc.

Giving himself up is looking like a bad idea.

A little camera with a blinking red light is positioned in the corner of the ceiling. They are watching him, making him wait. He changes his position in the chair.

No matter how he sits, he's uncomfortable. The chair was probably designed that way, just for police department interrogation rooms.

A clicking sound and the door opens. Two men and a woman enter: Hanks, who, as always, is carrying a yellow pad, a blonde woman dressed in a dark gray pants suit who is carrying a white pad and a large Starbucks cup, and a young man who is carrying a green steno pad. Charlie's betting the young guy is the secretary. It'll be his job to take notes.

The Bureau doesn't take recorded statements, never has. Instead, they have two agents take a statement. One asks questions and the other--the secretary--takes notes. The notes get typed into a Form 302 report. The FBI does this for two reasons--to manipulate the wording of the statement so it says what they want and to allow agents to lie to witnesses. Cops lie in interrogations. It's an essential tool in their toolbox. It's even been approved by the Supreme Court. Cops will say they have witnesses when they don't, they say they have forensic evidence when they don't, and they certainly like to claim the existence of non-existent informants. And these are all modalities of interrogation the Bureau is more than happy to employ. But federal employees are prohibited by law from lying or at least leaving a record of their mendacity.

Hence Form 302 and the need for a secretary.

The two agents drop into the chairs on the other side of the table and his lawyer sits next to Charlie. The woman looks at the camera and the light goes out.

"I'm Cathy Hunt, the woman says. I'm with the FBI. This is Agent Spender."

Charlie stares at her badge. It says ASSISTANT SECTION CHIEF. She's young to be an assistant section chief. She's accomplished. Probably very ambitious. No, definitely very ambitious. She'll want what he has in order to advance her career. That gives him leverage.

"I was in here so long, I thought you guys had forgotten about me," Charlie says.

"Oh, no," Hunt says, "we haven't forgotten about you, Mister McCoy. No, sir. Not at all. Quite the opposite. We are surprised you finally turned yourself in, though."

"I'm always looking to cooperate with the authorities. I heard you were looking for me. So here I am."

"You're in a lot of trouble."

"So I've been told," Charlie says. "I'm sure it's just a big misunderstanding."

"You're a suspect in multiple homicides," Hunt says softly. "Among many other things."

"Am I under arrest?"

"Not yet. You're being detained pending an investigation."

"Am I free to leave?"

"Not yet."

"Sounds like I'm under arrest."

Hunt slams down her pad.

"If that's the way you want it. Some fellas don't know when they're being given a break in life."

Hunt advises Charlie of his rights. She has a smirk on her face as she does it.

Hanks leans over, whispers in Charlie's ear. "It's not a good idea to make these people mad."

"You understand what's going on here," she says. "So don't act dumb. This isn't your first trip to the circus."

"That's fair to say. You've held me for forty-four hours total. And now you've got four hours to arraign me or you'll have to let me go. That's the law."

"We understand you want to answer some questions," Hunt says. "Is that true or are we just wasting our time here?"

Hanks says, "For the record, I've advised my client against this course of action."

"What can you tell us about Moe Baker?" Hunt asks.

Charlie leans back. He figures with what he has, they'll want to deal. It's just a matter of letting the process play out.

"I knew Moe," he says. "What can I tell you? He was kind of a moron, if you ask me. Always coming up with dumb ideas. Sorry to speak ill of the dead."

"Have you seen him recently?"

"A couple of weeks ago. He was trying to talk me into robbing Big Phil Adonis's house. Like I said, Moe wasn't too bright."

"Did you help him rob Phil Adonis's house?"

"Are you crazy? Does that sound like a good idea to you? I assumed he got somebody else to help him."

Hunt takes a sip from her Starbucks cup.

"We have you on tape. Talking about Moe Baker."

"I think I just mentioned his name. Because I heard he'd been killed. I thought the authorities needed to look into it."

"So you're claiming you didn't break into Phil Adonis's house with Moe Baker," she says.

"Do I look stupid?" Charlie turns to the agent taking notes. "Did you get that? I deny breaking into Phil Adonis's house."

"What if I were to say we have you on tape inside Adonis's house?" Hunt says. "And that we can match your voice with one of the burglars who was there."

Charlie shakes his head.

"I would say that's impossible because I don't believe I've ever been in Phil Adonis's house. Second, if I ever were, I never would've said more than twenty words. You'd need more than twenty words that match an aural spectrographic analysis of my voice and you don't have that. Because I wasn't there, of course."

Momentarily silenced, Hunt looks at her notes.

"We have a witness that puts you . . . near the scene of the Moe Baker murder about the time it happened. What do you say to that?"

Charlie smiles. The hesitancy in her voice tells him she's bluffing.

"It wasn't me," he says. "And eyewitness testimony is notoriously unreliable. What can I say? I'm a type. People always mistake me for somebody else. My suggestion on Moe is that you should find out whose gun it was that shot him. Run ballistics tests, that sort of thing. Then you'll find your killer."

Silence all around.

"And you know it wasn't me," Charlie continues. "Because I'm sure the gunshot residue tests you did on me came back negative."

"It was five days after the Baker shooting that you gave yourself up. Too long to get a valid response on the GSR.

Sorry. You even had time to wash off any residue from your escapades in Maine."

"Still, you don't have evidence I shot Baker. Or anybody else."

"Doesn't matter," Hunt says. "We have enough to charge you on Baker based on the witness ID."

"You going to charge me based on insufficient evidence? That doesn't sound fair." He turns to the young FBI agent. "Be sure to write down that she's trying to charge me based on insufficient evidence."

"Fair?" Hunt says, raising her voice. "That's where you go for ice cream on a stick. We talking fried ice cream here or something else? I'm talking cold-blooded murder. Your wife and her boyfriend were shot to death."

"It wasn't me. And I suspect you know that already."

"You've got an answer for everything. Who shot Niko Falcone?"

"Probably Little Phil Adonis. I'm guessing he found out that Falcone was an informant for the FBI and Little Phil made an executive decision."

She shoots the secretary a look. Charlie can tell what she's thinking. How the hell does this guy know this stuff?

"And who shot Adonis?" she asks.

Charlie shrugs. "Falcone, I guess. I don't know. I wasn't there."

"There was a gun found in Falcone's right hand, which is interesting considering he's left handed. I figure whoever shot Adonis put the gun in his right hand and squeezed off a shot, not knowing that Falcone is left handed. Ooops. I wonder who that could've been?"

Charlie says, trying to change the subject, "Wait until it comes out in court that the FBI had an informant inside the Adonis family and they allowed him to be murdered. That won't go over well."

Hunt laughs. "The jury will hear you're a convicted felon. As soon as they hear that, they won't believe a word you say."

My conviction was eleven years ago. It won't be admissible. Too long ago." Charlie elbows his lawyer. "Isn't that true, Hanks?"

Hanks mumbles something and nods.

Cathy Hunt leans over, looks him in the eye.

"Five men were killed at your former sister-in-law's house in Maine. You have an explanation for that?"

"And you think I did it? By myself? Five men? Really? Do you think I'm the fricking terminator or something?"

"You were a sniper when you were in the Marines," Hunt says, giving him the side eye. She seems to be enjoying this.

"You've been reading up on me," Charlie says. "Then you'll also know that was a long time ago, and that I washed out of sniper school."

"We know you didn't kill one of them," she says. "Maybe two. We're not sure about the others. Have you been at your sister-in-law's house recently?"

Charlie's thinking, this isn't going the way I planned. She's asking too many questions. They should be moving toward a deal by now.

"I was there a few days ago," he says. "She wasn't there, so I left."

He thinks, actually, every word of that particular sentence is true, give or take eight hours.

"Why did you go all the way to Maine?"

"I took my daughter up there to see her aunt."

Hunt takes another sip of her coffee.

"Where is your daughter right now?" she asks. "We'd like to speak with her."

"Look, let's stop beating around the bush. You're thinking I've got something you want. I'm here to find out how badly you want what you think I have."

"Why do you think we want it at all?"

"You'd be stupid not to."

"We don't need to make a deal with you," she says. "We have plenty of evidence against you. And do you know what the Bureau's record at trial is? We almost never lose. Wall Street bankers, hedge fund managers, Mafia kingpins. They all get their asses kicked by the Bureau. And we're talking guys who can afford thousand-dollar-an-hour lawyers."

She glances at Hanks. Charlie figures this is in case he didn't get the point.

"Go ahead and prosecute me," Charlie says. "Then you'll find out what I've got and it'll be very embarrassing. The tabloids will have a field day. You'll find I've got a CD with records of bribes going to an FBI supervising agent and--"

Hunt and the secretary both jump to their feet. She slams her fist on the table and the coffee cup wobbles. Hanks grunts in alarm. This is the first he's heard of the CD.

"No, you don't have any such information," Hunt says, pointing her finger. "That's a lie."

"You've got a high ranking agent named De La Torre in this office, am I right?"

Everybody looks at everybody else.

Hunt says, "We're not exactly sure of Agent De La Torre's status at the moment."

"He's probably on the lam because he's a big crook. I've got information showing he's been on the take from Phil Adonis. Who knows what kind of information he fed the Adonis family. And how many people died because of it."

He figures they haven't found De La Torre's body yet, which puts Hunt at a disadvantage. She think he's on the run. And the feds must have other evidence of his guilt, given her reaction.

Hunt doesn't say anything.

"That's what I figured," Charlie says. "I've got the bank routing number and the bank account number to prove that De La Torre was on Big Phil's payroll. And I got a senator and a former governor, some mayors, and a couple of congressmen, too. And a bunch of others going way back. Both parties, quite bipartisan. It'll be big for whoever breaks this case."

He recognizes a glimmer of acknowledgement in her eyes. Yeah, she's driven by ambition, all right.

"So, you can make your career," he continues. "Or all this stuff leaks out at trial. De La Torre will be our first witness."

Hunt's mouth settles into a thin line. "You think you're some kind of hero," she says. "But from where I'm sitting, you look like a sicko who dragged his little girl around as he tried to evade the authorities. To me you're the scumbag here."

"Stop with the histrionics, already. Is that tirade supposed to get me angry? I will make the FBI and the federal government look real bad in all this, I promise you. I have nothing to lose."

Hunt says, leaning forward again, "Do you know you're one weird son of a bitch?"

He remains silent. What do you say to a question like that?

"We'll need to see what you have," Hunt says. "Before we make any decisions."

"Then I'll want something in exchange."

"What do you want?"

"Immunity from these crimes you think I did."

"You've got to be kidding," Hunt says. "We--"

"And witness protection."

"--can't do that. No way. I'll never get authority. And I don't care about this dirt you say you have. I'm not going to be a party to covering up crimes committed by a Bureau agent. I say you should go for it. Let the chips fall where they may."

For the first time, Charlie's sure he's losing control. Maybe he pushed her a little too hard on De La Torre. She seems to be a real believer in truth, justice and the American way. Maybe her principles are stronger than her ambition. Wouldn't that be a turn up for the book? Or maybe she's bluffing.

Either way, he can't take a chance on spending any more time inside the federal lockup. But he has to find a way to move this negotiation forward.

He says with as much confidence as he can muster, "Don't you think you better check with your superiors first before you go making executive decisions?"

She glares at him but says nothing.

"What if I were to sweeten the deal?" Charlie says. "Give you something a little extra?"

She gazes up at the ceiling, at the non-operational camera.

"You've been staring at my coffee cup," she says. "You a coffee drinker?"

"I like a cup of joe now and then."

She turns to the secretary. "Agent Spender, go down to the cafeteria and get this man a cup of coffee. How do you like it?"

"Cream and sugar."

"Cream and sugar it is."

She waits until the secretary leaves the room and closes the door.

Hunt says, "I'm listening."

Chapter Seventy-Three

When the knock comes at the door, Charlie's just finished packing his clothes. He's going to miss this apartment. It's not much, but it was his home for five years, ever since he got out of stir. And, everything considered, it was more pleasant than his prison cell.

He figures he'll donate the furniture to the Salvation Army. But given the condition it's in, there's not much chance anybody's going to want to pay actual money for it.

The knocking comes again, louder this time.

He opens the door and Goran and two immense guys stand there. They're the guys who broke Charlie's hand.

"You mind we come in," Goran says, pushing his way inside.

He looks around, smiles. "Heard you were back in town, Charlie. Where you been?"

"Went away for a while. A short vacation."

"You didn't skip did you? To avoid paying Goran his money?"

"Of course not. Now I'm back."

"And you didn't call. We were worried something happened to you."

The two goons laugh.

"You thinking about going someplace again, Charlie?"

"I'm going to be leaving town again for a while," Charlie says. "Don't know when I'll be back."

Ivanov gestures to the two men.

"Milos, pat Charlie down. Make sure our friend's not wearing a wire or anything stupid like that. Boris, check Charlie's apartment with your little machine. Make sure there no bugs. And make sure nobody's hiding in the closets."

Milos gives Charlie a rough pat down.

"No wire, boss," he says. "Nothing in his pocket except a wallet, some keys, and a cell phone."

"Give me my stuff back," Charlie says, grabbing it and jamming it into his pockets.

"No bugs," Boris says. "And nobody hiding in any closets. We're good."

"We better close this window," Charlie says, shutting the living room window. "You're so scared about being overheard."

"So," Goran says, "back where we were. You forgetting something important? Like Goran's money?"

"I've got an idea on how to pay you."

"You want to pay me, that what you're saying?"

"Sure, I always wanted to pay you back."

"So where is it?"

"Twenty grand, right?"

"Twenty-five grand, now. You borrowed ten grand. You owed fifteen with the vig. Then you didn't pay when due, so it became twenty grand. Then you didn't pay when due again. Now it's twenty-five grand. Late fees."

"One hundred and fifty percent interest for less than a month? That's a pretty steep rate."

"It's what I charge everybody, nothing personal. I'm not bank. My borrowers aren't the best. Like you. There is significant risk of default. That's why I charge what I do." He shrugs. "It's strictly business."

"And if I don't pay, you break my other hand, is that it?"

Goran sighs.

"Charlie, we're way past hand breaking, now. I think a more dramatic message is needed, man. So you get the point. Finally."

"What are you going to do? Kill me?"

"I've done it before. You remember Mort Dranov, the bookie? He didn't lay his bets off and lost his shirt. I helped him out. He owe Goran hundred grand plus the vig. But he told me to go fuck myself. It was Mort who got fucked, but good. Now his body's out in the Pine Barrens somewhere. I don't know where, Milos and Boris here took care of it. You want to end up in Pine Barrens too, Charlie? Next to Mort?"

"You won't do that. If you kill me, you won't get your money."

"But everybody know not to screw with me. It'll be good for street cred, you know? And you're not paying anyway, so what's to lose?"

"I don't have the money."

"That's too bad for you. No more extensions, man."

"But I do have something else."

Goran looks bored. He picks a book off the table. It's The Book Thief. Charlie had bought a copy the day before. Goran thumbs through the pages.

"You saying you don't have my money?" he asks.

"You're not listening. I've got something else. Something better."

"Why should I be interested in what you got? Something better than money? Nothing's better than money."

"The thing I've got is more valuable. It belonged to the Adonis family."

Goran's expression changes from boredom to mild interest.

"What is this thing you got?"

"It's a CD with a bunch of information on it about bribes paid to public officials. Judges, cops, prosecutors, senators, governors."

"How does this help me?"

"I'll leave it to your imagination. I'm sure you can think of something. These are important people I'm talking about. They won't want this information made public. It's the ultimate leverage. So I give you the CD and you forgive the debt. Deal?"

Goran glances up at Milos and Boris. Everybody smiles.

"Sure," Goran says. "Why not? Let's see what you got. If it's like you say, I forgive debt. So let me see it."

"It's not here."

Goran tosses the book on the table. It lands with a thump

"Where is it?"

"It's at the bus station. Come on. I'll show you."

They go out the door and down the stairs. Milos and Boris in front, blocking the way forward, Charlie in the middle, and Goran right behind.

Charlie says, "Hey, Goran, you think you can throw in a couple of grams of meth into the deal? You know, a show of good will."

Goran says, "I didn't think you were a degenerate druggie, Charlie. You surprise me." He says to Boris. "Charlie wants some product. We got any in the car?"

"A half kilo," Boris says. "I was going to deliver it to Six-Pack later."

"You're in luck," Goran says. "It's your lucky day all round, man. We can spare couple of grams for you, my friend."

Boris pushes open the door. Outside, it's a brilliant summer day. Bright sun, blue skies, no clouds. But the sidewalk is empty. At the end of the block, a police cruiser is slanted across the street. Another cruiser blocks the other end. Two cruisers are in front, together with a black Crown Vic. Half a dozen guns are trained on them.

"Get down on your knees," Cathy Hunt shouts. "Hands behind your head. Now."

"The fuck is this?" Goran says.

"Get down, now! I'm not telling you again."

"Better do as they say," Charlie says. "They sound serious. And that little blonde gal is a one-woman war on crime. I wouldn't mess with her if I were you."

Goran, Milos, and Boris drop to their knees, but Charlie remains standing.

"What about you?" Boris says, as the cops approach.

"I'm with them," Charlie says, pointing at the uniformed men.

Handcuffs are snapped on Goran, Milos, and Boris and they are jerked to their feet. Boris and Milos are relieved of large caliber semi-automatic pistols, which are placed in plastic evidence bags.

"What is this shit?" Goran says. "I haven't done nothing."

"Give it up, Goran," Charlie says. "They've got you on tape."

"Not possible."

"It is," Charlie says.

"You're not wearing wire."

Charlie holds up the cell phone.

"The cops can switch on a cell phone remotely. Turn it into a bug. When I closed the window that was the signal."

Charlie walks behind Goran as he's led to a police cruiser.

Charlie says, "Extortion, loan sharking, murder, conspiracy to commit murder, drug dealing, and racketeering. It's all there on ten minutes of tape. Goran, I'm figuring they're going to lock you up and throw away the key forever."

He steps closer, close enough to get a good whiff of Goran's Drakker Noir.

"But it'll be good for you, Goran," Charlie whispers in his ear. "Make you a man."

He gives Goran a hearty slap on the back as he's dragged away, shouting.

Chapter Seventy-Four

Late March and it's still freezing cold. But that's Northern Maine for you, where even summer is really just two months of tough sledding. At least that's what the locals like to say. Snow is piled up two-feet high along the side of Main Street, and a gunmetal gray sky promises six more inches overnight. He could've gone somewhere warm, but he chose Maine.

Charlie checks his watch. Three minutes past four. He frowns. They're late. Then he sees it. A white Subaru Forester encrusted in dirt so thick you'd need an archeologist to excavate it. It maneuvers slowly down the icy street and comes to a sliding stop in front of the building with the ART STUDIO sign over the door.

Art.

What happened to writing?

Charlie picks up a pair of small binoculars and trains them on the Forester. Amy hops out and trots down the sidewalk, an artist's pad under her arm and wooden box with a handle in her right hand. She shouldn't be running.

They salted the sidewalk, but she can still slip and break an ankle. And she has an important volleyball game coming up. He'll be sure to catch that. Sitting in the top row, wearing a hat and sunglasses. One of the terms of his deal is that he's not supposed to get within twenty miles of Amy. Louise and Richard insisted on it on account of the five dead hoodlums that were found on their property. But so what? He only has one child. And he doesn't like the way the coach patted Amy on the rear that one time. Charlie's keeping an eye on that guy.

The door opens and Amy steps inside and the door closes.

He knows that it's wrong that Louise and Richard are taking care of his daughter. He wants to send some money, but there's not much left over when you're making $9.75 an hour driving a bread delivery van. She'll be going to college next year and how will that be paid for?

He scans the binoculars down the street to a rundown store front. The overhead sign says JEWELRY. He's cased the place a couple of times. They're holding some decent stuff on consignment. Mickey Mouse locks. A safe that was cutting edge technology during the Jerry Ford Administration. No cameras that he could see. An antiquated magnetic switch on the front door, probably a single relay. No doubt the same system is on the back door. He'd just have to cut a small hole in the wall in the back and then jump the circuit. It'll take three minutes and, hey, presto, he's in. He figures he'd clear fifteen grand easy, enough for a year of college.

Glancing back at the closed door, he whispers, "I love you."

He jams the ancient Ford E-150 into gear and pain shoots through his right hand, which never healed properly. A slapping sound comes from the engine. It probably needs a ring job, he thinks.

THE END

Printed in Great Britain
by Amazon

54470659R00231